ALSO BY LOIS-ANN YAMANAKA

Wild Meat and the Bully Burgers
Saturday Night at the Pahala Theatre

BLU'S HANGING

LOIS-ANN YAMANAKA

BLU'S

HANGING

FARRAR, STRAUS AND GIROUX   NEW YORK

Farrar, Straus and Giroux
19 Union Square West, New York 10003

Published simultaneously in Canada by HarperCollins*CanadaLtd*
Printed in the United States of America
Designed by Fritz Metsch
First edition, 1997

Grateful acknowledgment is made for permission to reprint excerpts from "Moon
River" by Henry Mancini and Johnny Mercer, with permission of Famous Music
Corporation. Copyright © 1961 by Famous Music Corporation. Copyright renewed
1989 by Famous Music Corporation.

Excerpt from "Blue Lantern" by Cathy Song with permission of Cathy Song.
Copyright © 1983

"The Most Beautiful Girl" by Rory Bourke, Billy Sherrill, Norris Wilson, with
permission of Warner Brothers Publications. Copyright © 1973 EMI Al Gallico
Music & EMI Algee Music. All rights reserved.

LIBRARY OF CONGRESS CATALOGING-IN-PUBLICATION DATA
Yamanaka, Lois-Ann, 1961–
    Blu's hanging / Lois-Ann Yamanaka. — 1st ed.
    p. cm.
    ISBN 0-374-11499-4 (alk. paper)
    I. Title.
    IN PROCESS PS3575.A434 B
    813'.54—dc20   96-42021
                                                        CIP

For John M. Inferrera, the Blue with stories, indelible memory, and for John T. S. Inferrera, your voice in every word I write

For Carla Beth Yamanaka, the one I adored, fearful child, the one I despised with equal possibility—the only one I love with such oblivion

I remember the music
at night.
I dreamed the music
came in squares,
like birthday chocolate,
through the window
on a blue plate.

—"BLUE LANTERN," CATHY SONG

BLU'S HANGING

I Love's king-size bread works the best, white, for Maisie, Blu, and me. The crust on the king-size loaf isn't dark brown and papery, but doughy and soft. We eat mayonnaise bread for a long time after Mama's funeral. It's been two months now and it's still our primary food. Poppy plays "Moon River" over and over on the piano he got from the dead deacon garage sale last Easter. He never cries for our dead Mama in front of the three of us.

Sometimes I put pepper from the rusted Schilling's can on the mayonnaise bread. Even down to the pepper dust at the bottom of the red can. Some days, we have paprika and red chili or yellow curry powder. I stick the fork handle into the Schilling's bottle, scraping chili or curry dust off the hard rock of seasoning.

We watch *Gilligan's Island* with our after-school snack, which is also mayonnaise bread; Poppy still plays "Moon River" in the background.

He sings aloud:

"Old dreammaker, you heartbreaker, wherever you're going, I'm going your way."

He makes me afraid.

I know where he wants to go.

And who the dreammaker is.

I turn up the volume on the TV. Even the castaways

eat better food than we do and they were stranded on a desert isle. All those coconut chiffon pies Mary Ann baked for Gilligan when they thought he was going to die from the rare tropical mosquito that bit him on the neck. Ten whole coconut pies.

❀

About a month later, I can't charge groceries at Friendly Market; the bill has run up too high. Poppy tells me, "Ivah, I gotta work the graveyard shift at Del Monte from now on. Straight from the school, I coming home for bathe and eat, then I going to the truck barn. You going be in charge of dinner."

The last things I bought on Poppy's charge were a jar of Best Foods, a pint of Malolo strawberry syrup, which I diluted 7 to 1 instead of 5 to 1, and three cans of Spam.

"You heard me? You going be in charge of dinner."

From now on.

Poppy shows me the fast way to make a hot dinner.

I cook a pot of hot rice, lots of rice. There are two things I can make from this: if the hen has laid eggs in the last three days that nobody ate, as soon as the button on the rice cooker pops I crack the three eggs right in the pot and stir it up with shoyu. Poppy says, "Just like the ole days, my madda made that for all us kids. Thass Japanee soul food, raw eggs on hot rice. Tamago meshi."

The other thing I make is cream-of-mushroom soup on the hot rice. Don't add any water. It tastes like gravy. I serve it right out of the rice pot with the soup ladle.

Poppy doesn't care. He comes home from the school full of chalk dust and the fine dirt from the dust mop that he pushes across the gym floor at the end of the day. He smells like Pine-Sol all the time.

Poppy says I'm the best cook in the house.

❀

Saturday morning, I saw my brother Blu gather eggs outside. He had two. I made them for him sunny-side up, and he licked the yolk off his plate.

❀

Poppy brought home cases of dry saimin that some-body bought for him from the Swap Meet in Honolulu. So I got good at making fried noodles:

Boil the saimin and drain. Chop Spam, green onion, and fried egg and mix with the saimin. Sprinkle the soup stock over the fried noodles for flavoring.

I also make regular saimin. And one day, I come home from school and Blu and Maisie are eating dry saimin sprinkled with the soup stock. "Taste like potato chips," Blu says, and Maisie nods.

It was getting pretty bad around the house. I saved a stick of Wrigley's spearmint gum that Evangeline Reyes gave me on Monday until Saturday. I felt funny every day asking Evangeline to give me a stick of gum from the PlenTPak stash that she had in her patent-leather white bag.

I stuck my gum to the bureau at night, and after I brushed my teeth in the morning, popped it back into my mouth. I figured the plaque would stay out and the spear-mint would taste fresher, longer. But the gum got so full of grit that it felt like fingernail crumbs until the gum and the grit stuck to my teeth like melted taffy. And that's when I threw it away.

I missed Mama for the loose change that she gave me for things like gum, and I missed her cooking. Pumpkin from the yard with shoyu, sugar, and dry ebi. Squash from the ravine with a small piece of pork belly. Or warabi and squash shoots with Spam. I wish I'd watched her cook so eating wouldn't be part of my dreams.

❀

Blu dreams:

"There was food in the house. Mama was in the kitchen. It was breakfast time. We had eggs (from the carton), Farmer John bacon, Florida orange juice. I smelled it all in my room! But when I woke up, it was only a dream!"

He's got his teacher ingrained in his head, Miss Torres, who makes every student write the same last line of every writing assignment. I had her in the fourth grade too. Curse on him. Now she's part of his talking.

❀

Today, Blu's class is going on an excursion and he has to bring a home lunch. I make the lunch for him. I look in the icebox and in the canned-goods cabinet for a long time.

"Get white bread," I tell Blu cheerfully, "and peanut butter and jelly. Get maynaise. Can make maynaise bread with whatever seasoning you like." Blu thinks mayonnaise bread is poor food even if he likes it a lot, especially with curry powder sprinkles.

One time I put cabbage instead of lettuce in his corn beef sandwich for Boy Scouts. Cabbage instead of lettuce makes a sandwich look poor, Blu says.

So I make peanut butter and jelly for him. I wrap two

sandwiches in tinfoil because there's no more wax paper or small Baggies in the house. I make carrot sticks too and put it all in a big brown grocery bag, too big for the lunch Blu packed, but it was all we had.

Blu's class goes to the Phallic Rock near the Kalaupapa Lookout for lunch. He says Miss Torres tells all the kids to gather around the huge cardboard box full of their home lunches. "Whose Superman lunchbox?" she yells. "Got some Kryptonite in there? Flintstones? Fred? Barney? No, it's Dino." All the kids start laughing. "Flying Nun? Oh, Sister Bertrrrilllle."

Then Blu says she grabs his paper package and yells, "Who does *this* belong to?" The package was smashed under all the other lunchboxes.

All the boys and girls laugh when Blu grabs his stupid lunch in the crumpled-up brown package. Blu tells me, "I went to sit by Scott Fukushima them. They all was busy unwrapping their frozen soda cans from the newspaper and tinfoil their mothers put around their soda to keep um cold till lunch."

Then I remembered. I *forgot* to give Blu something to drink. Scott tells Blu, "Where yours? No more? How come? No more nuff money? Aww, too bad. Thirsty?" Blu says Scott takes a big swig out of his green can of Diamond Head lemon-lime. Then he burps in my brother's face.

Scott probably told my brother to drink his spit like he tells all the kids at recess time when he's hogging the water fountain. "What, Blu? Thirsty? Then drink yo' spit."

Blu tells me, "Then they all take out their musubi with

nori and red ume in the middle. They bust out their fry chicken drumettes, egg rolls with green onion, and teri beef sticks. Kent Hayashi get one whole bag Chee-tos. I seen Scott, he had four Twinkies, so he gave away two. One to Darren Ota and one to Winston Wang. He gave um on the sly kind so the rest of us no see. But I saw.

"Ivah," Blu says, "they all was waiting to see what I get in my package. I no like eat already. Slow kind, I take out my peanut butter and jelly sandwich in tinfoil and I start to unwrap um. Some guys, they laughing, the white bread stuck to the tinfoil. Scott tell, 'Thass all you get, Blu? You made um yourself?' The peanut butter stuck in my throat. 'What else you get?' and he grab the package.

"He pull out the carrots and start acting like Bugs Bunny, 'Eehhhh, what's up, Doc?' All the boys laughing so hard, they holding their stomachs. 'How come?' Scott tell. 'You guys no more lunchbox with thermos inside at home? Your family no more sandwich Baggies your house? Not even *one* Ziploc? Thass why you gotta use tinfoil?' Pretty soon Scott throw my package back at me. All the carrots fall on the ground. But this time, nobody laugh. I picking um up one by one and wiping um on my shirt."

"Sorry, Blu."

"Not your fault."

I write this in Blu's marble composition tablet. Not even in his handwriting to trick Miss Torres, but my own. For him to see later on at school and maybe write back for me to read at home.

I write:

"ONE WISH" by Ivah Ogata　　(Fool!)

You know what I would wish if I could have one wish in the whole wide world? I wish my house was underneath Kaunakakai Groceteria.

In my bedroom there's a secret door up to the groceteria, which I could sneak into at night, after everyone went home. Then I can choose *anything* I want to eat when I get hungry, when all you, Maisie, Poppy, and I have to eat in the house is mayonnaise bread, peanut butter and jelly, or dry saimin.

And I would take Maisie and you with me too, so we can get all the ingredients we need to make the biggest laulau dinner, the whole works—day-old poi, lomi salmon, haupia, pipi kaula, and squid luau, just for the three of us, and Poppy.

That's my wish. My one and only wish.

2 We're wishing for rain, Blu and I, as we sit on our rusty banana bikes by the Kingdom Hall, Maisie on Blu's handlebars. Up comes this guy from the high school who lived three houses down with his married sister and her four children before he dropped out of high school and was sent to the Koʻolau Boys' Home.

Right up to the three of us in his olive-green Duster with smelly black seats. Right up to Maisie. "Eh, small girl, you know what is *this*?" Maisie looks into the car and nods yes slowly.

"And what about you, small boy?" Blu stares into the car, nods yes, and keeps looking. "Ten bucks says touch um and I'm yours, brah. Like ten bucks? Try come, try come. Get in the car. Ten bucks, brah." Blu slowly looks at me. Eyebrows go up: May I? May I?

The boy in the olive-green Duster takes Blu's pause as a no. "Fuck, no need then. Call your big sista over here. I betchu she dunno what is *this*. But I can teach her today."

"Ivah."

I look into the window.

In his hand, in the car that smells like old vinyl seats and red dust, a ten-dollar bill, and in the other hand: big, purple, full of red road mappings, and drops of liquid sugar. Rubbing himself.

"I like your bradda first. The fat kine feel like girls where I going. Call your bradda so I can practice."

"Run, Blu. Run, run, run!"

And laughing from the olive-green Duster. Gravel and tires spin. The boy with the purple penis does donuts around the parking lot of the Kingdom Hall. My brother and sister are stuck in the middle of dust and flying gravel; the boy laughs like an animal screaming. Blu yells, "Maisie, Maisie! Hold on to the handlebars, Maisie!"

I shout, "Blu, Blu!"

And Poppy has gone to work in the pineapple fields.

❀

Blu's eating again. He's gained a ton of weight since Mama died. So much fat that his nipples go in and look like two sad brown eyes pulling down on his fleshy breasts.

Maisie likes to make him eat with his mouth so stuffed with food that he looks like the *Five Chinese Brothers*, the one who swallowed the sea. Blu's mouth is full of mayonnaise bread. He pretends it's chocolate pudding pie or lemon bars that the church ladies make in the summer for Vacation Bible School.

The boys at school call him Cross-Your-Heart, 18-Hour-Bra-Boy, Totoy Boy, Boy-with-Breasts, and Tit-man. They don't know the reason he lies down in front of the TV. Poppy sings softly:

"Moon River, wider than a mile.
I'm crossing you in style.
Someday."

Blu eats Frosted Flakes with milk, bowl after bowl,

until he feels sick and full, rolls to his side, and closes his eyes till dinnertime.

Somedays.

❀

Blu defines crave for me.

"I *crave* for chocolate. All kinds, especially the kind with Rice Krispies inside like Nestlé Crunch and $100,000 bar."

This I know.

"I *crave* Mama come to see if Maisie and me sleeping."

I know.

"I *crave* for friends. Ivah, you my best friend."

Know.

❀

Don't tell anybody, Blu. Nobody.

Especially your teacher. I figured Miss Torres out a long time ago. Tell her what you *crave* three times and she knows how to pull your strings.

Write what you wish three times, and make her stronger than you. Blu's so dumb.

"I *crave* a hundred bucks to spend in Pascua Store."

He's going to tell her what *crave* means four times instead of three. This, I know.

❀

Pascua Store, words on an aluminum Pepsi sign rusting around the nails. This store across from Molokai Drugs sells the daily paper from Honolulu, cigarettes, soda, ice-cream drumettes, and candy. All the old men sit on the bench outside the store.

That's where Lerch squats and smokes his toscani,

scratches himself over there, and laughs when he sees us watching him.

Only a cane knife in his straw bag, that's what they say. His murky yellow eyes look up only on the sly. If Lerch comes anywhere near us on the main drag, we cross the street.

He lives in the abandoned house down my street, Evangeline Reyes says, in the old house hidden by African tulip and mango trees. Lerch sleeps on the dirty mattress Blu pissed on to bless for him.

One day we see Lerch coming down our street with his straw bag, so we hide in the bushes by Miss Elena Gaspar's house. He sees us and laughs. My brother turns to watch him: Lerch scratches his balls and smells his fingers.

"Must smell funny."

"*I scared.*"

"How you know, Blu, smell funny?"

"I get balls. I know what balls smell like when hot and you probly neva bathe for ten years."

"Why, you scratch your balls and smell your fingers too, thass why Lerch offering you some, hah, Blu?"

"Maybe yeah, why, bodda you, Ivah?"

"*I scared.*"

"Yeah, bodda me, 'cause Blu, you stupid-ass, ball-sniffing idiot with no friends. Maybe thass why you no mo' friends."

"*I scared.*"

"I get friends."

"Yeah, who?"

"Maisie. Poppy. And you."

"*There.*"

Lerch turns and walks toward the bushes outside of Miss Elena Gaspar's house. Reaches his hand into his straw bag and we run, never looking back.

But Blu tells everybody that Lerch pulled *it* out, waved *it* at Maisie, him, and me, and chased us up Miss Elena Gaspar's driveway. Now everybody has one more thing to say about Lerch. And Blu.

❀

Maisie's so scared. I tell Blu to stop making her scared in any way or I will have to kick his ass myself. Since Mama died, Maisie said about five things:

❀

I scared.
Sleep with me.
More.
There she is.
Mama.

❀

Maisie said very little to begin with and now her voice sounds dry from lack of use.

But Blu is scared of the Kuro-chan, more than either Maisie or me. The Kuro-chan with his dark skin, green eyes, and kinky gold-tipped hair always sitting on a rattan chair on his dusty lanai. Resting his chin on his dark arms. Smoking a cigarette, thick white smoke.

Mama used to tell Blu never to be bad to his sisters or Mama and Poppy or she'd call the Kuro-chan to take him away forever to his house with no springs on the screen door. "And what the Kuro-chan does to little boys like you, Blu . . ." Mama'd trail off like that and continue to

hang the laundry, which made Blu more curious in a kind
of sick way.

Blu would ask, "What he like do with small boys like
me, what you think, Ivah? Get something to do with my
dick and his dick, yeah, Ivah?"

I know what I think. My Mama told me about sodomy
between men and boys, but I don't tell Blu. The words
wouldn't leave my mouth.

"There she is."

Who?

Blu answers for Maisie. "The dog. The Kuro-chan's dog.
Maisie like bring the female one home next time she follow us 'cause she look all lost and hungry."

Skinny black and brown dogs come sniffing at us after
we cross the street. They're so hungry, they can't even
bark; their ribs are bony, and eyes, glassy. And there's
the Kuro-chan on his rattan chair, whistling for them to
come back to the porch.

"Mama."

We bring the black female home.

Poppy says, "How the hell we going feed that goddamn
dog when we eating tamago meshi for dinner? Shit, you,
Ivah."

It's not for me, I tell Poppy. It's for Maisie.

Something quiet comes over him. The black female
looks straight at Poppy and tilts her head to one side like
a trained dog on TV. Poppy looks at Maisie and he lets
the dog in the house. She sits on the woven rug in the
kitchen all afternoon.

"Sleep with me."

"You bathe her first. All three of you come with me."

It's a Saturday afternoon. Poppy starts the night shift at four o'clock. "Before I go to the truck barn." Poppy starts a march to the shed in the back of the house. He gets a rope and puts it around the dog's neck. "You guys three going come with me and do this right."

We walk to the Kuro-chan's house. Up the gravel driveway and Poppy tells Blu to knock it off. What the hell is he thinking, telling the rest of us about all Kuro-chans? "You like grow up prej-dist, dammit, Blu?"

Up the porch stairs, a knock on the door. From behind the dirty screen door reaches a hand with cigar-fat fingers. Out comes the Kuro-chan in a white undershirt and khaki work pants.

"Clarence, my kids took your dog. My small girl, she like um. What you think? You get plenny over here and the buggas all look hungry."

The Kuro-chan laughs. "You ain't kidding, Bertram, they all hungry. You know how much a twenty-five-pound bag of Friskies dog chow costs at Friendly Market? Yours, little girl."

And he reaches his big, black hand for mine. Says it's great to meet his fine young neighbors at long, long last. I don't know what to say. The dog's not even for me.

His face is smooth like the back side of a shiny piece of Hershey's. Brown, oily forehead. I don't even know what to call him, because I can't call him Clarence.

I start to say thanks, for Maisie. She looks faraway and scared. I say thanks and then there's a long silence. I don't know what to say. I stop and breathe in. I almost call him Kuro-chan.

❀

By now, I've seen three penises: Poppy's, which we've all seen. Blu's, well, since he was a baby, so big deal. The big purple penis of the boy in the green Duster.

The fourth one belongs not to the Kuro-chan but to an old man. Mama had seen his penis a couple of times before and told Maisie and me—but Blu especially—never to walk past his house even if it was the shortest route to town and the county pool.

But since her death, I've tested all her rules, and Poppy, too tired, doesn't seem to care. Or he's not even at home when the rules get tested and then rewritten by Blu and me.

This is how the skebe old man, Mr. Iwasaki, operates. He has Saloon Pilot cracker lids, about three or four of them, tied to the branches of his mango tree. Below are the cracker cans turned upside down. He's always lurking behind the tree with his unshaven face, old man white undershirt, and baggy khakis. And eyes so old and crinkled, they look all black.

When you walk past his house, he comes out from behind the tree and starts banging on the cans and the lids. If you look that way, startled by the noise, you'll be in for the shock of your life: Mr. Iwasaki playing with his old man's penis.

Penis. That's what Mama told us to call it. Evangeline Reyes calls it boto. Poppy calls the penis chimpo, and the balls kintama. Of course, when we were little, we called Blu's ding-ding or dinga-donga. At school they say pricks, dicks, or cocks. But Mama went along with what they teach you in kindergarten about words like flatus for fut and penis for dick and vagina for bilot. If we had to talk about any of it in our conversations at home, we would call things as Mama said, by their "bi-logical correct names": penis, vagina, anus, flatus, breasts, and buttocks.

❀

Blu tells Maisie perverted things under the house. He says it makes her laugh. Cool, fine dust under the house. Apple crates for tables. Hollow tile for chairs. Today he's the Teacher or maybe Mister Rogers:

"What is an exciting event that happened in your neighborhood?"

And Maisie never answers. So Blu talks like a baby and answers his own question.

"Well, the dog next door who just had a litter of puppies in the gully has breasts full of milk. The male who oofed her has a very red, shiny penis that hangs out of his penis skin all the time, big black dongas for balls, and a fat black buttocks. And we all were very excited in our neighborhood!"

Maisie giggles. He defines dirty words from the Webster's Dictionary. She giggles more. The two of them crawl out full of dirt and spiderwebs in their hair.

❀

Early that morning Blu had said, "Us just go walk past his house for go pool today, Ivah. He neva did show his boto to us like Mama said, so I dunno why you all worried. Plus, no biggie if all he like do is show you his boto. So what? We seen Poppy's."

"You know, Blu," I tell him, "you so ig-narant. You think I worried about me, hah? You think all he like do is show his penis to you? I doubt it. You the one gotta be scared, 'cause, brah, he like *you*, not me."

"Think I scared of one old man? I ain't scared. He bang his cracker can, I ain't looking. If you no look, then you not going see his shribbly old boto. We go, Maisie. Bring your dog, okay?"

"*I scared.*"

"Scared of what, shit? Tell your dog when Mr. Iwasaki show us his boto, go bite um off for beef jerky. We go dry um for your dog in the gully. Take only one day. Small, Mr. Iwasaki's boto. Damn old fut, he no like small kids like us. He like show his boto to old futs like Miss Gaspar and Mama."

"Penis," I remind Blu.

"Boto," he says, like he meant it.

"Sorry, Mama," I say for Blu.

"Sorry, Mama," he says, eyes on his dirty feet.

"You better be, Blu."

"*Mama.*" Maisie looks at her dog.

So off they go, Maisie leading her dog with the bust-up rope around its neck. I figure Poppy might kick my ass upside down if anything happened to Blu or Maisie. I watch them turn the corner of the street, then follow them slowly. Hide in the hedge by Miss Elena Gaspar's. Cross the street at the Kuro-chan's. Watch. And wait.

When I get near Mr. Iwasaki's house, I don't hear the gonging of cracker cans and lids, but the tinkling of bells in the light wind, the sound of the Buddhist temple down by the beach.

Maisie sits on a smashed can, her dog alert at her feet. "Where Blu?" I ask her, trying not to sound frantic. Maisie points to the side of the house and I strain to hear voices—my brother's.

"Blu! BLU!" And I run to the side of the house, where I see Blu with his hands full of Violet Crumbles, a $100,000 bar, and a box of Milk Duds. Dollar bills. His pants are below his briefs which are stretched down one hip.

"BLU!" He doesn't even turn to see me. Instead, he backs away with his hands full of chocolate bars and money. Mr. Iwasaki, an old man's stiff penis in his own chocolaty hand, makes slapping sounds, slurping sounds: gray-dry penis skin with a red-tip head, plenty of loose skin, and melted chocolate.

I grab my brother from behind as he tightly clutches the candy and bills. Mr. Iwasaki squeezes his gray rubbery penis and wags it at me. He doesn't speak English. My brother fixes his pants and says, "He gave me three candies for you, me, and Maisie. And the money is for buy soda from Pascua Store."

I have no words for Blu, no words, but I feel it all behind my eyes, burning. A stream of urine comes down my legs as I drag him quickly across the sidewalk. I yank Blu to the front of the house, under the mango tree, and smack him across his head, so hard that the candy and money scatter over the hot road. I run back to the front yard and grab Maisie.

But the dog smells the pool of urine, the shiny road mapping along my dusty ankles and feet, sticky urine on my rubber slippers, and right there, she pisses and shits, Maisie pulling at her rope, in the middle of the circle of Saloon Pilot cracker cans under the mango tree. Blu chases the dollar bills down the road. *Mama.*

3 There's so much time for thought.

Del Monte released some summer pickers and Poppy's been home all day, sad, playing the piano, or cleaning sand and shells from the ogo that Blu and he pick in the morning at low tide. Poppy acts as if each strand of ogo has to be washed and examined. Standing at the kitchen sink for hours. Humming sad.

I'm on my back with my feet propped up on the hassock with Hand, Hoof, and Mouth Disease again. Poppy's mad because it's highly contagious, the red dots surrounded by white-fat halos. I can't cook. I can't walk. I can't eat or talk. My hands and feet feel like prickly points of nerve endings.

And when they blister and pop, I look inside and see:

A white head, and if I push the flesh, it sinks deep like a root into my body. Blu dabs calamine lotion on each dot, whistling and counting.

"Blu," Poppy says, "you and Maisie go down Molokai Drug and buy for Ivah one small bottle Caladryl. That goddamn calamine from the clinic ain't doing shit for her feet."

"I can buy me one Violet Crumble with the change, Poppy?" Blu asks, and Poppy, so tired, says okay. "C'mon, Maisie," says Blu, "I half um with you. Ivah, you like something from the store?"

Blu's been filling in for me: washing the rice, washing the clothes, hanging them out to dry, picking the beans, sweeping the kitchen floor, and bathing Maisie.

"Watch out for Mr. Iwasaki," Poppy warns, "he shown his chimpo to the new haole lady across from Elena's house. Took her one bag Haden mango, knock on her door, and when the haole lady took the bag, there was his chimpo. Clarence told me the haole lady screaming and yelling and Mr. Iwasaki playing with himself walking across the street smiling like the cat who wen' eat the bird, the goddamn skebe. How you like that?"

Blu says nothing.

Maisie: "*I scared.*"

"Of what?" Poppy asks.

"Nothing, Poppy. Right, Maisie?" Blu hustles her and her dog out of the house.

❀

Poppy tells me that I could've lived in the cowboy days with all the diseases I've caught. I've had Hand, Hoof, and Mouth Disease twice already. Poppy says it comes from cows.

Once I was sick and developed trench mouth. Poppy said, "You the only person I know of since the Wild West who had trench mouth." White pus and raw. Sores leaking dead juice all over my mouth.

Poppy made me gargle with hydrogen peroxide when I had trench mouth and Hand, Hoof, and Mouth. Mama made me suck banana-shoot sap. She was alive the last two times when Poppy said I'd make a good cowboy full of real cowboy diseases.

❀

Clint Eastwood never had Hand, Hoof, and Mouth Disease in any of his cowboy movies. Most of the time, we see him on TV. Once in a while his movies come to the theater by Midnight Inn. *Hang 'Em High*, of course, was Poppy's favorite. Blu liked *Two Mules for Sister Sara*. And Maisie, she'd tag along for the Big Dip that she didn't have to share with Blu or me.

Of course, we all liked *The Good, the Bad and the Ugly*. Mama was good at whistling the Clint Eastwood music that came on when the bad guys walked all in a row down the dusty Main Street from far away. You could see them through the clouds of dirt and hear the whistling music in the background.

That same Clint Eastwood music Mama whistled when Elena Gaspar and her widowed sisters, Luz Matsumoto, Magdalena Keawe, and her youngest sister, Agnes Reyes, walked up our driveway with their leather briefcases full of Kingdom Hall pamphlets about "Premarital Sex: A Sin in the Eyes of Jehovah Our God."

My favorite is *The Beguiled*, which I've already seen twice. This is the one where Clint Eastwood is a Yankee soldier who's found by a house of Confederate ladies and they all get horny for him. But as I lay in the middle of the hot living room with Hand, Hoof, and Mouth Disease, I confuse it with *Gilligan's Island*.

Mitchell Oliveira, who I used to love until he went for Evangeline Reyes, would be Clint and I would be the young teacher who Clint really loves on a desert isle for a three-hour tour. Though Mitchell was Portuguese, he was from El Segundo and could talk really good haole English. He came to live with his Aunty Mary Oliveira one road above us in Ranch Camp. Once my hands healed, I would bake him fresh coconut pie with the recipe I saw on the can of Mendonca's frozen coconut milk and be Mary Ann, nursing the wounded haole surfer in my hut.

But I'm in the middle of the hot living room, not on the SS *Minnow*, with Blu swabbing Caladryl on my Hand, Hoof, and Mouth Disease, then washing the rice at the sink in his red felt cowboy hat with the cursive *Blu* stitched in white. Whistling the music from *The Good, the Bad and the Ugly*. Just like Mama.

❀

I have a calico cat. Hoppy Creetat. I found her in the gully by my house. It was the crying that made me climb down and find her with her paws slashed and whiskers cut off.

Hoppy Creetat, who Poppy called Hopalong Cassidy, walked on paws deformed by the slashing. She moved closer to the ground, as if she had longer paws, which gave her a sexier cat walk. Poppy says that they cut the whiskers so that the cat couldn't find her way home. He says they cut the paws for fun. Blu tells me he'd like to try that someday. On another cat, of course.

My brother has no friends and maybe that's good. He tells me one day when the Hand, Hoof, and Mouth is beginning to heal over, "Ivah, you know Scott Fukushima and Winston Wang, they was playing with one kitten by Kaunakakai School, then I seen them put the kitten in one extra-large milk shake cup from the Dairy Queen and shut um in, then throw um around the field like one football.

"And when they was pau with the kitten, they wen' run away and leave um there. So me and Maisie wen' go look, and you know what, Ivah, the thing was super stretch out and the eyes all Jell-O and the neck, the neck was backwards."

"So what you and Maisie did with the cat?"

"Maisie wanted for make funeral but I wen' get the tail part and swing the kitten until the tail came off. But you know what, Ivah? All this brown stuff came out the kitten's anus and wen' drip on me."

"Good for you. Thass what you get."

"I know."

❀

There's very little we don't know.

We know that Poppy's out of work.

We can't charge at Friendly Market and Kaunakakai Groceteria. It's all cash.

We know that cats won't crap in your yard if you fill Welch's grape juice bottles, the gallon size, with water, completely cover them with tinfoil, and then place them all around the edge of your lawn.

Hoppy Creetat's in heat. We know from the way she cries. We know that not even *one* of the *ten* Welch's bottles is keeping away all the tomcats that come around. We know from the way she cries late at night.

Every night, I let her in after Poppy goes to sleep, so Maisie and I can curl up with her and Maisie's black dog.

And every night, Maisie's black dog gnaws on Hoppy's ear before they fall asleep and the cat meows in a way almost human and content. My sister goes to sleep without crying.

The red felt cowboy hat with *Blu* in white cursive letters is from Disneyland when our cousins Lila Beth and
Big Sis from Hilo traveled to California with Uncle Myron
and Aunty Betty. Aunty Betty works at Fashion House in
the Hilo Shopping Center. Uncle Myron is the Ag teacher
at Hilo High School.

But Poppy doesn't talk too much about growing up
with Aunty Betty as his big sister. He says almost nothing
about her. Only about the shame he caused her and his
whole family. He cleans ogo at the kitchen sink. The water runs over the huge, shiny scars on his hands, as he
hums another tune.

I know where he wants to go.

And who the dreammaker is.

It was around three months after Mama died that Blu
began his fake fainting episodes. He even wanted me to
take a picture of him with the Kodak Instamatic camera
while he did it so that he could see what he looked like
while fainting. But we didn't have money for the flash-
cubes.

His fainting worked especially well if he did it after a
long day of picking ogo in the morning, running to get
the mail at the post office across town, swimming at the
county pool in the morning hours and in the afternoon
hours, and riding his bike to the Kingdom Hall parking
lot in the late afternoon.

He'd hold his breath in the hot shower and collapse.
Or he'd put his bed right behind him as he stood looking
into his bureau mirror, then hold his breath, and fall backwards on the bed. That way he could see himself in the
mirror as he was going down.

"Ivah, you watch and tell me what I look like when I going down. Please."

My brother has no friends whatsoever.

"C'mon, Ivah. Maisie. Please, please, please. Maisie, I going kick your dog's buttocks, I promise. And you, Ivah, I going cut off your cat's whiskers again. Please."

So Maisie and I, the black dog, and Hoppy Creetat watch as Blu holds his breath. Poises himself with his bed right behind him. Swoons, but instead falls forward.

Blu hits his forehead on the bureau but Maisie's dog cries the loudest, whimpering and whining.

Maisie cries too.

"Omigod, Blu." There's already a lump growing and throbbing on his head when Poppy walks through the back door.

Poppy cracked my head so hard, I was thrown to the kitchen counter and then fell to the floor. Blu pretended he had amnesia.

"What's your favorite food?"

"Duh."

"What's the capital of Louisiana?"

"Duh."

"What's your name?"

"Duh."

He's acting like Big Moose from the Archie comics with his "Duhs" and that empty stare.

"Sleep with me."

"Okay, Maisie," Blu says, yelling down the hallway. He stops, turns back toward me, and says, "Ivah, my favorite food is Violet Crumbles. My memory all coming back to me now."

❋

Our neighbors, Evangeline Reyes and her three sisters, make my brother's mouth water.

Blendaline, Henrilyn, and Trixi Reyes. They don't have a daddy, but they have lots of uncles and grandpas and grandmas. Always a big party at their house. And Agnes Reyes, their mother, looks like Cher, crooked teeth and all.

Evangeline smiles like Marie Osmond.

Blendaline always goes around saying she's half Spanish.

Henrilyn seems sad behind her long bangs.

Trixi's real dark and looks like Minnie Ripperton but without a huge Afro.

The secret is: *they're half Japanese and their father lives with Agnes Reyes' second cousin in Maunaloa.*

They make my brother's mouth water.

Blendaline told Blu that last New Year's their Uncle Paulo and their boy cousins from East End came for a party and caught cats in the gully. Some they put in burlap bags and threw against the hollow tile wall until they saw the blood leak on the outside of the bag.

Then they took the mother cat who was pregnant and shoved firecrackers up her ass and blew her up. Blendaline says the cat's ass got red and swollen. And brown juice leaked all over the road, the driveway, the garage, wherever the cat ran when it was chased.

Evangeline says she and Blendaline took one of the cats and drowned it in a metal washtub filled with water. "You know what? You shoulda seen the eye looking at us and the paws clawing the water. The bugga's eye. And then the cat wen' sink to the bottom and the jaw was going up and down, up and down, with the eyes wide open."

Evangeline tells Blu that she got a mayonnaise jar and busted it up in a paper bag. Then she mashed the glass as fine as dust. Evangeline says she took some hamburger meat from the freezer and defrosted it. She mixed the meat and the glass together and fed it to those stupid cats who keep her up all night, every night, from the gully.

Hoppy Creetat.

The next morning, there were six dead cats on the different ledges down in the gully.

"What Henrilyn and Trixi was doing when Evangeline and Blendaline was telling you all this?" I ask my brother.

"Henrilyn breathe heavy, and Trixi, she cover her ears. Evangeline said pretty soon Henri going handle and then they can work on Trixi. Trixi in Maisie's class, you know." Blu pauses. "I only keep on listening 'cause Evangeline said only wimps wimp out and I ain't one wimp, I one man, right, Ivah?"

I roll my eyes. "Whatever, Blu."

"You get one kala-koa cat, eh, Ivah?" Evangeline asks me one day after school.

Blu says yes. I say no. We say this at the same time.

No Welch's grape juice jar full of water and covered with tinfoil's big enough to keep Evangeline and Blendaline Reyes out of our yard at night.

❀

Blu says to Maisie under the house one day:

"Nobody like be my friend. I eight years old and I gotta play by myself. Ivah cooking all the time. And you in the house picking fleas off of your black dog. I like to wear my red cowboy hat and my silver cowboy guns in the plastic holster, but Evangeline and Blendaline tease me because I had to make extra holes in the belt with the ice pick so could fit around my stomach part. Henrilyn and Trixi behind them laughing small kind."

It's a confession, to a girl who never speaks. They sit under the house. An apple crate between them.

"So what if I fat? I saw a lot of fat cowboys in Clint Eastwood movies, even if they was mostly the cook. They think I look dumb, but I need somebody, just one guy, to be the bad guy. But Ivah in the kitchen, and Evangeline them hiding in the gully."

Maisie laughs uncomfortably.

He tells me what happened next. "Evangeline them was by the Portagee man's chicken coop smoking cigarette butts," Blu says, "so I sneak-attack them but they hear me coming 'cause the cinders by the mustard cabbage patch crunch when I walk. Then them four all run away.

"Somebody tell real loud, 'We go catch earthworms under the chicken coops,' so I go try find them by the old man's backyard, but I know they trying to reverse psy-co me. Every time I used to bite. I go where they tell (loud) they going be and when I reach there, only me stay with my Folger's can.

"Yesterday, Evangeline's Uncle Paulo wen' make one real cowboy hang-um-high noose and wen' leave um on their front porch. So I wen' steal um and make pretend I was the bad guy and the good guy wen' catch me. Then I wen' turn into the good guy again and wen' throw the rope wit the noose over one kinda high branch on our mango tree.

"But when I 'came the bad guy, I no could reach, so I 'came the good guy again and wen' pile the cement blocks that Poppy use for plant his orchids under the noose. 'You gonna hang, pardner,' I said with the good-guy voice.

" 'See you in hell,' I said with the bad-guy voice. Then I wen' look both ways, up and down the road, and I wen' give one last spit. And then I wen' jump.

"The rope wen' snap tight around my neck and I felt all the blood stucking in my head. 'Ivvahhh,' I wen' try yell. 'Ivvahhhhh.' But was one whisper. I was hanging for real, my feet was dangling.

" 'This is it,' I was thinking. 'I going die for real right here on the mango tree with my whole head turning pur-ple and hot like hell. Holy shit, now I did it for real and Poppy going kill me, but maybe he too late 'cause I going kill my own self.'

"I promise, my veins in my head was throbbing and my face was burning up fast. Then the branch wen' broke and I wen' tumble, branch and all, on the cement blocks. I no could loosen the noose, and I no could take the rope off the branch.

" 'Ivvaahh, Maiiisie,' I was yelling, but you guys neva come. So you know what I did? I wen' drag the mango tree branch, still stuck to my neck, all around Ranch Camp until I found Poppy, talking story by Mr. Bernar-dino's pigpen.

" 'You damn stupid kid,' he say, and he cut the rope off my neck with his pocketknife. And then Poppy wen' slap my head hard."

❀

Blu practices his cursive for Miss Torres:

I am eight years old. My name is Blu. I got no friends. I hang um high and no pardner to cut me down and bury my bones or wear my red hat to the O.K. Corral. I might never be a great cowboy full of cowboy diseases like my sister Ivah. And the moral of the story is, when you do have a friend or sister, find a hobby in common to keep you out of trouble.

❀

Through a cloud of swirling red pineapple field dirt, Hoppy Creetat comes running one day, in the back door, past my legs, into my room, where she curls up next to Maisie's black dog and cries when she begins to gnaw her ears.

In the gully lie Hoppy Creetat's first litter of three, eyes open just two days ago, two calicos like their mama and one soot black. I carried them in a shoebox to the garage. Hoppy takes them in her mouth back to the cool, tiny cave in the gully, where a fine dust settles over the ledge. Her breasts are full of milk. Again I move the kittens, and by night, they sleep together on the cool dust of the gully.

How can you tell a cat about sleeping in a box in the garage at a house surrounded by Welch's grape juice jars? In a day or two, I try to convince Poppy to let Hoppy Creetat's family in the house. How can you tell a cat to be patient and wait; that Poppy needs to see her Creetats and feel love for them first?

Four days later, two calicos and one black kitten hang from knotted rag nooses on the low branches of a huge kiawe tree on the Reyes side of the gully.

I walk into our bedroom. *"There she is,"* Maisie says

as she moves herself, pushes a cat and a sleeping dog to make room for me. "*Sleep with me*, Hoppy," she whispers to the cat whose breasts leak milk on our bed.

Blu crawls into our room, climbs up on our bed, and curls himself into my body. His feet are dirty and his breath sweet. And the moral of the story is: sleep together one and all. The cats are outside hanging.

4 Mama told me about Cat Haters. She said there's a breed who hate them because when cats get old, they know what you talk about, and they walk on hind legs like humans. They act like you, talk like you. Cat Haters, she said, are *Human Rats* like the Human Rats across the gully.

So Evangeline is Mickey Rat, their leader. Blendaline is the second-cruelest rodent, Minnie Rat. Henrilyn is Mighty Rat because here she comes to save the day, and she's so big-chested. And Trixi is T.T. I call her Trixi Templeton or Paul Lynde, the center square but never the secret square. Together they are the Reyes Rats.

I could tell Mama a lot of things that I learned since she died, about all the things she told me to do, and not to do. Especially what not to do in this life. And what I would say to her if I had the guts and if she weren't dead. But that's the trouble.

The cats are dead. Hoppy cries too much. Mama's dead. Poppy cries every night. Maisie too. So that's why you don't talk back to the dead. They may leave you crying forever.

This is how I try to remember my Mama. I remember all the things she told me about what to do in this life:

"Ivah, no stick your arm out of the window when I driving this Malibu or the traffic sign going rip off your arm. That goes for your head too."

If she weren't dead and I wasn't afraid of talking back to someone dead, I'd say, "My arm's not ever going be long enough to reach the sign unless you swerve the car on purpose over there so my arm get cut off."

Mama said, "Don't go around without a slip if you wear a dress unless you like all the boys see your panty. And please, always wear clean panty without holes in case you get in one car accident." When she swerves and my arm gets cut off, I suppose.

Be good to cats, she warned. They have a good memory. Cats exact revenge for the evil done them.

Leave the porch light on for me until I leave this earth. The light will lead me to heaven.

Don't touch my belongings for forty-nine days.

I stood in the sunlight in the living room. Last Sunday I stood there in the September light and asked Blu if he could see my panties if I spread my legs. Then I thought: Who cares?

At least I wear panties, not like Blendaline Reyes. That's what Mitchell Oliveira told me. He saw Blendaline Reyes waiting for her little sister Trixi on the swing at Kaunakakai School, with no panties and pubes.

"Yeah, right, how you saw pubes?"

"It was pretty dark, I must admit, but on one of her swings, her skirt must've caught an updraft, because I saw her cat with black, wiry fur." The guy speaks such perfect English, it's disgusting. Then he throws in the cat part to sound cool.

So at least I wear panties. And I have just one pair with holes. I would tell Mama, "The one you left on the washing machine overnight and you said cockroaches ate the crotch part."

Mama would sing: "Yellow on your panty, whadda you do? Yellow on your panty, whadda you do? Well, if you don't use regular Clorox, use Borax too."

And in life, after a song like that, who could say anything?

Mama said to hang the clothes on the line in an organized fashion so that the folding would be easier. I remember listening to the crunch of red cinders as she picked up the wet laundry and stepped to her right and then the whip of the clothes as she snapped out the wrinkles. The stiff, sun-dried towels folded like a dry chamois as Mama picked up the laundry while whistling the music from a Robert Redford and Natalie Wood movie, *This Property Is Condemned.*

Wish me a rainbow.

❀

No let one boy buy you clothes. Implies he *knows* your size, know what I mean?

No pass food from chopstick to chopstick. Bad luck.

No wear white, all white, or you going look like a goddamn snowman.

Eat the fish white eyeballs. Thass brain food.

No wash the colored with the whites.

No put too much water in the rice bumbye the bugga get mushy—buckshot better than sticky rice.

But no waste.

Sleep early.

Be good.

Steam, don't fry.

Turn off the TV.

No soda in the morning.

Be good.

Sleep tight.

Good night.

Good night, Mama.

Mama, you died and didn't leave me a damn clue.

Teach me how to be a mama too.

❀

Poppy teaches us the art of janitorial services. "Ivah, Ajax the toilet. Blu, Pine-sol the floors. Maisie, Crystal White the dishes and feed the dog and Hoppy. And take pride in your work, you hear me? Nothing's low-class in this world 'less you make um like that plus do a half-ass job."

Blu and I got a job ironing shirts for a haole school-teacher married to a Japanese man from Waimea. They live two houses down and have six children, all small.

We iron a laundry-basketful of shirts on Wednesdays since it's a short school day and get paid five dollars, one of which Blu immediately blows on candy and soda from Pascua Store and four of which I save. Maisie's not allowed in the house, says Mrs. Susie Nishimoto, originally from Bloomingdale, Ohio, who teaches Hawaiian Studies and PE at the high school. Maisie is a bad influence on her boys.

I don't know what she's heard or what Maisie's doing in school, but word gets around, Mrs. Susie Nishimoto says, as she digs in her wallet for a five. "Teachers talk," she says. "And you better get your father ready for a parent conference. Soon."

In the meantime, Maisie sits outside in the Nishimotos' garage with her dog, picking fleas and smashing them on the concrete floor. She's careful to leave blood puddles and fat blood ticks from way down deep in her dog's ear, alive, with a mate pulled from her dog's eyelid still holding on to a pink piece of eyelid flesh. So the blood ticks don't have to be alone.

❀

Among other things, Mama left us a few words. The Great Zabino or the Fantastic Zabi as a nickname for me. Once I learned some card tricks and palm reading from my cousin Big Sis and tried to be a magician. Mostly we liked the sound of Zabi. The *Ghhzzzabee* that only Mama could do from the back of her throat. No one calls me that anymore.

And Ivah Kinimaka, another name she made up because I look like the Samoan entertainer Mama saw when she went to the Waikiki Outrigger Hotel for an Amway convention. Except he's a man. "Kini, it's the hair," she'd say to me. The hair that's curly and long like Mama's.

Maisie was Carrie Pidgeon, for the cartoon bird who looked exactly like my sister. Pidge, all the time, "Pidge, come ova here, let me kiss your soft forehead." No one calls her Pidge anymore. And only Blu remembers to kiss her forehead.

And Blue Moon or Blue Hawai'i for my brother, whose real name is Presley. Change a letter—Parsley.

You can guess why he calls himself Blu.

Thank God she didn't name him Elvis. There's already an Elvis in our town. Sometimes I wonder if there's an Elvis in every town. Ours is Elvis Tomita, a short, scrawny Avon makeup salesman who may feel forced, because of his name, to pomade his hair so thickly that if a fly flew in his head, it would be jellied to death.

Mama invented people just to make us laugh. There was Hinalea Hammings, a big-talking haole who wanted to be Hawaiian. Vicky Ventura, stewardess for Malibu Airlines. Toiletta Paperu, so stupid, she didn't know how to wipe her own ass.

Mama would break into Hinalea Hammings, and tell us in a really convincing haole accent, "I'm a haole but I have a bowel movement fish first name. Oh, if you please, it's a Hawaiian name, nonetheless, but that of a tasteless bottom feeder. I'm just a haole who came to Kaunakakai and renamed myself with a Hawaiian name. Oh, you don't mind if I call my first boy, Jim, the Hawaiian equivalent, Kimo, do you? And my daughter Amanda, Alohanani, do you? Why, thank you." We laugh and laugh and beg Mama to do more.

Vicky Ventura, the stewardess for Malibu Airlines, sounded like she talked into an intercom. In the car, Vicky would remind us, "Ladies and gentlemen, your pilot, Captain Bertram "Wings" Ogata, requests that you fasten your safety belts and extinguish all cigarettes for the duration of our short flight. Mahalo." All the time, Vicky Ventura would comment on the scenery: "On our right, ladies and gentlemen, the lovely pineapple fields of Del Monte and Company. And on our left, the beautiful Pacific Ocean. Mahalo."

Toiletta Paperu made us laugh till it hurt. Cutting people down like the ladies in Elvis' *Blue Hawaii*. With a real Portuguese accent, Toiletta would pronounce, "All the hula girls in *Blue Hawaii* look so haole, I swear, and they sappose to be Hawaiian? And all the Japanee and Chinee chicks, them too looking all haole. *Oh, please, Louise.* Haoles with black hair and heavy eyeliner so that

they look like they get single eye. *Hel-lo.* Maybe they wen'
buy Avon eyeliner from Elvis Tomita. Like you seen
France Nguyen on *Hawaii Five-O* trying for talk pidgin like yours truly with her Chinee accent: 'I dunno,
McGarrett. You one dead mahimahi, you no watch out,
bruddah.'

"Please, France," said Toiletta Paperu, "you betta off
trying out for be Yuniyoshi's sista on *Breakfast at Tif-
fany's II,* or betta yet, Mrs. Livingston's aunty from Tokyo
on *The Courtship of Eddie's Father.*"

Mama made me laugh like nobody could.

Soon Hinalea Hammings came up with a new rule: "If
you want to come back to the seat you were occupying
while watching television prior to getting up to get a Diamond Head soda from the outside refrigerator, you must
place two fingers up your nose, lift it up like a pig's, and
say loudly so that we may all hear you, 'C-A-C-K.' Short
for 'Coming Back.' You must say this with a nasal-drip
voice."

Blu would chime in, "Mama, I said 'C-A-C-K' and Maisie
took my seat." This while sticking his fingers up his nose
and looking like a pig—before he got really fat like he is
now. Or I'd say, "Mama, I C-A-C-Ked and Blu came sit on
the orange chair." Which was the best chair in the house.

Blu, Maisie, and I C-A-C-Ked everywhere. At the dining-
room table, on the best side of the bed, the front seat of
the car, C-A-C-King for the orange chair.

Mama made it up a month before she died.

❀

That summer she was sick but still took us to see the
Moloka'i JayCees Fourth of July fireworks. I remember

there was a low tide, the mud popping and sucking as we sat on the wharf.

Mama wore Poppy's old army jacket, so big, she hugged Blu and Maisie inside it. She breathed deeply the smell of salt and sediment, an onshore wind. We all watched the huge, exploding balls of light, fireworks like giant chrysanthemums, one every half hour, while Mama ooohed and aaahhed, entranced by the fireworks hanging in the black sky, her face illuminated with light.

❀

I smelled her breath, sweet Choward's Violet Mints, all over the house. All around me, even with every window and door in the house open after her funeral, open, curtains pushing toward us, after we brought the urn full of Mama's white ashes back home.

Old dreammaker, you heartbreaker, wherever you're √
going, I'm going your way.

Open so she might pass through and depart.

She told me to fold all the mats in the house. Cloth mats, goza, and bath mat. The dead want clean floors. She asked me to wear her red dress, no matter what anyone said. Give all her T-shirts to Blu, and let Maisie wear her graduated pearls.

Mama gave her big cast-iron pots away: one to Elena Gaspar, one to the Buddhist church by the beach, and the last to me.

The night after the wake Poppy read her Will, the Last Will and Testament of Mrs. Eleanor "Ella" Yumiko Ogata, to the three of us at the kitchen table:

"I, Eleanor Y. Ogata, being of sound mind and body, do hereby bequeath my earthly goods and belongings to:

"my oldest daughter, Ivah Harriet Ogata, my Ponderosa Pines land just miles from the heart of Montana's business district, where she and her family-to-be can fish for trout in crystal-clear lakes and streams; a red dress with sequins for all occasions, and my ruby crown ring from Japan;

"my youngest daughter, Maisie Tsuneko Ogata, I leave to you a string of pearls, my Mings, topaz, and turquoise rings, under the condition that you stop biting your nails and cuticles;

"my son, Presley Vernon Ogata, my sapphire crown ring for your wife-to-be, my gold-filled teeth, and my Elvis Presley memorabilia from the Bradford Exchange, the best in limited-edition porcelain plates: 'Heartbreak Hotel' and 'Rockin' in My Blue Suede Shoes.' "

Mama left her sister-in-law, Betty, one of the expensive futons made of satin and silk from Japan and filled with kapok. But Mama said in her will that Aunty Betty couldn't take the futon until after the forty-ninth-day service.

"I be in the house with you for forty-nine days, so don't let Betty take nothing, okay, Bertram? I know thass your big sista but she gotta wait, 'cause I might get cold waiting for pass through the windows, know what I mean? I might need one good heavy blanket. She get her eye on all my stuff, I betchu."

Aunty Betty stayed a week after Mama died to help us around the house. Mostly to grumble about the "filth in this damn house, I swear, whassamatta with Ella? She no clean the toilets or what, gunfunnit, this place ain't fit for dogs." All the while Poppy sat at the dining-room table reading the obits and want ads and looking up toward the ceiling, into the corners of the room.

A week and a half later, she was putting all the futons in garbage bags, all of them. "I think Ella said for you to take one of um, not all, Betty," says Poppy. "We need blankets too, you know."

"Why, what you need this kine heavy futon for in Kaunakakai? Neva was a day or night I spent in this godforsaken hot-as-hell town that I eva needed one heavy futon like this. Whassamatta with you, Bertram? Came greedy and hoard all this good futon all these years? For what? I taking all of um home for Myron and the girls. Big Sis pretty soon going move out and she going need futon. Lila too. This her last year at Hilo High and she going need one heavy futon when she go mainland college. You no mind, eh, Bertram?"

Poppy was so sick, he motioned with his head and his tired hands: Take um. Take um all. They weren't even his to give. They were ours. The one we slept with every night too was squeezed into a garbage bag by Aunty Betty from Hilo.

A week and a half later, not forty-nine days later, Aunty Betty boards Aloha Airlines, stopover at Kahului Airport, with her two suitcases full of Mama's eelskin wallet, Chanel No. 5 unopened, a leather handbag, a string of amber beads, and a paper shell necklace. All of that and four garbage bags of the rich-man futons Mama received as gifts from Japan. Everything Mama owned in her whole life.

Once home in Hilo, Aunty Betty slept with Mama's futon, the silk fabric smooth against her clean feet. But that night, something choked Aunty Betty; the futon seemed to pull up toward her neck, bunch around it, a heavy, rich-man futon, then futon and hands were over her mouth. Aunty Betty screamed, but no one heard, so she choked. Suffocating and gagging from satin and kapok shoved down her throat. She woke up sputtering.

And by the morning of the forty-ninth-day service, Poppy had driven me down to the post office to pick up four garbage bags, filled with futons, from Aunty Betty.

"For the kids. Better them than me. Keep in touch, Betty."

Of the Human Rat species, Aunty Betty was Speedy Gonzales Rat. Fast to send back what wasn't hers.

❀

I could tell Mama a lot of things that I learned since she died, about all the things she told me to do, and not to do.

Always make your musubi triangle, not round, which is *ma-ke* man style.

Black cats cure sadness. Calico cats bring good luck.

"You remember all this, you hear me, Ivah?"

Blu said, "I write um all down in my tablet for help Ivah rememba, you like, Mama? What you said, Mama? Again? C'mon, you guys. Okay, tell me what to write, Mama. Tell me what I gotta do. We can write um all down. Thass how you remember important things, right, Ivah?"

I nod yes. And that evening in the lamplight, I rub cocoa butter into the shiny rivers of scars across my Mama's belly and back. They would map my way home to her body, I was sure, should I ever get lost. I didn't want them to fade into the smoothness of her skin, but she wanted no trace of them. I rubbed the warm oil on her with a finger coursing tributaries, humming as she lay naked beneath me.

Humming.

Wish me a rainbow.

And wish me a song.

❀

Today, Maisie says, "*Mama. More.*"

I know who the dreammaker is.

❀

I take the money that I make ironing shirts with Blu on Wednesdays for Mrs. Susie Nishimoto down to Friendly Market for a five-pound bag of Ralston Purina dog chow and a five-pound bag of Purina cat chow.

The Human Rats killed my black kitten. The one I wanted to put on Poppy's stomach to stop the crying. I buy a five-pound bag of cat food so when I find *the* black cat and bring her home, Poppy's got nothing to say about "We ain't got no money to feed this dog, Hopalong, and now this goddamn black cat."

I've been ironing shirts for cat food, listening to what Mama said:

Good things come to those who wait.

I wait for my black cat.

But in the meantime, I call the black dog to sit at Poppy's feet as he lounges in the orange chair, and she nuzzles Poppy's ankles. Poppy reaches down and slowly pets her, saying, "Now, now."

Then Hoppy Creetat crawls through the hole in the screen door that Poppy cut out for her yesterday. The windows and doors remain open. The curtains pull in toward us. The porch light flickers off and on.

5 The light is out in the classroom. I can hear her as I walk outside with Blu. The first one I want to kill. Yelling so loudly, the whole kindergarten wing stops moving to turn their heads and eyes to the sound.

"What did I ask you to do, Maisie Ogata?" asks Miss Tammy Owens in her Texas drawl. "Yet you continue to defy me day after day after day. Now I don't know what the hell is going on in that manipulative little head of yours—but if I say read, you read. If I say share, you share. If I say change your underwear, then you—"

"Maisie!" I scream. My sister runs to me with a look on her face I will never forget. Wild, scared eyes and red-faced. And something in me, a rage I have never felt, courses through my body and rises up to my mouth.

"Why you yelling at my sista? Why you making my sista scared for, you fuckin' haole?"

"Ex-cuse me," Miss Tammy Owens sneers. "And who in God's name are you?" She must see my eyes ready to burst out of their sockets, my face and hands burning. She shoves her way past Blu and me. "Filthy-mouthed kids with limited vocabularies. Good, real good. Git me a bar of Lava. I'll be back. Y'all wait right here." She clomps down the wooden hallway in her teacher high heels.

"Run, c'mon, run."

Maisie doesn't say anything when Blu and I stop by the

baseball backstop, catch our breath, and start firing questions at her.

She only started talking at four and a half years of age. Then a few months later, Mama died, which is when Maisie stopped saying anything.

What Blu and I gather from her, we gather from "playing" 20 Questions, fast before Miss Owens can call our house. We run home. I sit my sister in the garage next to the black dog, whom Maisie holds as big, fat tears roll down her dusty cheeks.

"You no wear panty to school because you got none?"

"Stupid, Blu, she got plenty. I just bought her one whole Days-of-the-Week set from Imamura's."

"You wear panty to school but you take um off?"

Nod yes.

"You take um off 'cause hot like Blendaline Reyes?"

"You so stupid, Blu, of course not, right, Maisie? You not taking off your panty 'cause you hot, hah?"

Nod no.

"See you, Blu. Go on. You take um off 'cause get dirty?"

Nod yes.

"Dirty from playing outside?"

Nod no.

"Dirty from, dirty from—Maisie, you pissing in your panty?"

Nod yes.

"Every day?"

Nod yes and lots more tears.

"What you doing with your wet panty? How come you get panty every day?"

She lowers her head.

"You using dirty panty?"

"Cannot be, you stupid Blu. You washing your own panty? No wonder I no see too many of your panty in the wash."

"Why you neva tell us, Maisie? We not going scold you."

Sad, so sad.

I'm not stupid. Blu's not stupid. She cannot talk, so she cannot ask like this haole wants the kindergartners to ask, "Teacher, may I please use the lavatory?"

"Finish, Blu, finish."

"So Miss Owens make you take your wet panty off, and 'cause you do um every day, no mo' extra panty in your cubbyhole?"

Nods yes slowly.

My heart squeezes tighter and tighter.

"So you gotta go around *all day* without panty?" I ask Maisie. Everything else, the part I heard about not reading and not sharing, means nothing. "Maisie, I sorry. I suppose to give you extra clothes if you need um. Thass what said in Miss Owens' Welcome to Room 3 letter she gave you on the first day of school."

"I know something, Ivah," Blu starts. "I neva think nothing of this when Trixi Reyes told me 'cause I thought was just bubbles, but Trixi, she nice to Maisie, you know—"

"What, what?"

"You know on the playground recess time, Maisie stand by Room 3, right? I told you I always see her there."

"C'mon, move on. Tell the story, shit."

"The boys in Maisie's class and some first- and second-grade boys too, Trixi said—" Blu pauses. He knows how I hate all the Reyes sisters. "Trixi, she fight for Maisie, you know, Ivah. She stand by her and kick the boys' head when they make-pretend fall down by Maisie and look up her dress. I neva think nothing 'cause I do that too sometimes. I like see the girls' panty. But from what Maisie tell us, that mean that—"

Maisie squeezes her legs together, holding on to the orange-painted pole. Flecks of shiny paint stick to her sweaty arms. Boys falling down on the broken sidewalk, looking at her, see her under there. Hold on to the pole and squeeze.

She looks at me, then at Blu. Nods yes. And her lips quiver.

"And Miss Owens got her rotten haole ass in the Teachers' Lounge smoking cigarettes and drinking coffee. She no even let the class in till the eight o'clock bell, and they the only kindergarten class running around the playground. Even on cold and dark mornings. And she hate them, you know, Ivah. She only like Jonathan Nishimoto and Thomas Mooney."

"She make you stay all day without panty?"

Yes.

"Sheez, why?"

"She make you clean up your own piss with the mop?"

Yes.

"And Pine-Sol?"

Yes.

"You scared, Maisie?"

Yes. This time, her eyes in mine.

Mama told me, "Always take care of your brother and sister."

Now I lay me down, down.

Mama, I want to kill, feel my fingers squeezing tighter and tighter around a white, freckled neck.

❀

At long last, Maisie, Blu, and I name her black dog, Ka-san, which comes from somewhere in my memory. "Remember when Mama use to make-pretend be Ka-san, Maisie?" Blu says. "She talk like one old lady Japanee, and bow her head, and shuffle her feet in small kine steps, and make like she get buck-teeth?"

"O-kasan," I tell Blu. "And she played O-kasan for make us feel spoil, you mento Blu, like how the Japanee old ladies take care their kids on hand and knee." Mama was O-kasan on my last birthday. Just for me.

"But we cannot name our dog O-kasan if that was our Mama," Blu says.

"Ka-san," says Maisie. Blu and I both stop and stare at her open mouth. The dog nods and rests her head in Maisie's lap. Maisie looks deep into Ka-san's eyes, which glow blue at first, and then red.

"This dog understand English, I tell you," Poppy says. "The bugga nod when you talk to um. You seen um do that, Ivah?"

"Yeah, Poppy."

Poppy has started a night job three times a week with Felix Furtado cleaning the Bank of Hawai'i. Once a week, they clean the office of Molokai Motors, a used-car lot full of a fleet of six clunker cars. He gets home at about nine o'clock. And it's the dog we send down the road to greet him.

I remember Mama telling me, "You know what I learn from the Filipinos? Well, besides how for cook ono stuffs with bay leaves—I learn about the inu." Mama touched the scars on her hands and face.

Weird scars.

Like Poppy's—on his hands and face.

The scars that disappeared when water ran over their hands, doing the dishes together, and then shone like the shiniest skin. Scars that Maisie, Blu, and I never had on our hands or faces. But hands that Mama and Poppy hid in their pockets. And faces turned down, shamed eyes.

As Mama touched the scars on her hands at the sink, she talked about the inu. "I know inu is Japanee, but was the Filipinos who tell that you take the makapiapia and tears from the dog's eyes and wipe that mucus in *your* eye and you see spirits."

I won't tell that to Maisie, who wants to see my Mama so badly, spirit or not, that she'd put dog tears in her eyes, follow my Mama, a spirit with no legs, like a ghost's long hair around the house.

❀

Early one Saturday evening, Elena Gaspar walks up our driveway, her eyes afire, without her Kingdom Hall leather briefcase. I hear her talking to Poppy. "Yah, you know. Somebody been take my punty off de clothesline. Eberry night, I no mo' one or two. Only mine one gone."

Poppy says, "Ai-ya, manang, somebody in lub with you, like keep your private with him, I think."

"Not funny, you Berrtrram. Bumbye you daughtas no mo' punty too, and den what? Ai-soos!" She crosses herself.

"Ai-ka shame por you, Elena, maybe Mr. Iwasaki keeping your panty inside his house, whatchu think? Old man gotta catch his thrills, eh, take your panty and then—" Poppy makes a motion with his hands as if he's sniffing them.

"You think you so bery punny, you Mr. Ogata. More betta I talk to the schoolteacher next door. What for I talk wit you? Eberything is one joke but only you laugh." Elena Gaspar scoffs and starts to walk away.

"Hang um inside your bathroom, manang," Poppy calls after her.

She waves him off with a flick of her hand.

Poppy closes the door behind him and says to me, "Somebody teaching her a lesson for hanging her parachutes on the clothesline. No mo' shame, that wahine. What kine fun that, steal one old lady's panty? Somebody desperate or Elena lying. Sheez, this Christmas, go buy her one package Hanes from Misaki's."

❀

As if we don't have enough trouble, Blu starts wearing underwear with the initials E.E. on the label. I see the briefs in the wash.

E.E. is Blu's friend. Well, sort of. I call him Ed the Big Head. Blu calls him "Bob." For Pep and Bob. The two of them, I guess, wearing each other's underwear. Blu and his new best friend Ed the Big Head Endo.

Blu says, "You like know the reason why I Pep and he Bob, hah, Ivah?"

I say no, but Blu goes on anyway.

"Okay, after we pau swim on Saturdays, me and Ed go down Pascua Store and we no mo' plenny money, right? So me and Ed, we split the chips and soda. He take one drink, I take one drink. Then he take two chips and I take two chips, know what I mean? So anyways, I buy the Pepsi. Thass why I Pep. And he buy the bob-be-cue chips. Thass why he Bob. Get it? Pep and Bob."

I don't even have the heart to tell him that Bob should be Barb, which is more like it to me. You know, a barb, a thorn, a prick is what Ed the Big Head is to me. I know that Ed makes Blu pay most of the time. And Blu, he's so desperate for somebody to like him, he probably doesn't even mind.

Ed the Big Head comes over, showers at our house, and uses the bottle of Herbal Essence that Blu hides in his BVD drawer. The one he bought for *his use only*.

He's greedy, so greedy. He used the whole bottle I bought for the family in a frenzy of one big lather. So into that empty bottle, I put water and green food coloring and pretended to have purchased more shampoo. I waited as he poured himself green. And scratched his head to make lather. He was using the Herbal Essence as body soap.

Blu's been acting like a real spendthrift, as Mama would say, with our ironing money. It's his half that he's spending, but I keep telling him that the money should be for emergencies only.

Like this Pep and Bob thing. I know a lot of his money goes into that friendship, because they go to the store after school. And Blu's been ordering all kinds of junk from the back of the "Betty and Me" comics. It's the only one we all like. The best Archie comics are "Betty and Me," "Laugh," and "Betty and Veronica." Twenty-five cents for the giant issue and twelve cents for the regular issue.

Blu says, "You no wish comics could last forever? When I reading um, I try for *not remember* what happening so that the next time I read um, is like I was reading that comic for the first time. No work."

Blu and I act out all the parts. Maisie and Ka-san watch and laugh because we're real good, "Blu and Me." Acting out the parts makes the comic good another time through.

I'm always Betty. Betty who loves Archie (Mitchell Oliveira) but can never have him. "Oh darn! Darn! Darn! Archiekins, why can't you break your date with Veronica? If you want me to fix ole Betsy so she runs for the Valentine's Day Sock Hop, then you stay here with me. Pass me the wrench, Archiekins."

Somebody like Evangeline Reyes is Veronica. Somebody sassy with black hair and evil mouth. "Gasp! D-did you hear what that hockey puck ASKED? IMPORTANT? Every Lodge that ever lived was important!" I do this at the top of my lungs.

But I'm always Betty. Blond, good, kind, sweet, and who Archie really should love and smooch but doesn't. "Eeeek, I feel so depressed, Ethel! I'm a miserable failure as a teenage girl. All week long Archie used me to tune up ole Betsy, and now on Saturday night, he's going out with Veronica. Sigh!"

Blu always plays both Archie and Reggie because they

have lots of lines. Blu says, "Yo, Arch! The Winter Wonderland Dance is just around the corner. Who are you taking? Hey! I got a groovy idea! Why don't we double-date?"

"I don't know, Reg," Blu answers himself a note higher and nicer, "I mean, I wanted to spend a quiet evening with Ronnie and after din-din, cuddle up to the TV." Blu's such a dip with lovey-dovey lines.

Sometimes he's Jughead, if he's in the mood: "Standing around the Choklit Shoppe is a drag! (Yawn!) Where's good ole Arch?"

Or Mr. Weatherbee: "Oh good grief! Hold on, young man, there shall be no running in the hallowed halls of Riverdale High."

Or Mr. Lodge: "No! By George, no!! Smithers, remove this harebrain from the Lodge premises." And especially if they get real mad, Blu loves to yell the lines. Anger is the easiest emotion for him.

"Miss Torres would make one good Miss Grundy," Blu says.

"Miss Owens mo' betta, Blu. She match. Haole to haole. Witch to witch." Maisie doesn't laugh.

Blu became an official member of the Archie Fan Club after sending in his dollar. They mailed him a cheesy bookmark and a button that was a punched-out piece of cardboard with Archie's face on it, along with a certificate that said something like "Official Member of the Archie Fan Club," with the Archies in the background singing "Sugar, Sugar," according to the caption, and a blank that said, "Fill in your name here."

Blu joined the Olympic Sales Leadership Club from the

last page of the comics to sell Christmas cards. He called the Captain "O" operator and became an Official Salesman. He was trying for the Spalding Tennis Set (he doesn't even play tennis), the Unisonic World Calculator Clock, and the Tasco Roc-Binoc.

Before he was done with his half of the money, Blu bought a Secret Compartment Book, which looks like a fake plastic book on the outside but is a safe on the inside. He couldn't even figure out how to open the safe. And no burglar would think that was a book, it looked so cheesy.

Then he purchased a Sea Horse Family *and* the Amazing Sea Monkeys, which turned out to be the same thing. Ed the Big Head made him do it, he said.

In the comics they were all smiling—Mama Sea Horse (with apron), Poppy Sea Horse (reading the newspaper), Big Bro Sea Horse (sidewards baseball cap), and Li'l Sis Sea Horse (pigtails, blond too).

But these were dried-up miniature sea horses, smaller than the ebi Mama used to cook with; if you put the Amazing Ones in water, they all floated to the top.

Blu says, "I no give a shit what you say, Ivah. I one member of the Archies Fan Club and one member of the Olympic Sales Leadership Club. I belong to something that mean something to me. So there. So shut up."

Now he's spent all of his money. He's under the house with Maisie stirring the dried-up sea horses in a mayonnaise jar with chopsticks. Watching the swirling water.

❀

Spinning out his Datsun truck in the gravel down the hill, Evangeline's Uncle Paulo heads back from the store.

Maisie and Blu look up from the jar of dead sea horses, and I peek out the kitchen window. He has black lace tied to his radio antennae under the orange 76 ball.

"For every virgin he poke," Evangeline told Mitchell, who told me, "like one flag, my Uncle Paulo tie one lace to his car antennae for one week. Or till the next one he scratch and sniff. And no tell nobody before my Uncle Paulo broke your ass." But Mitchell told me.

Evangeline's Uncle Paulo looks like Davy Jones from the Monkees. He knows it. And all the stupidest intermediate girls in low-section classes and the sluttiest high school girls, a new one every week, ride Da Sun, the Datsun truck with the "t" sanded off the tailgate, black lace riding the wind.

❀

The phone rings.

"Yes, yes, yes. I will be there." Poppy talks in perfect English. "I'm very sorry. Yes. Yes."

When he hangs up, he says, "Ivah, you go talk confrence with Maisie's teacha tomorrow. I no can get off work jes like that. Sheez, I lose pay, I take off. Plus I gotta work with Furtado tomorrow night. I neva tell her this, but I send you in my place. You the one look over the kid's work anyways." And then my Poppy looks me in the eye. He's mad at himself for kowtowing: Ve-lee so-lee, ve-lee so-lee, Missy Owens.

"I no can handle haoles. Think they so holier-than-thou with their fast-talking mouth and everybody mo' brown than them is dirt under their feet. All the lunas all haole before on the sugar plantation—they mean sunnava-bitches with bullwhips for hit the kids and all. And they live in the biggest, most nicest house made special for the plantation bosses. Then they made some of the Portagees lunas. The damn Portagees was workers like us, but they was the closest to white."

"Poppy, Mama said not all haoles *haoles* to her," I tell my father softly. He's madder after thinking back to his days in Hilo. "She said some of um like reg-la people. They was born here and no act like they hot. And some, she said, help the sick. She said she knew some real good haoles. Only the real haolified haoles you gotta watch out for."

"Sick"—Poppy pauses—"and dying. Yeah, them haoles your Mama was talking about was damn good haoles."

"Hah? Who was sick?"

"Nobody." He catches himself. "A haole is a haole to me."

Tell me, Poppy, tell me.

"One in a hundred you can trust as one friend. I told you all this before. The rest of um see your Jap face and you be sitting at the worse table in the place. Talk circles around you till you know you the stupidest jerk in the room. Think they so goddamned betta than the rest of us. I ain't talking to Maisie's teacha. You go, Ivah, but be like your Mama. No talk wise, bumbye we get mo' trouble."

I guess Miss Tammy Owens didn't tell Poppy how I swore at her that day in the hall. *Thank you, Jesus.* For that, I know I would've been sent headfirst into the kitchen counter. Why didn't she tell? She's saving it to make the effect greater when she meets with Poppy in person. But *what a shame,* Poppy's not going to be there.

Mrs. Nishimoto says Miss Owens hates it here on Moloka'i. "That's why we have so much in common," she says. "You know, when you're from the Midwest, Hawaii sounds like a paradise. But once you're here, oh for heaven's sake, the heat and the children are just so, so, oh never mind."

The next day after school, I walk with Blu to Maisie's classroom. She's sitting at her desk, so I send Blu in to gather up all of her books, papers, and wet panties into her straw school bag. Maisie wraps her wet panties in drawing paper.

They go to sit on the steps of the kindergarten wing. When I look out the door, Blu turns to look at me. My brother puts his arm around Maisie and she curls into him.

"Will your father be here soon?" Miss Owens asks without even looking at me.

"No. Just me."

"And why is that? Should we reschedule the conference for another day?"

"No need. I mean, no can. My fadda no can come ever 'cause he gotta work. So he wen' send me for take his place. I here to talk with you about Maisie, then I gotta tell him."

"Can we set a few ground rules—what's your name again? It seems to have *slipped* my mind."

"Ivah."

"Ivah, that's right. *Unusual* name. Well, *dear*, we need to speak to each other in standard English for the duration of this conference. I find the pidgin English you children speak to be so limited in its ability to express fully what we need to cover today. Am I clear?" Miss Owens turns her back to me and erases the chalkboard. She mutters something about "the darn lyin' recruiter" and a "lousy teacher's cottage in paradise."

I nod my head.

"Well, first of all, as you probably well know at home, Maisie's rather uncommunicative. Has her hearing ever been tested?"

"She not deaf." Miss Owens gives me a sneering smile for my pidgin. I don't even care.

"Has she ever been tested for Special Ed?"

"She not stupid. She understand everything you say."

"She can't even tell me she wants to use the bathroom. We're talking an accident every day. Nobody wants to sit near Maisie and my room smells like a *janitor's* nightmare." She talks mean. That's how she must talk to my sister.

She catches herself. She *knows* about Poppy's jobs. Miss Tammy Owens and Mrs. Susie Nishimoto are best buddies. You see the two haole teachers all over town and on picnics and at church. That's how Miss Owens knows about us. I should've put two and two together when Mrs. Nishimoto told me to be ready for a parent conference.

"And she's been exposing her vagina and buttocks to the boys in the schoolyard."

"How you know?" She's never there. She's smoking cigarettes and drinking coffee in the Teachers' Lounge.

"Word gets around and I have seen it myself."

Word gets around. Mrs. Nishimoto's exact words. Two rotten haoles. Go home to the Midwest. Who told you to come here?

"Maisie has on a number of occasions been forced to stay in school without underwear because of her constant wetting. It was on those days that Maisie exposed herself to several of the boys in our wing."

Why, why, why didn't you call me from the intermediate campus? Or Blu in the next building? You wanted to humiliate her, that's why. Make the boys fall on the broken sidewalk outside of Room 3 and see my sister, her thighs squeezed together, the wind lifting the gathered skirt of her plaid dress, and take turns around her.

"Well, Ivah? What have you got to say? These are incredibly sociopathic behaviors we're seeing exhibited in a very young child. Do you have a mother?"

How come Mrs. Nishimoto never told her that my Mama died? Or is she playing with my head? "No, Miss Owens."

"No, what?"

"No. Mother. Dead. Just. Us."

"*Oh?*"

"Dead and my sista no talk."

"*Oh.*"

She wanted me to say the word. *Dead.*

"In any case, I'm glad we met to talk things over. I'll be putting in a request for Special Ed testing. Maisie has social, emotional, psychological, and academic problems that need addressing. Thank you for coming, Ivah." Miss Owens gets up and starts shuffling papers on her desk. Then she starts to close the windows. "By the way, Ivah. I've informed the VP of your profane, racial remarks in the hall the other day. He will be calling your father any day now. Am I clear? You will inform your father, won't you?"

I look at Miss Owens, and think: *She's show. All show.*
Acting like she's in control. With fists clenched and teeth
gritted, I nod my head once. Tammy Owens smells
scared, she can smell it herself, so she turns. I stare hard
at her. Red eyes, right inside her.

Read my mind, haole: *I don't care. I answer all the
phone calls anyway. My Poppy's never home. My mother's dead.*

I walk out the door of Room 3 into afternoon sunlight
that might burn the skin right off a freckled haole. Blu
and Maisie scuffle after me. There's dust in the beams of
sunlight that cut across the wooden hallways. It looks
like pixie dust. But it's red dirt from the pineapple fields.
That's all.

❀

Back home, Blu talks to Maisie on the porch and shares
with her, for once, a small bag of David's sunflower
seeds.

"I give me and Ed our own Pep and Bob. All we can
eat and drink. I give me a large bottle of Herbal Essence
all for myself (and sometimes Ed) from Molokai Drug,
the best store for stuff like shampoo. I give me, the number one Olympic Sales Leadership Club member, a Tasco
Roc-Binoc. I give me ironing money, lots of it, to buy four
packages of Days-of-the-Week panties for you, Maisie."

She puts her head in his lap, little Pidge.

"That's twenty-eight clean panties you can take to
school to last a whole month. This all the gifts I would
give myself."

He strokes her hair and spits seeds, one after another.
Then he tells Maisie about the magic bag that never ends.

❀

On *Bewitched*, the magic never ended. There was the first Louise Tate in black and white. Then the second Louise Tate who (poof) became younger so that old fut Larry Tate could have a baby named Jonathan.

There was the first Mrs. Kravits with the buckteeth, also in black and white. Then the second Mrs. Kravits with a face like Elena Gaspar.

Of course, the first Darrin. Dick York. Then the second Darrin. Dick Sargent. Must have been planned, the names, Dick to Dick.

You still got confused. But you got used to it in the end.

Especially if you could pretend that the first Louise Tate, Gladys Kravits, and Darrin Stevens never happened.

Kind of like a haole from Bloomingdale teaching Hawaiian Studies. If you close your ears, you won't hear her mispronounce Kamehameha and Kaunakakai wrong every time she uses it in a sentence.

And a Tammy Owens, another haole forcing Maisie to hold on when the trade winds come: Close your eyes, there's nobody there looking up your dress. You have your underwear on. It's just a little boys' game.

I sit on the porch that evening after my conference with Miss Owens. I close my eyes and imagine that Maisie is not in Special Ed. Blu is a rich Christmas card salesman. Ed the Big Head Endo is my brother's best friend. Elena Gaspar has all of her panties. Poppy ends "Moon River." Mama's in the kitchen steaming mullet.

There are no Human Rats. I *can* be a Mama too.

That evening is the first time I do this. I will remember it for all of time to come:

The night darkens. The smell of pakalana on the vines

s upwind. I leave the porch light on. Ka-san sits with
)utside as I take her tears and rub them in my eyes.
ay inside of Ka-san's red eyes, I see her in there:
мama. In white. Spirit mother in a long dress.

*Send me out. Leave the porch light on. I'll be coming
home.*

I hear these words but they're already inside my head.

Then who do I see? Her long hair and feet that touch
the ground. Do you know that they're good if you see
their feet?

Mama, come back. Mama.

It's only for a moment.

I watch the black dog walk down the dark street and
turn once to look for me. Into the mock-orange hedge
outside the Reyes' house and gone.

In the middle of the night, I hear Ka-san squeeze
through the opening in the screen door. Climb onto our
bed. Snug into our bodies. And sleep. *"Mama."* That's
Maisie. How did she know?

In the morning, all over our street, all over the kindergarten wing, down the main drag of town: black lace
panties, ripped at the crotch, lots of them. Black lace
bras, red bras, beige bras, white bras, purple bras, slips,
girdles, pink satin pillowcases like only haoles use,
teacher high heels ripped and slashed. Leopard-print
panties, red lace panties, peach lace, lavender, zebra
print, and pink baby doll panties, they smell like urine,
they smell like a powdery haole, strewn all over the
streets of Kaunakakai.

6 It's so hot in this town that babies wear diapers only, men go without shirts, windows and doors stay wide open, and people seek out the shade of a mango tree, or a lanai where there's breeze. Inside, ceiling fans whir and standing fans with blue-cool plastic blades collect oily dust in a blue-gray blur.

That's why Mama said steam, don't fry—it's so hot here that when you're standing over a pan of bubbling oil, your sweat rolls off your eyebrow, lands in the hot oil, and wham, it shoots you right in the face. *Teach me how to be a Mama too.* I'm learning the hard way. Never reach for the salt over a pan of frying chicken. Hot oil spat at my underarm for doing that.

I needed to practice cooking chicken for our Thanksgiving dinner, so I took two dollars from my ironing money and went down to Friendly Market to buy a tray of Tyson's drumsticks, which are the cheapest chicken parts.

I know only one way to cook chicken, and that's the way Poppy taught me. Salt and pepper, roll it in flour, and fry. Even the school lunch chicken tastes better than this way of cooking chicken, but never mind. Good practice for Thanksgiving.

"Maisie," Blu says, "Poppy coming home early tonight. Maybe he give you money buy Hartz shampoo for your dog. I no mo' too much money or I would give um to you. We go ask Poppy, then we can bathe Ka-san and Hoppy Creetat too."

"O-kay," Maisie says. The voice sounds light.

"Ivah, you *heard* what Maisie said? She said 'Okay.' Ivah, Ivah, you heard?"

I nod and smile at my sister.

"Good girl, Maisie, you wen' talk," Blu says. "We can make plenny bubbles in the bathtub and scrub-a-dub-dub them, okay?"

Talking because Mama took care of Miss Owens, I know. Miss Tammy Owens, who made the janitor pick up her panties in the kindergarten wing. I let Maisie watch before leading her into her classroom: Miss Owens pretended the panties weren't hers, nervous, standing in her doorway.

"Now say, 'I love you, Blu,'" my brother continues. "C'mon, you can talk, Maisie." She turns away. I take the fried chicken off of the oil-soaked *Parade* section of the Sunday paper and put the drumsticks on a nice plate. All the legs face the same way. I squeeze out all of the water from the boiled won bok and place the cabbage flower in the middle of the drumsticks.

Mama told me that presentation is just as important as eating the real thing. Somehow it tastes even better when it looks good. "Thass half the deal," she said to me. Mama made a slab of tofu look like a dish for the shogun himself with bonito flakes, minced green onions, and grated ginger.

Poppy comes through the door. Hoppy slides in between his legs and Ka-san whimpers happily. He throws down the mail and sits on his dining-room chair, the marbled yellow vinyl one with red electrical tape holding in the cotton. "I got one letter from Aunty Betty. She says this and that, how's the kids, hope you doing okay." Poppy pauses, then looks at all of us. "Look like we going Hilo for Thanksgiving. She wen' give me four airlines ticket."

Aunty must still feel the hands around her neck.

"So I guess we gotta go. I mean, she made reservations and all. She must think we all pitiful or something, what you think, Ivah?"

Poppy rubs his forehead and closes his eyes. "To me," he says after a while, "would be good for spend time with family. I mean, more than just us."

"Ka-san and Hoppy?" I ask. Maisie looks frantic. I feel her panic, and it shortens my breath. I feel it in my neck.

"What you said, Ivah?" Poppy asks. Then he sees Maisie's face, her white lips. "I gotta figga out what we going do with them. They ain't coming with us. We get coupla days for think on this. No panic, eh. Whass this chicken? How we got the chicken?"

"I was practicing for Thanksgiving."

"Oh."

There's a long space of silence.

I sit down at the table. "What we going do, Poppy?"

"I dunno."

Nobody looks at Maisie.

Poppy picks his dirty fingernails.

"Poppy," Blu says all of a sudden like he's figured out a solution, like he knows how to take away Maisie's scared feelings, "I know what I was going tell you."

Maisie looks at Blu with relief all over her face. Poppy too. We all hold our breath for Blu's answer. And then he says, "Maisie and me can have money for buy Hartz shampoo for Ka-san and Hoppy?"

Everybody stares at him, he's so off-the-wall. Off-the-wall. Stupid. Stupid, dumbass, selfish Blu. I look at Maisie. She's stunned. She *thought* he had the *answer*.

"Ka-san and Hoppy," I tell Blu. "She thought you knew what we was going do with them, you stupid jackass. Maisie—"

But it's too late.

Maisie screams, high-pitched and frantic. Porch lights go on and old ladies stick nosy heads out from their screen doors.

❀

The next day after school, I take Maisie and Blu to Molokai Motors to meet Poppy. The lot's full of dark oil stains that eat the asphalt right off the ground. There are no trees and the steps are dusty.

"I would buy this car 'LOW, LOW 1,995.00.' Nice, yeah, this Datsun, Maisie?" Blu says. "Me and you go cruise down East End." He's been trying so hard. "And we go take off the 't' from Datsun and make um Da Sun like Evangeline's Uncle Paulo, okay, Maisie?"

Poppy pulls into the lot, parks the Malibu, and walks over to us. "Okay," Poppy says, "I figga we do this. Maisie, you listen to Poppy. It ain't the end of the world, you hear me? I wen' ask Clarence take back the dog for coupla days. He said easy, no problem, and she should do okay, be with all her old friends and braddas and sistas. See, then Ka-san spend Thanksgiving with her family too.

"The cat. Now thass another story. I dunno what the hell we going do with her. But I figga like this. Cats, they survivors. She kill one bird, last her the whole weekend. Maybe she get her own Thanksgiving dinner too."

"What about the Human Rats, Poppy."

"What you said, Blu? Speak up, boy." Poppy's pissed.

"Ivah," Blu starts, "we cannot let—"

I put my hand over his mouth. "Okay, Poppy, see you at nine. I take care of things." Maisie's got her face in her hands. Sitting on the steps of the Molokai Motors office, crying so hard, there's no sound, only heaving shoulders.

I carry her from the used-car lot. Maisie's getting tall. She wraps her legs around my waist and puts her face on my shoulder. "I got all my ironing money here, Maisie. ✓ And some of Blu's too."

"Huh, what, Ivah?" says Blu.

I carry my sister to Friendly Market. The air-conditioning smells like a meat and produce market and the tiles feel icy on my bare feet. We go to the pet-food aisle.

"Price the twenty-five-pound bags good, Blu."

"Twenty-five pounds? You nuts or what, Ivah? Okay, okay, I get it, twenty-five pounds for the two of them to share, right? What we going get—dog food that the cat like eat or cat food that the dog like eat?"

"A twenty-five-pound bag each."

"Each?! C'mon, Ivah. Our *whole* stash going to Purina pet food. No. No way. Gimme my share back."

I shove him into the bags of Gravy Train. "Stupid, what if the Kuro-chan give the other dogs some of Ka-san's food too? What if we give him just one Tupperware-ful and he give um all to the whole pack of them fuckin' dogs on the first night? Then what, hah? You *know* who our dog is? Neva mine, you too stupid."

"I know." Maisie.

I stare at Maisie for a long time.

"Mama," she says.

"Who?" Blu asks. "Who's our dog?"

But Maisie doesn't answer.

I look way down into my sister's eyes:

I see my Mama in there.

"Who's our dog?" Blu asks again.

Maisie looks at me.

"I know you know."

❀

Now I lay me down, down.
Be with our dog and cat this Thanksgiving.

❀

Maisie puts the rope around Ka-san's neck. Up the gravel driveway to the Kuro-chan's house. "Clarence," Poppy yells. Out of the broken screen door comes the Kuro-chan. "Give um the bag, Ivah."

"Whoa, twenty-five pounds. How long you plan on bein' gone, Bertram?"

"Just couple, three days, Clarence."

"Well, I be sure your dog has a super Thanksgiving."

"Thanks eh, Clarence. Say thank you, Mr. Briggs, you kids."

"Thank you, Mr. Briggs," says Blu like a robot for all of us.

The hungry dogs sniff the bag of Purina dog chow. A brindle-colored male sniffs Ka-san's anus. She growls and turns. She's alert and fed. The glassy-eyed ones back away from her. Ka-san follows us to the end of the drive-way. The other dogs follow her and another black female rubs her face to Ka-san's.

"We be back, no worry," I tell her. We take a few steps. I turn to Maisie. "No worry. No dog fuck with Ka-san. Promise. She eat um alive, I know."

"Okay," says Maisie. And Poppy's so amazed, he lowers the hand that was about to crank my head.

❀

I hoist the bag of Purina cat chow on top of the washing machine. Then I get a kitchen knife, which I grip tightly in my hands, and slice a deep cut into the bag. "Not all in one sitting, okay, Hoppy Cree?" I pour water to the brim of an old Cool Whip container. As I walk down the driveway, I turn around to see the cat on the washing machine, nibbling on cat chow, licking her slashed paws, cleaning her face. Then she looks straight at me.

❀

There's a tile wall, straight back, all the way around Aunty Betty and Uncle Myron's house on Kinoole Street near Ando Store and Andrews Gym. A tile wall the three of us play on when we first get to Hilo.

Poppy's inside with Aunty Betty and Uncle Myron, drinking coffee around the small Formica table in the kitchen. Aunty's making the sekihan for Thanksgiving dinner tonight, the macaroni salad, and lomi salmon. The turkey's in the oven. And ham. I can smell them both.

Aunty Betty brags about our cousin Lila Beth. "She take the SAT and maybe she make National Merit Scholar, you know," Aunty Betty says. "And you know,

Bertram, I think she going be the first one from the Ogata side go mainland college, how you like that? She getting *gooood* grades her senior year and plenny people tell thass when the kids burn out, but not Lila Beth. And she get job too at Lanky's Bakery."

"Nah, for real?" Poppy asks. "How Big Sis doing?" She's our oldest cousin, whose real name is Faith Ann Fukuda.

"She okay. She one mo' year at Hilo College and then she student-teach in the fall. Then law school at UH. I tell you, Myron been one teacha twenty-five years, and we know how hard the life. I mean, we get nice house, but teachas ain't the richest job in the whole world, you know what I mean? But Big Sis, she tell thass what *she* like do. I feel like tell her, then if thass what *you* like do, then *you* pay the tuition. But sheez, thass only Hilo College, know what I mean? I working on her still yet."

Outside, I run to the tile wall. I don't want to hear any more, so I tell Blu that I'll be Olga Korbut and he'll be Cathy Rigby. He gets into this right away and says, "How come you the gold medal winner, hah, Ivah? I like be Olga Korbut." Sheez, we're in Hilo and I don't want to fight in front of Aunty Betty.

"Okay, big brat crybaby. Be Olga, who cares."

"Thanks, you silver medalist."

We dip our feet into the air beneath us, pirouette, balance on the balance beam tile wall, which gets taller as we move toward the back of the lot. We're the same height as the papaya treetops. Turn around and finish the routine all the way to the short end of the wall. Dismount. Two feet together, no bobbles. A 9.8.

"C'mon, Ivah. Again," says Blu.

"Nah, I going in. C'mon, Maisie."

"No, one mo' time, please, please, please."

I don't want him to make a scene and he seems poised to make one in front of Aunty Betty. New audience. Full-blown scene, starring Blu.

"O-kay, shit." I jump on the wall. We go to the tall end and Blu gets really fancy, dipping low and spinning.

He says, "C'mon, Cathy. You the silver medalist, what the heck, you ever like win the gold, or what? I making one betta routine than you."

On the dismount, I start running on the tile wall. Blu's on the ground already, watching me. I figure I'm on the short end of the wall anyway. "Watch this and weep," I yell.

Then I slip.

I remember my face hitting something. The wall? The ground? And blood. I get a cut in the valley part of my upper lip on my first day at Aunty Betty's house. Blu yells, "Poppy, Poppy, come quick."

Out of the house come all of the adults and our cousin Lila Beth Fukuda. Poppy grabs me off the ground, dusts my ass, and cranks it for good measure. That was the most embarrassing thing. "I expect this kinda shit from your bradda, but not you, Ivah. What you trying fo' prove? That you one stupid ass with no brain, hah, Ivah?"

Aunty Betty's grumbling too. "Damn stinkin' kids. First thing you come and you making humbug. Stay off that wall, you hear me, Presley, Maisie? Bertram, they give you hard time or what? She need stitches? Jeez, first thing they come and they making trouble. I can just imagine what must be like at home if this is how they act away from home."

No, you cannot imagine.

Lila Beth laughs from the top of the stairs. She leans on the doorframe licking something off of her fingers. From behind her comes Big Sis, our other cousin. "Stupid Ivah wen' smash her lip," I hear Lila Beth tell Big Sis.

"Shut up, Lila." Big Sis comes down the stairs.

"Take her inside and put one Band-Aid on this, Big Sis," Uncle Myron says.

Big Sis takes me to the bathroom. She says nothing until she finds the Bactine. "They say on TV that this bugga no sting, but every time I put um on my cuts, the bugga burn like hell. Close your nose. Hold your breath." The spray goes all over my mouth.

Lila Beth comes to the bathroom door. "Put Mercurochrome, Big Sis. Burn Ivah's mustache right off her lip. Stupid punk. You in Hilo. No act dumb."

"Eh, fuck off, Lila," sneers Big Sis. "You such one asshole. Why no go play clarinet with your stupid band geek friends."

"Dyke."

"Bitch."

"Butchie."

"Fuck you, slut." Big Sis flips her the bird.

"Fuck me?" Lila acts cute.

"You wish."

"Don't they all?"

"Yeah they all do," Big Sis says with a smile, "but what they don't know is that they all been dipping their sticks in use oil that smell like rotten butterfish."

When Big Sis finishes, I have a huge Band-Aid over my whole upper lip. I walk into the living room and Blu laughs the loudest, then tries to make like he's the most concerned. "So-wa, Ivah? I sorry, okay?"

"See, Ivah," says Aunty Betty. "Presley is so concerned with your well-being. You wasn't on the wall with Ivah, hah, Presley?"

"No, Aunty Betty."

The fat liar.

"I not stupid," he says. " 'Cause if I was stupid like Ivah, I would look stupid like her right now with one Band-Aid mustache."

Everyone laughs, including Poppy, which makes Thanksgiving dinner light and funny. Blu gets laughs at my expense along with all the attention and plenty of white meat.

❀

The next morning, I take off the big Band-Aid for good. The skin above my lip is raw and dark. When I get to the breakfast table, Blu looks up from his plate of Portuguese sausage and rice covered with shoyu. "Eh, Ivah—Hi Hitler." There's a striking resemblance. And for the rest of the morning, "Hi Hitler," with the heels snapping together and the raised arm every time Blu sees me come down the hall, in the kitchen, or at the doorway: "Hi Hitler." My brother wants all the eyes on him.

I may look like Hitler, but Lila Beth's eyebrows are so overplucked she looks like a Japanese doll with penciled-in ridges and tiny red lips.

When I look at her, I remember Mama telling me about the art of eyebrow plucking. That you never pluck from the *top* of the hairline, or else when you raise your eyebrows in surprise or wonder, there'll be meat that goes up where the eyebrow should be, but no hair. That's what Lila Beth looks like: penciled-in eyebrows under the meat line.

But who am I to talk? Now I have a circular Band-Aid over my mustache cut. Big Sis and I drove to Long's to get smaller Band-Aids, and on the way back we ate hot dogs in steamed buns from Itsu's and shave ice. But I didn't feel better; every time I opened my mouth to eat, the scab ripped open again.

Beneath Lila's penciled-in eyebrows is jade eye shadow, and she always reeks of strawberry musk. Everything's visible on her body—her belly button (an outie) because she has on rust hiphuggers, and breasts because she has on a low-cut halter top and a lumber jacket slung over her shoulder. Dr. Scholl's (ivory) on her feet, of course.

"You going out with Marvin tonight?" Uncle Myron asks.

"Yeah, maybe, why?" Lila Beth's so sassy even to her father.

"I thought you guys was pau, liar," says Big Sis from the kitchen.

"Eh, at least I get boyfriends, not like somebody I know acting all high and mighty. Queen of the chicks. Fuckin' butchie."

"Betta butch than slut, how you figga, Dad?"

"Nuff," says Uncle Myron.

"Eh, Bertram," says Aunty Betty, "I told you that Lila Beth was senior class attendant for Hilo High homecoming this year? Yeah, you know. She get her ways, but she make us proud as parents."

"Big deal." Big Sis sits down on the recliner with her legs spread on the arms.

"It *is* a big deal. And Lila Beth going be Queen of the

Winter Ball next month. And you, Big Sis, wouldn't hurt for you be a little more feminine, you know. You so god-damn otemba with that short, short hair, and T-shirt every place you go."

"There your ride," says Uncle Myron. "Come home early, now. We get house guests."

"Yeah, yeah, yeah."

Then Aunty Betty gives it to Lila Beth good. "You betta not use the fifty-dollar gift certificate from Joanne's that Marvin gave you if you broke up with him, you hear me, Lila? And return his TV and Pong game before you broke um and we gotta buy him another one. Why you gotta use um every time? You no even love him.

"And what about this dozen rose? Throw um away already. Shame, you know, you broke up with him and we still get um on our coffee table. And no use the rice pot Marvin gave us—you going break up, thass why. Neva mine thass one Deluxe Sanyo with Warmer Button.

"I seen you in front the house with Marvin in his car last night. How come you no talk to him? Why you press your face to the passenger window? I no blame Big Sis for telling me all this. We *all* was looking, even Uncle Bertram them."

"Eh, no get me involve in this," Poppy says.

Aunty doesn't even hear Poppy.

"Yeah, Ma," says Lila, "Marvin saw all you guys staring at us and he piss off to the max."

"What you talking Marvin seen me looking? I was watching KIKU-TV and side-eyeing through the jalousies. He ask me, I tell Marvin straight I-no-was-looking-what-the-hell-he-talking-about?

"And I seen what you had when you came in the house. Why you took the Mings ring when you know you like break up with him? Give um back, Lila Beth, or you going be one typical low-income-housing girl with no class whatsoeva. Take what you can, when you can. Goddamn Portagee style. And give him back that goddamn rope chain.

"And you," Aunty says to me. "Yeah, you. Stop smirking. Nobody asked you for the two cents you get written all over your face. You just like your madda's side of the family. Hopeless, neva there when you need um most. Not like us Ogatas. We was *there* when Bertram needed us. But not your madda's useless family. Maybe *you* would keep all the stuffs. 'Cause, I swear, you three kids no mo' manners and you rude like hell."

Poppy looks toward the kitchen. He doesn't even back me up. We're all separate nobodies around Aunty Betty.

"But lucky thing Lila Beth like me, yeah, Lila? You just like me. You one good girl who going do whass right, yeah, Lila, 'cause you *just like me*. And I always do whass right."

A big black moth lands on a picture of Aunty Betty on the TV. Nobody moves to kill it.

I know who the dreammaker is.

Aunty Betty gasps. I know she feels her shallow breath in her throat. Someone holding on to her neck, shoving futon kapok in her mouth, and she's screaming but nobody hears.

She knows who the dreammaker is too.

"Get that shit moth outta this house," says Lila Beth.

"No!" It's Maisie.

"Oh, so the deaf-mute can talk," Lila says. "I going, Ma.

Marvin and Roger waiting outside." As she begins to walk out of the living room, the moth flies, flutters around the big light overhead, then lights on Lila Beth's head. She swats like a long-armed gibbon monkey, screaming, "Fuck, fuckin' moth," and runs out of the house. Good for her.

But it flies back to the picture of Aunty Betty. The wings slow in rhythm to my heartbeat. "You know what the Japanese say about those big black moths, eh, Bertram?"

"Yeah, thass the dead."

"You know who that moth, then, right, Bertram?"

"No say nothing bad about Eleanor," Poppy says all of a sudden. "She right here, you hear me, kids?"

Nobody said anything bad about Mama. Only Aunty Betty.

Maisie has faded back into the wall. She hasn't eaten anything except lime Jell-O mold. Her eyes shine like glass.

❀

The Hi Hitler thing got old fast. "Eh. Theodore J. Mooney," Blu says, "pass me some pistachio nuts." He's eaten so many from the crystal dish on the coffee table that the tips of his fingers are stained red. When I don't respond, he says, "Sergeant Schultz, this is Colonel Klink. Pass me some pistachios. Say 'Ya-voldt, Commandant.' " Aunty Betty and Lila Beth laugh so hard, Blu feels a rush of power. I see it in his puffed-out chest. Poppy sighs.

"You act so lame, Presley," says Big Sis. "Why you like make your sista shame in front all us? You just like Lila. Where get one audience, you like be the star."

"Fuck you, Big Sis."

"Fuck yourself, Lila."

"Knock it off, both of you." Aunty Betty puts her hand on Lila Beth's leg, taps her lightly. Big Sis sees this and shakes her head.

"See, Presley. You like you and Ivah come like me and Lila? I don't think so."

Blu swallows hard. Somebody cut his line.

But Big Sis makes up for it quickly. "We go Onekaha-kaha Beach. I take you guys to the smallest, junkest zoo in Hawai'i. Stay right by the beach. You like? We go. I treat you guys plate lunch from Hilo Lunch Shop. The best macaroni salad."

"C'mon, Maisie." I take my sister's hand. "We go, Blu, no need be mad with me." Lila Beth and Aunty Betty can't stand it when we stick together, that's what I think.

"Ho, big spenda, eh, Big Sis. Everybody going have their own plate lunch. Whoa, big time. She musta make big tips last night at Green Onion, yeah, Ma?"

"You know what, Lila—soon as I get my teaching degree, I going take a coupla dollars in tip money, plus that diploma, and shove um all the way up your ass. You so wise—"

"Yeah, two-bit degree from Hilo College. Whoopee-do. I going Washington State or Portland State or Seattle University or Creighton and you going see me shove my mainland degree in your face."

"Good, good, talk is cheap."

"Like the drinks and pupus at Green Onion. They neva ask you put the tassels on your tits yet, Big Sis?"

"Eh, why no take out the fuzz you get stuck between your front teeth and then shut your mouth," Big Sis says. Blu laughs the loudest.

Before Aunty Betty can scold anybody, Big Sis shakes her head and takes all three of us out the door. Through the picture window I see Aunty Betty waving her arms, ranting and raving, probably about Big Sis. Poppy leans back on the recliner staring at the walls. Uncle Myron walks out of the room. Lila nods her head, *I know what you mean, I know what you mean,* watching her mother's face.

❀

"Your fadda always so sad and quiet? I no rememba his face always so down." Big Sis's face is handsome with her short hair, smooth skin, and strong cheekbones. We all squeeze into the front of her truck. "Presley, you cannot be one little shit to Ivah. You no mo' madda. Ivah all you got. What the hell the matter with you, man?"

"I dunno. I said sorry."

"Sorry don't mean shit, 'cause one day you going wake up and you going be talking to Ivah just like how Lila Beth talk to me. You like be all ugly like us? Fuck, man, thass no way to be with your own blood."

Big Sis would be my favorite teacher if I had her for math. "Blu just getting silly, but he normally no act like this, yeah, Maisie?" I ask.

"Yes."

"Eh, you all right, Maisie. I take you see the junkest zoo in Hawai'i, okay?"

She nods.

The zoo's all right for a bunch of peacocks running loose, a goat pen, wild pigs, one coatimundi, and three gibbon monkeys. Lots of loose chickens, iguanas, and land turtles that people have autographed their names on.

When we get to the Onekahakaha Beach, Blu takes off his shirt and runs to the water with the inflatable raft that Big Sis bought for him from Itsu's. His stomach jiggles—layers on layers of cellulite.

"He was always that fat? Shit, Ivah, I no rememba him being so round. Jeez, he can greez the kaukau like one grown man. The last school picture Aunty Ella sent, he was skinny."

I don't want to tell Big Sis that we don't have good food to eat like Aunty Betty's and that Blu's probably making up for lost dinners. I don't want to tell Big Sis about the half loaves of white bread full of mayonnaise and curry powder that Blu eats in front of the TV. Too ashamed to say.

"He came real fat after Mama died," I tell her. "Thass all he did was eat, eat, eat from right after the funeral. We brought all the leftover food from the service home —was all meatless kine stuff, but he ate um all. And he neva stop till now, he still going."

"You gotta cook all the meals?" she asks.

"Yeah." I don't want to go on. I feel it all rising in my throat, what I want to say, I want to say it to Big Sis. It's harder than I can ever explain, holding it all in. No Mama, no Ziplocs. No Mama, no vitamins. No Mama, no Pledge. No Mama, no wonder.

Maisie starts filling in a plastic cup with dirty sand and makes cup after cup of sand molds until she's surrounded by them. She sits in the circle of sand and watches Blu.

"You gotta take care them two? Bathe um, take um school, dress um like that?"

"Yeah."

"Sheez," Big Sis says. "You know what, Ivah. My friend Nancy, her fadda one old Japanee guy had her late in life, the old man, thass one of my best friends too, he tell me, when you get all sad and no mo' no place for put um no mo', you go find you one black cat. Not any old black cat, but *the one*, know what I mean?"

"I know what you mean. My Mama told me the same thing. I got a cat, but she calico."

"Good luck."

"How you know, Big Sis, all this?"

"The one who come to you, Nancy's fadda tell me, thass the one for help you. And you put that black cat on your stomach and the bugga pull all your sadness into herself. I take you down the Hilo Pet Shop after this. We go find your black cat."

"How I going take um home?"

"No worry. We buy one kitten carrier box and you take um on like one carry-on bag. Ivah, everything be okay." Big Sis puts her arm around me and I feel the weight of a huge animal fall off my shoulders.

She'll be a good teacher someday.

❀

I want *the one* to come to me.
The black one who absorbs all sadness.
Starting with Poppy.

❀

The last night in Hilo, we're all lying down on Big Sis's bed. We slept with her the night before and she helped me bathe Maisie. She's got lots of trinkets, cologne, and lotion in small bottles in her drawers and she's giving them all to us, taking turns.

Shalimar—Ivah.

Love's Lemon Scent—Maisie.

Brut—Presley.

Jergens—Ivah.

Avon miniature lipstick—Maisie.

Aramis sampler—Presley.

It's about nine o'clock and we hear Marvin's car peel out of the driveway and Lila run into the house. She comes into Big Sis's room and shuts the door.

"Get outta here, you small scrubs," she says. She just got off work at Lanky's Bakery and still has her pink dress and white apron uniform on.

"They ain't going noplace," Big Sis says.

"I gotta tell you something—" It's then that I see all over Lila Beth's neck: purplish-maroon hickeys tinged with red dots the size of silver dollars, right around her neck. A hickey necklace.

"What the fuck I going do, Big Sis? Ma going kick me outta this house. What I going do?"

"What you was thinking when you did this? With who? Marvin?"

"No, was Roger first. Then when Marvin came pick me up, he seen all this on my neck and the fucka, he wen' pin me down in his car right in the Hilo Shopping Center parking lot and did this." Lila Beth turns her face and all over her cheek, stork marks, suck marks, dark and wide. She lifts the sleeve of her uniform and they're under her arm too. Then she unbuttons the first few buttons of her uniform: all over her breasts. Maisie stares at the wall. Blu cowers behind Big Sis.

"Stupid ass."

"Rememba the hickey contest us had at Lanky's last month? I was still going with Marvin but us lost to Mari Mukai and Dwayne Robello? You know why I lost, right, Big Sis? And I had mine all over my ass and back. You know how hard for make hickeys on the ass, right?"

"No. I don't know."

"Shit, I made um back there, and I mean all the way down, 'cause had hundred dollars in the pool. But I neva like Ma and Daddy see. Shit, Mari won 'cause she had um all around her mouth and all on her tongue, rememba? Dwayne wen' suck so hard, you know the small meat that connect your tongue to the bottom of your mouth? The bugga wen' rip off little bit from Mari's mouth. But nothing—thass how all the girls wen' figga out that you no really need that small meat under your tongue."

"Yeah, so what this got to do with you?"

"Big Sis, I told all that to Marvin last month. When he seen me tonight after what Roger did to me, look what Marvin did." Lila Beth opens her mouth. All over her tongue, swollen, red and purple welts. And when she lifts it up, the small meat under her tongue is torn. There isn't any blood. "What I going do, Big Sis?"

I want to smile but I don't; my scab might rip open. "What the fuck you smiling about, Ivah?" Lila snarls at me. I wasn't smiling. "Take the fuckin' bandage off your cut, bitch."

"So you can cover *yours*," Big Sis says. "I don't think so. Too late. And too much."

❀

Uncle Myron loads our bags into the car. "Next time, me and you go drink with Big Sis down the Green Onion, you hear me, Bertram?"

Poppy nods and smiles. "Thanks for everything, Myron."

"Look for your black cat, okay, Ivah?" Big Sis holds me. "And you, be nice to your sista, you hear me, Presley? You guys is blood." She punches both his arms and then hugs his head. "And you," she tells Maisie, "talk."

Maisie hugs Big Sis.

Inside, Aunty Betty is furious, arms flailing and smacking Lila Beth across the head and face, over and over. "You look like you get one disease all over your goddamn body. You make me sick. Your body full of disease."

You just like me.

You just like me.

Poppy pulls his scarred hands deep into his lap. He says to Uncle Myron, "Must be Lila Beth's red welts make Betty rememba the shame I brought our family—"

"Stop, Bertram," Uncle Myron says. "Thass all in the past. Thass why nobody talk about *that*, eva. 'Cause it's all pau and we all moving forward, you hear me?"

Scars I know nothing about.

7 We pretend that Aunty Betty never happened.

It's just us again. Like it always was. At home in the house in Kaunakakai. Nobody says anything about Hilo —except once in a while Blu, who talks about the good food. But nobody talks back, so he shuts his mouth.

Right after Thanksgiving, the Portuguese in our neighborhood, the Oliveiras, the Pachecos, the Souzas, and the Barbozas, bring out their plastic lighted candles, snowmen, Santa Clauses, and lighted reindeer pulling jolly Santas in sleighs that straddle rooftops.

Rudolph's nose blinks on and off and outdoor Christmas lights hang all around the house and the garage, lights that don't come off until Easter of the following year. Baby Jesus sleeps in a flashing manger, Mother Mary looks on in neon blue, and wise men glow in yellow light. It's a Christmas competition, in which the family ✓ with the most decorated yard wins.

This year, the Souzas add huge golden garlands around their plumeria and puakenikeni trees. The Pachecos hang a humongous blinking star over their Jesus scene, stringing the electric line low over the manger. Mary Oliveira hand-paints the Seven Dwarfs on giant wood cutouts and makes a North Pole Toy Shop scene with colorful floodlights on the dwarfs' faces. And the Barbozas buy a Snoring Santa and Snoring Mrs. Santa from the Lillian Vernon catalogue and put them on a wooden platform right next to their wrought-iron gate. Coils and coils of orange extension cords.

All of this for the lines of people who walk by with baby carriages and children and stand in front of the yards. Crowds of people ooohhing and aaahhing night after night. I take Maisie and Blu this year as soon as the Barbozas and the Souzas display their yard ornaments.

At the Barbozas', Blu reaches his hand over the gate to touch the velvety sleeping Santa. Then Mrs. Irene Barboza screams from the garage, where the whole clan drinks beer and waits for compliments: "Zha-zoughz, you keed, yeah, you, you little Japanee. Keep your han's off the merchandise. Ai-kooreesh, the way these keeds ack, you tink they dunno we spent thousands of dollas for all this in our yard. Look, but no touch."

And that's how we spent this first Christmas without my Mama. Looking, but not touching.

Poppy never brought a tree home. No time, he says, to go up to Halawa and cut one down. "We no mo' one tree stand anyway," he says. "I dunno where your madda wen' pack um."

"We can put the tree in one coffee can with rocks," I tell Poppy. "Even a small one would be okay."

"Yeah, right. And then what. The bugga going tip and we be stuck with scrubbing rusty water off the rug for the next two months."

Looking, but not touching.

The presents we wouldn't be getting. "No expect nothing from Poppy, you hear me, Maisie and Blu? He not going take your whining for this and that."

"So how we going get presents this year?" Blu asks me. "And no try trick me that Santa going bring me something. No mo' such thing as Santa. You ain't fooling me. I not writing letters to the North Pole." He pouts for a long time.

"No?" Maisie asks. She hadn't talked for a long time and she said the word with such sadness.

"See, you mento ass Blu. See what you did?" I yell at my brother, who snubs me. "Get Santa only for good kine kids like you, Maisie, and the rotten ass ones like Blu, no sense they believe in Santa anyways, 'cause they ain't getting shit outta his sleigh."

"I going make sure I get presents, man," Blu says. "I going buy me some stuff down Misaki's and I going wrap um myself and put on the tag 'To Blu, From Blu.' I ain't going suffa. Maybe I buy something for you too, Maisie. Yeah, I buying presents for me and Maisie. I no care. And I not putting on the tag 'To Maisie, From Santa.' I taking all the credit."

"Just wait, Blu. I figga something out."

He doesn't believe me. I see it in his sad eyes. Mad eyes. Can't get a thing from nothing.

Look but don't touch.

No Christmas dinner can compare with the ones Mama planned and cooked. "Make the Cool Whip, cream cheese, and can blueberry on shortbread crust," Blu says.

"I dunno how for make um."

"The sweet potato stuffing in one small turkey, Ivah, thass easy."

"I dunno how."

"Sekihan with plenny azuki beans, sprinkle um with roasted sesame seeds and salt," Blu says.

"Dunno how."

There won't be enough money anyway. Not a thing. Looking and wanting.

"Look, Poppy ain't getting us one tree," I finally tell Maisie and Blu. "We gotta get out the aluminum one that Mama bought us from the dead deacon garage sale for the Christmas she made every July. You rememba, Maisie?"

Maisie nods yes.

"The one with the missing branches?" Blu screams. "I no like that ugly tree, Ivah." He's even stomping his feet for emphasis.

"You no like that ugly tree? Then you no mo' nothing. We all no mo' nothing. You go hang out by the Barbozas' and wait for them throw you some scraps from the garage."

Blu runs down the dark hall. I make mayonnaise bread with paprika for Maisie, and she sits on my lap as we watch TV when Poppy comes in the door. He sits down heavily. "Eh, Maisie, Ivah took you see the Barbozas' and the Souzas' yard?" Poppy takes off his dirty work shoes. "The Oliveiras' one coming up too. You seen um, Maisie? Ho the nice, you know."

She nods yes slowly and swallows a big wad of bread.

"Just like Christmas already, yeah?" my Poppy says, closing his eyes and leaning back in his chair. "Feels just like another Christmas."

❁

It was Christmas in July when Mama died. She put up the aluminum tree before she went into the hospital. And by the time we took it down, its branches were filled with red dust from the pineapple fields.

To buy us Christmas gifts, she took extra jobs cleaning houses or ironing, worked as a substitute salesclerk at Imamura's or Misaki's in town, and took in sewing for the schoolteachers.

All of this and her regular job at the Airport Snack Bar selling hot dogs, candy bars, and loaves of Kanemistu bread for visitors who forgot to buy omiyage while in Kaunakakai town.

Last Christmas, Maisie got a Baby Tender Love who, never mind that she had white-blond hair and could never be Maisie's real baby in a million years, had the softest baby arms and legs you ever felt on a doll.

That and a big Mrs. Beasley from *Family Affair*, a doll just like the one Buffy carried around the house while Jody and Mr. French talked about a walk in Central Park. You could take off Mrs. Beasley's glasses and put them on Baby Tender Love too. Mama sewed two miniature quilts for Maisie's babies from scraps of cloth.

The last real Christmas, she gave Blu two of the best ✓ presents he ever got in his life. She always knew what to buy that would last a long time. Nothing he'd put away in an hour and then watch TV. She bought him a Mouse Trap game, which was a gigantic booby trap with a ball bearing, trapdoors, chutes, and a cage that came sliding down a pole at the end of the line to catch the mouse. We played this for weeks.

That and an Easy Bake Oven. Blu made cake after cake until he used up all the mixes, so Mama bought him a roll of Pillsbury frozen cookie dough. And if you had an Easy Bake Oven, only then would you know how long it takes to bake a single cake with the 100-watt lightbulb for heat.

Hours and hours of Blu and Maisie waiting for their cakes and dough to bake, poking toothpicks in the center of the tiny cake pans just like Mama told them to do. Then finishing the cakes in one bite each. This was her present to Blu.

But Christmas was never happy for me, and Mama knew this.

My birthday was December 27, and every year, we were so broke from Christmas that I barely got a cake two days later for my birthday. I figured it was *the worst* time of year to have a birthday.

So Mama always gave me three presents on Christmas morning. Two presents from her and Poppy. And one for my birthday. The last Christmas with Mama, I got Dutch clogs with apples stitched in the leather. Muslin smocks she sewed with apple appliqués on the pocket. And a golden bracelet, thin gold, an apple with a bite taken out of it for the clasp, and the words "I Love You."

Mama said, "I mean it. Though we never say it in this family," as she put the bracelet around my wrist. "Happy Birthday, Kini." And I believe her, what she said about love. We just never say it in this family.

❀

The day before the intermediate school's Christmas dance, "Walkin' in a Winter Wonderland," I start feeling sick. It happens in school during PE first. I feel like I might have diarrhea, so I run into the locker room and sit for a long time on the toilet, pushing and pushing, cold sweat and sore stomach.

It goes away, but after school, Maisie, Blu, and I walk by the gym and I feel the cold sweat coming again, the pain in my stomach, and I can't wait to get home. "Go in the gym," Blu says, "go, Ivah. Hurry up," as I run into the bathroom and sit on the toilet, push hard, but nothing comes out. There are brown stains on my panties.

This goes on through dinner. My pale face, white lips, and more brown spots. "You feeling all right, Ivah?" Poppy asks.

I wonder why my anus leaks diarrhea when it never leaked before. "Maybe you betta not go school tomorrow. Only half day anyway."

And then I know.

"Go sleep early. You feel betta in the morning," Poppy tells me.

Right before I sleep.

How alone I feel.

No Mama for me.

Nobody to help me with this blood.

Blood.

Nothing in the house.

I go into the kitchen after everyone's gone to sleep and take out the stack of napkins I've been saving from Dairy Queen to make a pad like the pads they showed us in "Time of Your Life," grade four.

I check again. There's nothing under the bathroom sink. Mama left me without a clue: how do you stop the bleeding?

❀

"Ivah, you feel betta, right, Ivah?" Blu says at the kitchen table the next morning. "You guys get one dance today, yeah? Ho, I dunno why the elementary school wasn't invited too. Not fair. Next year I going join Student

Gov and protest how come we no mo' dances too. We only get junk kine homeroom parties and the principal said no can join classes for make one real big party."

"You do that, Blu." I wasn't even listening. The bleeding's heavier today. But I want to go to the dance. Mitchell Oliveira might slow-dance with me if Evangeline Reyes stays home from school. It's a double dream for me. But I don't care.

I stayed up all night thinking about my rags: Why me? Paper napkins from the Dairy Queen only go so far. Toilet paper too. I need to buy Kotex or Modess, but I can't. I'm too embarrassed. Everybody might see. Go to the store three minutes to closing. Go to the store right when it opens. I cannot do it. Go to the store for one box of pads? No, buy other groceries and hide the box underneath a twenty-five-pound bag of dog food, a bag of rice, leafy vegetables, and a family-size bag of OreIda Crinkle Cut Fries.

I feel dirty. There's lots of blood. I walk with my legs pulled in tight. I might leak on my panties. What if it runs down my leg? Mama: Help me.

✿

I figure it's only a half day. If I take another wad of paper napkins, I can flush the used one down the toilet at recess and use the new napkins until the bell rings. Then I can go to the dance.

Intermediate dances are in the cafeteria. The "Walkin' in a Winter Wonderland" committee shuts all the wooden jalousies and puts black bulletin board paper over the windows above the doors. So it gets hotter and hotter inside. The teachers don't let us out to drink water or use the bathroom because we might smoke cigarettes. The lights start spinning and all of a sudden it smells like toe jams, sweat, wet PE clothes, and sour cafeteria milk cartons.

The girls sit on one side and the boys on the other side. I dance mostly with the short Japanese boys like Earl Nishi, Eugene Endo, who is Ed the Big Head Endo's brother, and Kerwin Yamada, who are pretty much the only Japanese in intermediate.

I'm waiting for Mitchell, who's been my friend ever since he moved here from El Segundo. Teaching him to not even *attempt* talking pidgin with his haole accent to *anybody ever* should be reason enough for him to ask me for one dance. I saved his haole ass, for heaven's sake.

And then he walks over. It's a slow dance.

Things like this happen only on TV or in a dream.

"Ivah, would you like to dance?" he says as he reaches out his hand. He's the only one who speaks English when asking the girls to dance. Most of the other boys head-jerk the girls and grunt.

The shiny mirrored ball spins.

And I reach out my hand.

As Evangeline Reyes screams, "Ai-sooos, I smell somebody's rags. Somebody on this side get their rags, I can smell um." All the girls scream and laugh. The boys scatter. Mitchell lets go of my hand. Evangeline starts sniffing around and all the girls start crab-skittering away. Even me.

Until she stops.

And screams, "Oooohhh, thass you the one, Ivah. No lie. You get your rags, shit, I could smell um."

I don't know what to do. Run. Hide.

She says, "You!" one more time.

I say, "Not me."

She says, "No lie," and sniffs near me. She can't smell shit, she's such a liar. She just didn't want me to dance with Mitchell. No, maybe she *can* smell the blood on the paper napkins. I don't know.

I get up and shove her face away. "You fuckin' cat killa, Evangeline. You wen' kill my cats, eh?" I don't know where that comes from. Where inside me? I save myself from her sniffing.

"I neva kill your fuckin' cats."

"Liar, you did. You wen' hang my cats."

The whole intermediate school gathers around. They gasp on hearing about the hanging. We start pushing and shoving, but the VP and the shop teacher break in and pull our yelling faces away from each other.

"Cat killa," I yell.

"Rags," she yells back. This word shuts me up.

❀

Blu had a good idea for Christmas.

"Darcy Malama told me that his family do this 'cause get too many cousins and sistas and braddas and nephews and nieces—they pull one name each from one hat at Thanksgiving and you gotta buy Christmas present for only that person."

"We go buy Mama and Poppy one present each," I tell him.

"We get the ironing money and split um five ways," Blu says. "Thass pretty fair."

"And we buy Mama and Poppy's one together but the

one we buy for each other is one secret till Christmas morning," I tell them.

Maisie's excited. And I'm glad, now that she's wondering whether there's a Santa or not.

I write our names on small pieces of paper and put them in a small margarine container.

Maisie gets Blu.

Blu gets me.

I get Maisie.

On the day we decide to walk to town to Christmas-shop, I remember the air feeling cool as if it really was Christmas. We start at Molokai Drugs for Mama and Poppy. There's not much choice on our island. Most of the rich girls go to Honolulu for a day to shop. But after walking aisle after aisle, we finally decide on two statues.

One says "BEST MOTHER IN THE WORLD . . . WE LOVE YOU," with a lady with red hair, an apron, and a loaf of bread in her hands. The other one says "BEST FATHER IN THE WORLD . . . WE LOVE YOU," with a bald-headed man with a pipe and glasses, a suit with a vest, reading a newspaper.

"Poppy going be happy if thass what we think of him," Blu says. Maisie votes with Blu and that's that. I thought it was a cheesy present but Blu says, "Two to one, you lose, Ivah."

The statues are dusty. They've been sitting on the drug-store shelf for *years*.

Then we split up to buy each other's presents. "Meet back here in one hour," I tell them. "Maisie, you stay on this side of the street only, okay?" We all go our separate ways. I watch Maisie and Blu run down the street as I cross to Imamura's. And in an hour, we meet back at the drugstore.

Once home, I dust each branch of the aluminum tree. Turn the bald spots against the wall and we put our presents under the tree. It feels like Christmas. It really does. The next morning, Poppy gets up before us. Poppy and Blu. Sleepy-eyed, Maisie and I walk into the kitchen. "Merry Christmas," Blu says. "Happy Birthday, Ivah. Poppy and me made French toast and hash brown plus hot cocoa for our Christmas breakfast. And scramble eggs thanks to the hen."

Blu puts one candle in a piece of French toast and lights it. I don't know where he found the candle. And my family sings Happy Birthday to me.

"Sorry I neva buy you guys nothing for Christmas," Poppy says. "This breakfast is it. But I see you guys wen' take care of each other. Finish your breakfast, and then we open your presents." Poppy looks at me like I pulled it all together, but I shake my head. It wasn't just me.

We all sit around the aluminum tree.

"O-kay, who's first?" Poppy asks.

"You and Mama," Blu says.

Poppy slowly opens both presents. The dusty statues who in a million years would never look like our Mama and Poppy. But his eyes stay on the words at the bottom. "She was the best," my Poppy says. "Thanks, you kids. Go put this on the TV, Blu." Poppy opens his statue. He looks at it and smiles. He rubs the words "BEST FATHER IN THE WORLD . . . WE LOVE YOU" with his thumb. "Thanks. Who next?"

"Youngest to oldest," Blu says again. "Okay, Maisie's

turn." Blu reaches under the tree. "Here get one 'To Maisie, From Ivah.'"

Maisie pulls the wrapping off of the present. She's holding out as long as she can. "What you get, what you get?" Blu says. And Maisie pulls the package out of the tissue paper. "Panties," Blu says, excited. "Wow, nice kine, Maisie. Thass bikini kine. Oh, wow." Maisie smiles.

"Try wait, try wait," Blu says. "Get one more present for you, Maisie. This one says 'To Maisie, From—'" and my brother pauses. Maisie's eyes get wide, her face happy, she wants to say: Hurry up, hurry up. "To Maisie, From Santa?" Blu says. "Maisie, you got one present from *Santa* when you was sleeping last night. See, I was wrong," Blu says. He's only trying to make up for being such a punk before—but my sister believes him. I know she does. "See, Maisie? Get such thing as one Santa. He brought you something."

She opens her present and holds up Goody ribbons and barrettes and a deck of the good Old Maid cards and Crazy Eights. She's so happy, she puts her presents in her lap and waits for the next one to be opened.

"Blu's turn," I say. "Here, 'To Blu, From Maisie.'" It's a huge box covered with Christmas wrapping, which Blu tears open like an animal. Under the wrapping is a Kraft macaroni and cheese shipping box all taped up. So Blu busts that open.

Inside the box, he pulls out one by one: a small bottle of Herbal Essence shampoo, a can of Pepsi, and a package of barbecue chips. Then Blu pulls bar after bar of chocolate candy. "Wow, Maisie, thanks," he says. And he really means it.

Blu passes me my gift from him. It's huge. And across the top, Blu writes, "OPEN IN PRIVATE. ONLY IVAH CAN SEE." He writes this with a thick marsh pen. There's an envelope taped to the present. It says, "Secret Present for Ivah, From Blu. Open letter FIRST."

"Go, Ivah. Go inside the bedroom and shut the door," Blu says.

"Why?" asks Poppy. "Open um here, Ivah."

"Yeah, why?" I ask my brother.

"No, 'cause I said no!" Blu screams.

"Okay, okay," I tell him. "This betta be good, sheez."

I go inside the bedroom and throw the present on the bed after ripping the envelope off of it. The folder paper says:

Dear Ivah,

Merry Christmas and Happy Birthday. You might think I bought you the worst present ever in the whole wide world. But I really had think about it for long time. Ed (also known as Bob) or Ed the Big Head Endo as you call him told me that his brother Eugene (your classmate) said that you had your rags. Which I didn't know what that was, so Ed told me all about it. He said that when his sister Elsa had her rags or periods as Ed call it, she use to come sad and cry and punch her vagina 'cause she was shame. So Ed mother Mrs. Edwina Endo had talk to Elsa about birds and bees and periods and go buy the pads and sanaterry belt for Elsa so that she no be shame no more and buy it herself. So when I check under the bathroom sink, I saw that if Eugene was right and you had your rags then you had no pads and you probly was like Elsa which was shame! And since us got no mommy to go buy it, I went to Friendly Market and look for sana-terry belt and pads. (Isle 4 near the Charmin and MD.) I not shame and I no care 'cause you got no mommy to tell you about birds and bees. So here my Christmas present (Kotex) and birthday present (Modess) to you. Only had two kinds so wasn't that hard. And I will buy for you again if you want me to.

Your brother,

Presley Vernon "BLU" Ogata

I sit on the bed. I remember a golden bracelet, thin gold, an apple with a bite taken out of it for the clasp, and the words "I Love You," and I take it out from the box of treasures under the bed. I remember Mama said, "I mean it. Though we never say it in this family," as she put the bracelet around my wrist last Christmas. And I still believe her, what she said about love. We just never say it in this family.

8 *Bla' Futha' ?* These days, he's fast with his hands: "You goddamn kid." Blu gets slapped across the head. "Stop hitting your sista with those meaty hands before I broke your fingas one by one." Poppy sighs deeply, but he doesn't stop. "I sick and tired of hearing you pickin' on Maisie, fighting, fighting, fighting, and I swear, Blu, one of these days, you going make me lose it." He puts his face in his hands.

Meaty hands. When Blu slaps Maisie or me, it feels like a piece of hard rubber whacking your thigh. Meaty hands that always aim for the thighs. Like rubber on rubber, and the sting echoes on your leg forever. Blu's meaty hands.

"Teach your damn bradda to keep his hands to himself, Ivah," says Poppy, frustrated. "Or I going teach him myself." All the time, now, Poppy takes everything one step further. " 'Cause you going see him get slam on the wall, if you no start your lessons fast. I not home to take care things like this. Why you no can step in and help out, shit? You cannot even teach your goddamn bradda some basic kindness."

It's not fair. Poppy isn't around to see Blu carrying Maisie's bag in the morning and later home from school.

Poppy doesn't see Blu walking with his head up high

to the Special Ed building to take Maisie to her new class every morning.

Doesn't see Blu waving at her in the cafeteria.

Doesn't see Blu waiting there after school and all of his stupid classmates calling him the brother of the mental girl.

Doesn't see Blu spending his ironing money on Maisie for Violet Crumbles at Pascua Store.

Doesn't see.

Doesn't see.

He sees us differently ever since we went to Aunty Betty's in Hilo, two months ago. It's Aunty Betty in him. It's Aunty Betty in all of us. Even Blu.

"So you get meaty hands, eh, Blu? Wait till you feel my meaty hands upside your head." Poppy stares at the TV, tired eyes, but I swear, he's not watching it at all.

❀

Poppy stares hard at me. I catch him all the time. "What, what you like, hah, Ivah? I owe you money? Then what you looking at me for, hah?" I wasn't looking at *him*. He was looking at *me*. He went from sad to mad. I mean really mad. Every day. All day. Some days, nothing I do is right.

Black cats cure sadness; we're too late.

"Poppy, wanna read something real nice?"

"No, not really, why? Not unless I gotta. Why?"

"Neva mine."

Maisie has a real nice Special Ed teacher, Miss Sandra Ito. Short and cute and young. Maisie writes all kinds of letters to Miss Ito. Some days, there's only Maisie and Henry Kama in Miss Ito's kindergarten Special Ed class. And Maisie doesn't wet her panties anymore.

This is what I wanted Poppy to read:
"Dear Maisie,
Who do you love?
Yours truly,
Miss Ito"

✿

DeaR MiSS iTo,
DaDDY THe BeST
IVaH CooK
BLue SHaRe
MY Ka-SaN aND HoPPY
MaMa STiLL HeRe
YouRS TRuLY,
MaiSie o.

✿

Then Blu reads it and writes in Maisie's black marble composition tablet:

✿

Dear Maisie,
I share with you *everyday* and *anyday*. Violet Crumbles the BEST candy. Now can you talk alot more?
Your best brother,
Blu Presley Vernon Ogata

✿

But over and over, Poppy picks on Blu. Is this a father-and-son thing? I don't say anything or Poppy might turn his mad eyes at me for cooking cream of mushroom on rice for the third day in a row.

We get a free lunch now with the tin-type tokens handed out by the teacher in the morning. Most of the Japanese and Pakes don't get tokens. Most of the Portuguese, Hawaiians, and Filipinos do. I'm the only Japanese who gets a free lunch token, but I don't care. It's the best meal of the day for all of us. Poor Poppy, he has one meal. And that's the one I cook every night.

"Blu," Poppy starts at dinner, "what I said about eating so damn much? You get stink ear or what? I no like you be one fat shit, you hear me, Blu? You no shame or what?"

Poppy hesitates, as if he wants to stop himself from being so mean. But he's in this far, and he can't back down. "Try look around this table—nobody one fat shit here, eh? Damn deaf ear, you listening? Ivah, from now on, you serve Blu one serving only, and if this bugga still gain weight, then I know he making stink ear, no listen, and I going haf to make things clear to him with one guava branch."

"Poppy, I think—I think that—"

"Ivah, you no Poppy-I-think-that me, you hear? Or you get deaf ear too? And you," he snaps at Maisie, "you eat everything on your plate or we going start giving your food to the damn dogs—get plenny Pake children starving in China, but this food ain't even fit for them. I going give um to the starving dogs in Kaunakakai. Get plenny of them at Clarence house. You better listen to me, I telling you now, Maisie. And you too, you stink ear."

Poor Blu, eating away all the sadness until he's so full that he feels numb and sleepy. Plate after plate of hot rice—it's what there's plenty of at dinnertime. Eating all his school lunch and wanting more. Warm food and chocolate bars until his stomach hurts and his eyes glaze over. Just so he doesn't feel Mama gone so far away.

❦

It's hard to walk away from the money. I hate ironing for Mrs. Nishimoto, but Blu, Maisie, and I need the steady cash. Now Mrs. Nishimoto lets Maisie come into her house. Ever since Maisie was sent to Special Ed, she's been prying right into our life with questions that she asks Maisie and Blu.

"So how's your *new* class, Maisie? Do you like your teacher? How's Miss Ito treating you?" I usually grab the money, gather Maisie's small toys, and rush out the door. Mrs. Nishimoto's still rapid-firing the questions as Blu wraps Maisie in his arm behind me. And we never give her an answer. "Thank you, Mrs. Nishimoto. Bye. See you next Wednesday."

She wants to know about Miss Ito so badly. It's because Miss Ito is young and has all the young male teachers on the island over at her teacher's cottage. Miss Owens shares the cottage with Miss Ito and that's how Mrs. Nishimoto knows all the so-called bad stuff, like the fact that Miss Ito's a Buddhist and drinks a screwdriver after work.

But talk about the *miracles* she works on her kids, some teachers say, and how she *loves* them so much, the parents at church say. She has her students to her house to sleep over and some of them don't want to go home. So old bucks like Mrs. Nishimoto get red ants up their ass.

Pretty soon, on Wednesdays, Mrs. Nishimoto asks if I'd like to babysit her middle boy, Jonathan, age five. Wednesdays are short school days at Kaunakakai School and the teachers normally have meetings. We get an extra two dollars for watching Jonathan. Their oldest, Christopher, goes to baseball practice. Michael and Richard are in preschool, and the two babies stay at the sitter's.

Maisie used to be in Jonathan's class. When we babysit Jonathan, I make Blu rush to pick up Maisie first at the Special Ed building, then we walk over to the kindergarten wing to get Jonathan. Miss Owens doesn't even look up when she sees me come into the room. Sometimes she's caught off guard, so she puts her hands on her hips and stares at me and head-jerks Jonathan out of the room. I just stare right back. Then her eyes look scared for a moment, so she shuffles papers on her desk.

What the hell, I know what color panties she wears, like everyone else in this whole town. Miss Owens watching the janitor pick up her panties outside the kindergarten wing and taking from him the ones with *Tammy* stitched in gold.

❀

While we're eating dinner, Poppy says, "Ivah, you seen wana growing from Blu's underarm yet? I hope you wen' explain to him why and how he going get wana way before he sprout some fuzz and he get all confuse, shit. On top of everything else, I going get one fat shit son who dunno why he getting sea urchin growing on his underarms."

I can't take another bite. I look my father straight in the eye and he looks right back. I'm scared, but I say, "Why you gotta make things so hard, Poppy? You neva was. You neva use to. You neva use to make so mean to us. Poppy, you gotta—"

"I gotta stop pickin' on you, Blu." For a moment, I think he means it; I want to believe what he tells my brother.

"Yeah, Poppy," I say.

But then it seems like he can't back down. He's in this

too far. "Yeah, Poppy, yeah, Poppy. Gimme this, gimme that. Buy me this, buy me that."

My father doesn't get it. The effect of his words on Blu, as if he has Aunty Betty under his skin.

❀

Dear Ivah,

My friend Nancy's father died.

He used to show me this gray cat he had. And that cat would be scratching his arms all over. I never know why he love that cat. Every time used to run away when he try for hug um. When the cat ma-ke, Nancy beg and beg the father for get um checked by the vet.

But he said no sense 'cause the cat dead. But Nancy keep begging. So he took um to the vet in a shoebox. Then the vet said, "Your cat is dead." Then he told Nancy, "You goddamn wahine, cost me $45.00 for the vet tell us the cat dead. I coulda told you for free." The cat never even had a name. All his cats, and he had plenny always making babies under the house, *not one had name.* But he love them all.

He went sleep. And he never woke up. Was over. Just like that.

Ivah, I sorry I had to tell you all this. But way deep down, I knew you would understand. That day on the beach, I didn't have the words that I wanted to say. Now 'cause of this, I maybe don't need words the next time I see you. You know what I miss most of all? And I will miss him *forever* for this. His *kindness* to me. That's all. *Kindness.*

Love,

Big Sis

I keep Big Sis's letters in a shoebox under my bed with my own precious stuff like Scout Finch in the movie *To Kill a Mockingbird*. When I take the box out from under the bed and hold the letters that smell like her cologne, the malachite stones she gave me, pink quartz, her Avon eye shadow and small lipsticks, Shalimar, a Snoopy charm, a small gold tennis racquet, a pearl in black sponge in a small plastic container, Maisie's baby teeth, Mama's reading glasses—I can hear the music that's whistled at the beginning of *To Kill a Mockingbird* when the camera shows you Scout's spelling bee medals, a rock, chewing gum, and a broken watch. A little girl humming. Crayons and letters.

"Somebody in this house get itchy fingas. Who took the two dollas that was under the telephone? Shit, one of you three betta own up fast. You, Ivah, you the itchy fingas?" Poppy's so mad, I see his nostrils flaring.

"No, Poppy, I got my own money from ironing."

"You, Blu. Shit, if you the one hawk my money with your itchy ass-scratching fingas, yours I going broke one by one, then hang you by your balls till you turn purple, Blu."

"Uh-uh, Poppy, not me. I got my own money too. I no steal, Poppy."

"Yeah, right. Maisie, you taking Poppy's money?"

Nod no and so scared.

"And one of you jackasses been snooping around in Mama's drawer. I no like you looking in there and reading anything or touching nothing or taking something that not yours, you hear me, you damn itchy fingas for rotten kids? Leave your Mama's stuff alone. We get all kine personal stuff in there that I no like *nobody* eva see, neva again, and if I eva lose um, and I gotta go back down—" Poppy stops and looks scared too. "And if I catch the one who steal and no can own up," he says, soft but mad, "I going squeeze your neck to kingdom come."

❀

Blu sings his rhymes to Maisie under the house. She draws faces in the fine dust with a stick. Sweat rivers etched in red dust run down their faces.

"Blu is my name, itchy fingers is my fame. I stole some-thing from Poppy. But I dunno know who touching Ma-ma's drawer. No tell, Maisie. Big secret. No say not one word, swear to God the Father, the Son, and the Holy Ghost. Ssshhhhh.

"Blu is my name, and meaty hands is my fame. If I use my meaty hands on you, he going slam my head into kingdom come. Where kingdom come?"

Maisie giggles.

"Blu is my name, wana underarms is not my fame. I figured this out, but sure took me long time. When people (mostly man) have bushy underarms, look like the purple sea urchin stuck to your underarm. Wana underarms, get it, Maisie?"

She nods.

"Blu is my name, stink ear, doo-doo ear, and deaf ear is my fame. I get too much wax. I can grow carrots and taro in here. Remember Mama use to say that before she take the Q-tip and clean out my wax? I get wet wax like Poppy. You and Ivah get dry kind wax like Mama. You get the matchstick or bobby pin. Me and Poppy get Q-tip."

Drifting, drifting, both of them in some strange tide.

"So the moral of the story, Pidge: If Ivah tell, come here, Blu, I going clean your ear, be kind and go, even if she wrapping pieces of cotton ball around the match. Better than growing carrots and taro in your deaf ear, whatchu think?"

"Kind," she says, and he holds her tight.

❀

The sky is black, the days in February short and cold. Some days, there's obake rain, when the sun and the rain come together; look for the fox wedding across the rainbow, Mama told me that. No foxes in Kaunakakai, only mongoose.

Maisie wears my old white sweater, so old, there are fuzzballs on the elbows and the cuffs; the pearly buttons hang limply, facing different directions. I wear Mama's sweaters. Big Sis writes that the Japanese claim wearing the clothes of the dead brings good luck. Nancy's father taught her this. Nancy wears her daddy's clothes too, and she found a new job as bookkeeper at Irene's Liquors in Hilo. So it must bring good luck.

And it does bring good luck. I found another job for a lady at church who owns the world's largest number of cocker spaniels. Mrs. Ikeda says if Blu, Maisie, and I come every Saturday morning to help her with the dogs, we get to split ten dollars. Ten dollars every Saturday! "But it's a lot of hard work and you have to be at my house by seven in the morning."

Seven every Saturday. So many dogs. The old breeders

in rusty cages in her basement. Stacked up like a poor man's doggy motel. And full of feces, blood ticks, fleas, and male ticks on their eyelids, and all around their anuses and vaginas. Even on their penises and balls. All the way down their ears. Talk about stink ear.

It's so damp and hot down there in the doggy motel that their ears get caked with wax, so stink, the ears red and swollen, the urine and the feces stuck all over their buttocks.

When we walk to Mrs. Ikeda's house, if there's a kona wind, the smell of dog comes to us from a block away. "Ivah, I think about those dogs," says Blu. "Thass not kind, what Mrs. Icky-da do to them. They all messed up. We go steal um, Maisie. For make friends with Ka-san."

Maisie nods, then looks at her hands. They get dry and peel from the Sulfodine that Mrs. Ikeda makes Maisie use to bathe the dogs.

Our first job: get the old dogs out of their small cages one by one and prepare them for grooming and bathing. Start on the mauka side of the basement. It'll take six Saturdays to take care of them all. We can only do three dogs every Saturday. Open the cage and lift the dog out. They've been in there for so long, waiting to bathe, that some of them cannot walk right away. It's like they developed arthritis of the legs.

And the smell.

"Omigod, Ivah. Kingdom come."

"Shut up, Blu."

"Mama," says Maisie as she reaches her small fingers through the wire.

The smell of dying.

But their eyes. I carry them in my arms and I don't care about the smell. Looking at me with a cocker spaniel's eyes, so sad and so old, the lower eyelids sag way down and I see the red veins going up to their eyeballs, the black folds of membrane.

Blu waits at the washbasin on the side of the grooming table with Mrs. Ikeda. He and Maisie scrub the dog after we finish the grooming. All the dogs have human names. Today we start with Chloe.

Part of the reason Chloe and the old ones cannot walk is that the hair under their legs is so long that it gets matted together in wads about the size of tennis balls and it pulls their skin when they walk.

Wana underarms.

The skin is so sensitive that if it were you, you'd probably keep your arms down and not move them too.

I feel them crying, all of them.

I take an X-acto knife and cut the matted hair into slices so they can be combed out piece by piece. I pull at the sore skin with a comb until it's red. But Chloe doesn't whimper; she's happy to be touched.

Mrs. Ikeda shaves her down with the Oster hair clipper. If she bleeds, Mrs. Ikeda sticks her finger in this white powder, I don't know what it is, and dabs it on the cut, and then goes on shaving; we've got so many dogs to groom. Same with the toenails. This is the part all the dogs hate. They bleed and get more white powder.

Into the washbasin, and scrub with Sulfodine dog shampoo. Some have huge scaly gray spots; others, like Chloe, have juicy lesions all over their bellies. And one by one, Blu's job is to pick off the blood ticks and fleas, and drop them in the Folgers can of turpentine on the washing machine.

Maisie gets to walk the freshly bathed dog in the yard, and Mrs. Ikeda makes her pick up the dog shit in a Baggie. I don't know why. Her yard is full of dog shit and tiny flies anyway. But she doesn't pick up the shit when she lets the house favorites out, she makes Maisie do it.

Then Chloe can spend an hour or so in the house with Fiona, who had four black puppies three weeks ago. Desiree is pregnant. Augustus is the house stud, and Rowan, his son, the stud-to-be. Ready to be sold, so they can eat and eat, and develop shiny coats.

I pray to taste someday the food the house favorites eat. Boiled eggs, sliced. Fresh beets, pureed. Cottage cheese and grated carrots. Chicken and tofu simmering in chicken broth. No turkey, which causes pancreatic cancer. Brown rice and fresh green beans.

Today, we finish Chloe, the old white; Simon, blind in one gray eye; Gunther, who had ticks way inside his foreskin. And Prudence, whose eyes are scared and who is deaf. We get to play with them in the house for an hour before they go back to the basement. I tell Blu and Maisie, "No give love to Fiona, Rowan, Augustus, and Desiree. They get it all the time from Mrs. Ikeda. We ain't seeing Chloe, Gunther, Simon, and Prudence for more than one month. They not coming out ever."

Blu says, "Tell Icky that we take the old ones for walks free, anything, Ivah. I come myself. You like come, Maisie? Ivah, we gotta steal the old ones."

"Stop it."

It makes me want to die. Hold on to Chloe and Prudence, whisper things to them to make them hang on for a month or so.

Be strong, clean yourself every day, be kind always, talk to each other through the wire, and cry every day if you have to.

Mrs. Ikeda takes them all down. "C'mon, c'mon, you geriatrics ward patients. C'mon, Chloe. Simon. C'mon," she says as upbeat and happy as a circus trainer. "Pruuuu-dence," she almost sings it. "Gunnn-ther, you all had your fun."

And when they don't come, I hear the dogs getting hit in the basement, the howling as they're pushed into their cages. *Be strong, hang on.* The door closes. Suffocating, damp, Kaunakakai afternoon heat, the air so thick, they cannot breathe. A closed window and one night light.

Fiona's babies go to Honolulu next week. Two hundred dollars each. That's eight hundred dollars. Marcella's last three litters were born all deaf blacks. I don't know what happened to the puppies. Marcella mated with her brother Augustus. She's in the cage by the night light, waiting for her bath.

Mrs. Ikeda hits the old dogs all the time. When she feeds them dry dog food and they don't wait nicely, she whacks them or flicks them on the nose. *Her meaty hands.* "Be nice, be nice, you can wait."

It's the last thing we do. Clean the cages and feed the old ones. Chloe whines and turns her body to the door of the cage, pressing hard. She wants to be touched through the wire. Prudence, deaf, whines loudly and doesn't even know it.

The smell is so bad that Blu lifts his shirt to cover his

nose. *I'm sorry. I'm sorry.* It's like this every Saturday. He acts as though it's the smell, but it's the crying he can't stand. He drops the bowls of dog food all over the floor of the basement. He can't walk the old ones, wave hello when he passes Mrs. Ikeda's house, buy them Milk-Bones from Friendly Market, hold his head up high. He cannot do a thing. Blu runs home without his share of the money every Saturday, while Maisie sits in a human ball outside in the garage. Counting on her fingers, over and over.

❀

The night is cool with the mild odor of Ka-san's dog blanket and puakenikeni near the gully. The moon is a sliver and a television can be heard from far away. The thud, thud, thud of Ka-san's tail on the porch as I scratch the right spot on her that I know by heart. I bathe myself after working at Mrs. Ikeda's and still Ka-san smells the dogs on me.

Ka-san, give me your eyes so that I may truly see:
Kingdom come,
thy will be done,
on earth as it is in heaven.

Mama is a speck of white way inside our dog, walking and thinking, saying my name over and over. I see her mouth saying, *"Ivah, Ivah, Ivah."*

I rub the mucus all over my eyes, Ka-san's tears on the inside of my eyelids.

Thy will be done.

"Open your eyes, Ivah." I hear my Mama in my head as clearly as can be, real words.

See, all around me, Mama. All around Ka-san, clouds

of smoke, dogs, black cocker spaniel dogs, dancing and jumping, no matted hair under their arms to pull at tender skin; no infected ears that are rancid, red, and swollen; no blood ticks in the softest places, bodies without itchy lesions, and no deafness. They're dead and happy, dogs without rusty cages. The dogs who followed me home.

Dead and happy, Mama holds her arms out to them. But it doesn't make sense. If this were true, then Mama would go to heaven.

9 Blu's happy.

"I happy when I take good care of Maisie," he says to me. "But if you talking real happy, then thass when Maisie and me camp in the living room in the blanket we pin together with clothespins even if in the morning the pins all over, even under our so-called sleeping bag, no, Maisie?" My sister nods. Happy too.

Happy so rare, I listen to Blu and Maisie under the house. "I happy when Ivah said maybe we can buy Blu *and* Maisie school pictures this year with the ironing and dog money."

Blu licks his dirty fingers to turn the pages of the Walter Drake catalogue for Maisie's birthday present, a birthday almost the same day as Mama's. Dusty fingers over shiny pages on the apple crate table.

"Ivah said I can pick something for me too with the dog money," he whispers to Maisie, then claps for himself. "And you going get cupcakes for your class because . . ." He pauses. "Because you in—because you get only three students in your class."

They come inside. He's sitting with her on the orange chair. "I getting cupcakes for my birthday this year, Ivah? Thirty-five for my whole class plus Miss Torres?"

"No."

"See?" he says to Maisie. "Tightness."

Maisie and Blu lie on their stomachs in the middle of the living room with the Walter Drake catalogue and a bowl of Haden mangoes I cut for them. Blu shoves three huge chunks in his mouth. "Pig, why you gotta be so oinky? Thass why Poppy get mad with you, Blu."

"Sorry," he whines, "I said sorry. Maisie, you like?" He puts a chunk in her mouth. "Here, I found your present, Maisie. Look, Ivah." I squeeze myself next to them.

"Hey, no breathe my air. Move, Ivah. Here: 'A wallet your child will be proud to own. Choose our purple wallet with rainbow accent for a precious little girl.' You the precious little girl, Maisie. Up to ten letters." Blu counts on his fingers, "M-a-i-s-i-e, space, O. Thass eight letters, he fit. Thass for all your dog money, Maisie. She get plenny money, you know, yeah, Maisie, 'cause she not spending her money on Liddle Kiddles and stuff like that, yeah, Maisie?"

She nods yes.

"Okay, okay, I found something for me," Blu says after flipping a few more pages. "Here what I like for me. 'The Quick and Easy Donut Maker gives you perfect taste-tempting treats every time!' I like this, Ivah. We can make our own pastries. See, it says, 'You'll just have to try the sixteen recipes included.' See, sixteen different kine donuts. Please, please, please, Ivah."

I'm thinking about Blu's fat. Fatter and fatter and Poppy getting madder and madder at Blu. He's eating until he aches all the time. "But look the picture, Blu. Gotta fry the donuts in Crisco oil."

"So what? What you saying? Thass fattening or something? Maynaise bread is fat on fat. We fry chicken drumsticks in oil. And lumpia and sunny-side-up eggs, thass fried in oil. And what about malasadas? I seen Mrs. Oliveira in the Portagee booth at the Country Fair frying malasadas in big barrels of oil. And the Okinawan booth—the andagi, thass donuts in oil right there except no mo' holes in the middle. So what if we gotta fry our donuts in oil? Sheez, Ivah." Blu puffs up big because Maisie's nodding in agreement.

"You going have one good birthday, Maisie, I promise," says Blu. "I going make homemade donuts for you, okay?" I watch them filling in the order blank and start counting the money in my head. The money it would take to get all the stuff I need for a cake and ice cream, frosting and candles, hot dogs and buns, and Walter Drake presents. I want Blu to shut up, to settle down, to stop making this into such a big deal.

But Maisie has already written her own card: HaPPY BiRTHDaY To Me.

❀

Miss Sandra Ito writes to Maisie about four times a day. She's the cutest teacher at Kaunakakai School; if they had a Hoss Election for teachers with the category "Cutest Face," she'd win, and she's the most mod. And for a Japanese, she would also win "Best Smile," I think, because of her pink frost lipstick and bright blue eye shadow. The only thing I might suggest is that she wear false eyelashes, but she seems to be the natural type.

She's the only teacher who wears culottes and Dr. Scholl's to school every day. The only one who doesn't look like she's sweating in her dress as if her slip is stuck to her thighs or wedged up her buttocks. The other teachers wear hot nylons and heels. Like Miss Owens. Mrs.

Nishimoto said that Miss Owens and she hate Moloka'i —the heat, the mosquitoes, the brown windward ocean, and the brown people all on welfare.

"And this is paradise? Oh well, we must've read the wrong travel brochure," Mrs. Nishimoto says over the phone to Miss Owens as she digs in her bag for a five for Blu and me. "Sandi said *what*? When did she call you this? No—I can't stand that word. I mean, it's so racist. And try calling *them* anything short of O-R-I-E-N-T-A-L and the locals blow a fuse. Tammy, you don't have to stand for that. Next time, you give it right back to her."

Other things we've heard about Miss Ito from the teachers, like Miss Torres talking to Mr. Shaw at the first recess by the swings: "Well, of course she can be the world's greatest teacher—she only has four kids in her class. And the young ones got all the energy. Give her a couple of years and she'll burn out like the rest of us. I used to be just like her when I first started teaching. Gung ho. Gimme a break."

Or Mrs. Ota to Miss Torres at lunch duty in the cafeteria: "My sister-in-law at Kalihi Elementary was Sandra Ito's supervising teacher when she did her student teaching. You know, she barely passed because her grade point was so low. That's why she ended up here on Moloka'i, you know, because none of the Honolulu schools wanted such a dummy."

Or Miss Owens to Mrs. Nishimoto, one Wednesday at the Nishimotos' house: "She's a lush, I tell you, Susie. Drunk as a skunk every night with every local yokel from the damn janitor to the whole PE department. And talking that pidgin of theirs so that I can't understand what they're saying. And Sandra lays it on thick whenever she's talking about me. We're talking every night. She's a lush and a whore."

❀

Miss Ito's classroom is full of books and bulletin boards that you want to look at and terrariums and plants all over the place, apple crates for tables and shelves, a couch and rug by a fake but nice cardboard fireplace, lavender gingham curtains, guinea pigs who have smart names like Einstein and Ophelia, parakeets with the best bird toys, a fish tank, and bookcases without any dust on them. Sometimes I see Miss Ito at PE time for the small kids, running on the field with her class, while all the other teachers fan themselves in the shade.

Maisie writes to Miss Ito. Maisie writes to Blu. And Blu has gotten into the act by writing letters to Maisie that Miss Ito helps her read and the three of them write back and forth.

❀

Dear Maisie,

Fill in the blank. I am happiest when . . . If you get stuck and maybe you will because I did get stuck too, repeat the line I am happiest when . . .

Yours truly,

XOXO Blu

❀

DeaR BLu,

i aM HaPPY WHeN You SiNG HeY DiD You HaPeN To See THe MoST BuTiFuL GiRL iN THe WoLD.

LoVe,

MaiSie o.

Dear Maisie,

Will you be buying your school pictures this year? Please, may I have one for my room? Do you have any special pictures? May I see them one day?

Sincerely yours,

Miss Ito

❀

DeaR MiSS iTo,

i GiVe You a PiCTuRe oF Me. BuT NoT SCHooL oNe. i HaVe a PiCTuRe oF MY MaMa i TooK FRoM HeR DRaWeR. i iTCHY FiNGeRS.

SiGNeD,

MaiSie o.

❀

Dear Miss Ito,

How do you get my sister to tell you all of these things? Are you helping her to spell the words? I guess the answer to that is yes. How come she tells you all of these things? Do you know that she hardly never says nothing at home? Does she cry? Help me please.

Signed,

Confused

❀

Dear Confused,

Your family reminds me of my family when I was growing up. My mother passed away when I was a little girl too. I had to care for my three sisters. I would like to invite you, Maisie, and your brother to spend a night at my house this weekend. Then I will show you how I work

with Maisie! (All the secret tricks!) Just kidding. Ask your
father and let me know by Friday.

Yours truly,

Miss Ito

❀

How did she know it was me?
I was pretending to be Blu.

❀

Saturday comes and Poppy makes things clear. "Ivah,
you go pick one whole bag green beans for Miss Ito and
cut couple mustard cabbage from the tarai. And buy one
pound Farmer John bacon and one dozen eggs for you
guys' breakfast plus two cans Exchange orange base. You
kids listen up—neva go someplace empty-handed, and if
you no mo' nothing for take, then no go, is what I say.
'Cause we ain't no haole family showing up for one barbecue with one loaf of bread and nothing else.

"And you," he tells Blu, "mark my words, you get
greedy and start acting like one pig without no manners,
then, Ivah, you call me up and I bring Blu right home.
I tell you, sometimes, your eyes mo' big than your
stomach—and right now, your stomach getting mo' big
than your ass. Blu, you betta cut down your eating."

Blu pulls his mouth sideways into his cheek. "How
come only me get scoldings, Poppy?"

" 'Cause only you make shame for this family."

❀

Still, Blu's happy. Where does he find it?

He's at the kitchen table drawing Happiness Is cartoons with bubbles for thoughts, cartoons that Maisie
tapes to the refrigerator.

"Happiness Is no shame for this family. A father, a mother, two sisters, a brother, a dog, and a cat. Only thing missing is a mother but otherwise that is what Happiness Is.

"Happiness Is Gunther, Chloe, and Simon after they groom and bathe and stay in the house for one hour of love and play with their friends. When dogs happy, they dream. I seen my dog dreaming she was chasing a rabbit in her sleep. I love dogs."

It takes all morning. Like the morning he cut little circles, colored them with Smile Have a Happy Day faces, then taped them all to our bedroom wall.

"Happiness Is all good foods and money. I heard that money can't buy love or something like that. Paul or George said that but it's not true. Money can buy food and if there was plenty, I wouldn't love it so much.

"Happiness Is a friend like I used to have. But now Ed also known as Bob stick with Winston and Darren so he can eat his own Twinkies and Ding Dongs every day and not share a Pep and Bob with me.

"Happiness Is my sister Maisie who is the BEST in all the whole wide world next to Ivah when she don't have evil mouth."

This one Maisie folds up and tucks away in her pocket.

❀

Saturday, noon.

The sun's high and I pack the laundry basket with our clothes and toothbrushes, the writing tablet, a bag of green beans, two heads of mustard cabbage, and all of the breakfast foods. A horn toots from outside, so Maisie and Blu run out of the house. "It's her, it's her!" Blu starts jumping up and down, and Maisie waves from the porch as Miss Ito pulls up in her mustard-colored Toyota Corolla.

"Hi, everybody, you ready?" She takes off her bumble-bee sunglasses and tucks them into the neck of her T-shirt. Poppy walks into the garage from the garden. "Hey, Mr. Ogata. I'll bring them back tomorrow noon."

"Thanks, Sandi, you no need do this, you know. Even my own family wouldn't take these three for sleep-ova. They one handful, I tell you, so any one of them get outta line, I like you whack um one first, then call me, and I pick up the naughty one in two shakes, you hear me, Blu?"

Again, my brother pulls his mouth into his cheek. Then he jumps into the front seat. "See what I mean?" Poppy says. "This Maisie's teacha. You get your ass in the back seat right now."

"Bye, Poppy."

"Bye."

Miss Ito has an 8-track in her car. The seats smell new and piney. And air-conditioning dries up the sweat right off my upper lip. Maisie sits in the front with her hands in her lap. She's so scared to be good; she doesn't want
✓ to be sent home.

We pull into the row of teacher's cottages that all look alike with white paint, green trim, and large porches. All of the houses have red hibiscus hedges in front of them and kiddie pools, marble-swirled plastic balls, tricycles, and sandboxes on the lawns.

Miss Owens slams the screen door of the cottage and hauls an overnight bag to Mrs. Nishimoto's car, waiting in the driveway. Jonathan yells from the car, "Hi, Blu!" He really looks up to my brother, who could treat him like a piece of shit, but doesn't.

"Hi, Jonathan. Next Wednesday when not my turn to iron, I challenge you Battleships. I know your favorite spot, B-14."

"Okay, Blu. And yours is C-17."

"Stop yelling in my ear," Mrs. Nishimoto tells Jonathan. "You're making the babies cry. Sshh." Everyone looks sweaty in their car. All six kids and Mrs. Nishimoto with her pink face.

"All yours, Sandi," Miss Owens snaps. "See you tomorrow after church. You know, Sandi"—Miss Owens turns and tightens her lips—"you can't save um all like they were yours to save in the first place. Surely the Lord's work can't be done overnight? All these sleep-overs— they do have to go back to their lives, wretched or no. That's why prayer works better." I think of strangling her freckles off of her head again.

"Thanks, Tammy, for the wonderful Christian advice." Miss Ito grits her teeth. "That's one thing I notice about haoles and especially haole Christians," Miss Ito says to the three of us behind her—and then she turns and faces Miss Owens—"you have lots of talk about charity and goodness, but nothing you say really happens. I'll keep them out of your room."

Miss Owens looks at Mrs. Nishimoto, and Mrs. Nishimoto gives her a look that says: Give it to the Jap. I've seen that look before a lot of times. *They're just Japs.*

"I resent being called a haole, Sandra. It's like me calling you a Chink or a Jap, which I would never do." Miss

Owens' voice trembles so Mrs. Nishimoto steps out of her car and puts an arm around her. "I've treated you like every other person I know, even when there were empty bottles of beer all over the living room and peanut shells all over the couch on a Sunday morning before I left for church. I've never stooped to making any racial remarks whatsoever."

"You're so condescending, Tammy, it's pathetic. I'm a Jap to you. And my friends are all brownies. It's written all over your face every minute of every day. I've had to put up with your judgment of us and your snide remarks for months now. I'm no dummy, so don't you ever talk down to me, you undastand"—Miss Ito's pidgin English comes out. I've never heard her use it. " 'Cause you keep acting stupid, Tammy, you keep on lifting your haole nose in the air at me and my friends, you going hear worse things than 'haole' come out of this Jap's mout'."

Miss Owens takes a deep, angry breath. She gets into Mrs. Nishimoto's car and slams the door. "I expected better from you," Mrs. Nishimoto says.

"Haoles *always* gotta have the last word. And thass what *I* expect from *you*." Miss Ito gathers Maisie up in her arms. Maisie turns and I see in her face, her scared eyes. *Wet panties and fingers washing sticky urine from thighs, cold water.* Blu and I sit on the wooden porch. I lower my head, but Blu gets up and stands next to Miss Ito as the station wagon pulls out of the driveway. Nobody says a single word.

"Well," Miss Ito asks as she turns to me sitting on the porch, "why so glum? Screw it. If we let Tammy get to us like she wanted to, then she's spoiled our weekend. That's what she wanted. But we have party plans, don't we? We only have five hours before the best birthday party you've ever seen."

"Birthday party? Maisie, c'mon," says Blu. "We go hurry up, bumbye we no mo' time for whatevas we going do with Miss Ito. By the way, what we going do first?"

"We're going to see how Maisie talks."

❀

In the green kitchen that smells as if it doesn't know whether it's haole or Japanese, the three of us sit at the table. Miss Ito tapes a paper chart to the wall with the directions from the Betty Crocker yellow cake mix written in big, bold letters. Blu stands nearby as Miss Ito reads: "Mix three eggs with two sticks of butter. Maisie, it's your cake, you read."

Just like that, like it's every day of her life that my sister reads aloud upon someone else's simple request: "Your turn now, Maisie."

Blu looks at me, stunned. He's panicked. His eyes say: Don't force her to talk. Save her, Ivah, she can't do it. It's still for a while. She hasn't spoken but single words, one a week, for almost a year now. And every night, I've prayed to God to give my sister her voice back. I've prayed for the day I hear her say my name.

"Maisie, this is delicious cake," Miss Ito tells her. "Help us read the directions so we can make it. We need your help. You can do it."

Blu looks at Miss Ito. You're hurting her, his eyes say. Don't make her do this. He walks toward me, nostrils flaring mad. He wants to cry. Then he turns to Maisie and says, "I no like eat cake. C'mon, Maisie, we go watch TV."

Her face stiffens and then her mouth slackens. She

lowers her eyes and stares at her distorted reflection in the tabletop. "No need make this dumb cake," he says again, flicking the box with his hand. Then Blu looks at me. He wants blood to run thicker than water.

After a long moment, I say, "I dunno. This cake look pretty tasty to me." I put the box near Maisie's absent eyes. "And made into a birthday cake? Might be the best cake I eva ate since it's Maisie's birthday and she's my best Pidge in this whole wide world."

No one moves or speaks. "Mine too," Blu says at last.

"Help us read the directions, Maisie," Miss Ito says easily, no pressure. "We just need your help, all of us."

"C'mon, Maisie," Blu says. I hold my breath.

"Mix . . . three . . . eggs . . . with two sticks of . . . butter." The voice is raspy and low. She sounds like Mama after her last cigarette smoke late at night when it's cool, and there's no wind.

She doesn't look to us for approval. I feel my body start to quiver. Blu presses his face to my back and wraps his arms around my neck.

"Good talking voice, Maisie. Mix in one and a half cups of milk. Then three hundred strokes. Can we all help her count this high? Maisie, can you read the instructions for us?"

And then, for the first time, she looks up at me. She has come back from some strange dream wandering in and out of a shiny riptide. She recognizes me. *Where have you been, my little Pidge?*

"Ivah," she whispers.

I push Blu toward the paper chart. He wipes his face with both hands. Miss Ito continues reading the directions. Then with some hesitance at first, Maisie repeats each line as Blu points to the words, mouthing them as Maisie speaks them.

He wants to cry. His body wants to crumble. But he holds on. "Whass my name? Whass my name?" he asks over and over.

For the girl without words, there is laughter for what is light, gesture for want, and tears for all that is dark. There is not much more. Names are nothing but extravagance.

I listen to the teacher speak each word as my sister repeats them slowly. I keep each word as I would a precious stone. These are gifts from God. Listen to the voice that hangs in the air.

After we put the cake in the oven, Miss Ito brings a soda box to the kitchen table, which is covered with construction paper, pens, glitter, Elmer's glue and magazines. "We need a few birthday cards for our party. Everyone —make Maisie a card. But I want you to write a short something for Maisie inside that you remember about her. Something nice. And, Maisie, you and I will work together on a card for Ivah and Blu."

Blu writes:

"One time, we was in the car and you got sleepy, so you put your head in my lap and fell asleep. It was the first time I touch your hair like a Mama. Happiness Is, XOXO Blu." He makes the Malibu on the front with glitter. A big glitter heart with a doily inside and his name in blue glitter.

I write:

"I remember your spongy forehead when your were

small and I kissed it so many times it turned red. All I
want to do is hold you, hold you, hold you, even now,
my pretty Pidge. Always, Ivah H. Ogata." Hearts all over
the place in all shades of red and everyone's name in a
heart. Mama, Poppy, Ivah, Blu, Maisie, Ka-san, Hoppy
Creetat, Big Sis, and Miss Ito.

Maisie writes:

"iVaH iS Ma WHo PuT Me SLeeP. BLu THe oNe WHo
SiNG TiLL MY eYeS CLoSe. Ka-SaN iS HeR. HoPPY
iS LuCKY. PoPPY iS FaR. i LoVe eVeRYBoDY. LoVe,
MaiSie o." She's got words, just words on hers.

"Okay, Maisie," Miss Ito says. "Now we need to learn
how to write the words to your favorite song." Miss Ito
goes into her room and brings a phonograph to the living
room. She presses a red disk into the center of the 45
and puts it on the turntable. It's the Charlie Rich song
that Maisie likes so much when she hears it on KKUA as
we sit outside picking fleas off of Ka-san just before
dinner.

"I asked my sister in Honolulu to get it for me from the
House of Music in Ala Moana Center. I got it last week.
So listen good." Miss Ito plays it three times. The third
time, we're all singing, even Maisie.

Over and over, pick up the needle, and mouth the
words so we don't forget them. Miss Ito puts a quarter
on the needle when it starts to skip. The cake bakes in
the oven, the frosting cools in the refrige, and the glitter
on the cards dries on the counter. "Take it slow.
Maisie?"

"Hey. Did you happen to see the most beautiful girl in
the world?"

"Good talking voice. Now write it down in your tablet."

"Spell beautiful, Miss Ito."

"B-e-a-u-t-i-f-u-l."

※

Green beans and ham, rice and macaroni salad. Just like a real party. Balloons hang from the lights. A yellow cake covered with Avoset and canned peach frosting waits in the refrige. Six candles and one for good luck.

Miss Ito and I wash the dishes together at the sink. "Ivah," she says, "I talked to some of your teachers and I pulled up your school records—you're a good student and your teachers have a lot of nice things to say about you." She pauses. I don't know where this is going. I get nervous and run my hands under the warm water.

"I really want you to consider applying to Mid-Pacific Institute in Honolulu."

"Whass that?"

"It's a boarding school—we'll talk more about that later. See, when my mother died, my dad struggled with the four of us girls. But one of my teachers helped me get a scholarship so I could get out of my small town and attend a good college-prep school with Honolulu kids.

"When she said I had the potential, I didn't believe her at first. Sometimes when you're from a small town, you think you're a nothing, you know? But I got in there with all those haoles and rich Japanese and Chinese kids. I helped my three sisters get in—it made a big difference for all four of us."

I peer over my shoulder at Maisie and Blu. "I dunno if I could—"

"Well, will you think about it? I have an application waiting for you. My sister picked one up for me."

What about Blu?

What about Maisie?

What about Poppy?

I don't say this.

I rinse my hands.

I feel panic.

And then she says, "Sometimes, you've got to let go. Otherwise, what you're holding on to suffocates and dies. You kill yourself and the ones you love so much. You think about it, okay?"

I nod my head. And Miss Ito puts her hand on my head that I find is resting on her shoulder.

❀

After the dishes are washed, we gather in the living room. Blu, Maisie, and I sit on the sleeping bags Miss Ito has taken out of the hall closet. There is one for each of us, real sleeping bags, with pillows and clean-smelling pillowcases, and no blankets with clothespins. Miss Ito drags her futon out of her bedroom. "You sleeping with us tonight, Miss Ito?" Blu asks.

"Yeah, why? This my house. You think I want to miss out on my great ghost stories? Maisie, why don't you read your cards?"

Maisie reads each birthday card, even the one that Miss Ito made. Hers says:

"You are my STAR. Next year, I promise, you will be in Mr. Shaw's first-grade class with the rest of your class-mates. Boy, will I miss you. But I will never forget you. Love and kisses, Miss Ito."

"Maisie, the Walter Drake stuff never come yet, so we no mo' presents for you from me and Blu."

She shrugs her shoulders.

"I got something for you," Miss Ito says. "You remember I wanted a picture of you? I paid for your picture package so that you could autograph pictures and write letters to all of your friends and family. And there's a picture of me with your class in there, Leroy and Rodel and the others. Open it."

Maisie pulls her picture out, the big eight-by-ten. She looks at herself for a long time. Then she writes on the back:

"BeauTiFuL. MaiSie o."

"Okay now, who's ready for cake?" Miss Ito walks into the kitchen and comes back with the cake and candles lit. "Turn off the light, Ivah," she says to me as she starts the singing, "Happy Birthday to you. Happy Birthday to—" She stops because Blu's not with us.

He's singing, "Hey, did you happen to see the most beautiful girl in the world?" All by himself, my brother sings for my sister over the radiant candles on her birthday cake, her favorite Charlie Rich song in his voice, so soft and smoky that it hangs in the air.

10 The voices over the airwaves sound staticky at first. Blu and I sit at the kitchen table, after dinner, after a bath and homework, adjusting with fine fingers the dial on the radio so AM KKUA Honolulu comes in clear and strong; cool nights work best for the electromagnetic waves to travel across the waters of the Moloka'i Channel and into our little radio. Tonight, Poppy and Felix Furtado clean the Bank of Hawai'i. He'll be home past nine.

Maisie lies on the living-room floor drawing in coloring books that arrive in the mail—Skipper and Friends, Josie and the Pussycats in Outer Space, Connect the Dots, and Letters and Numbers. All that and a 64-pack of Crayolas from Big Sis for Maisie's birthday.

Big Sis sent me a huge box of Lila Beth's old clothes that look just like new. Everyone says that in Kaunakakai we're five years behind Hilo, and Hilo's five years behind Honolulu, and Honolulu's five years behind the mainland. So if you ask me, the clothes that Big Sis sent me, not even faded clothes, are right in fashion at my school.

"Quick before Poppy come home. We gotta finish the words to 'Colour My World,' Ivah. Maisie, we go ask Miss Ito if her sista can go buy us 'Colour My World' and 'Goodbye Yellow Brick Road' tomorrow. I go spend my dog money. You like half-half with me?"

She nods, looking up toward the light over the kitchen table.

"Mento you, Blu," I tell my brother. "What you going play your records on? We no mo' phonograph." I'm still thinking about what Miss Ito told me about Mid-Pacific Institute. *Want to make the way.* I don't want to wear out the favors we ask of her on stupid records.

Want to go.

Need to let go.

"Yeah, we no mo' phonograph, no? Why, why, why—I can play um in Miss Ito's room after school, yeah, Maisie, me and you when we waiting for Ivah, we can listen to our records, yeah?"

Maisie nods again.

I give up. I flip through the pages of Maisie's composition tablet. She and Blu have started a running game of Hangman. Nobody's hanged yet. The farthest Blu and Maisie got was a whole body and two eyeballs. The word was HAPPINESS. Blu writes: "Maisie, choose your vowels first before you hang." He writes to her so that she can learn to read as they play their games of Hangman.

I flip a few more pages. There, next to the words for "The Most Beautiful Girl in the World," Blu hangs. On two simple words: a whole body, two eyes, two ears, a nose, and a smile turned upside down. Hanging on COCONUT ROPE. Blu writes in the margin: "Maisie, YOU WIN!"

Then Blu breaks into my reading. "Eh, Ivah," he asks all of a sudden, "who you think could kick whose ass— George of the Jungle or Lancelot Link and Matahari on one team?"

"Stupid, George of the Jungle, of course," I answer,

I slam the tablet shut. My brother constantly pon-
stupid subjects, then gets mad if we don't indulge
.....

"Thass what I thought. George of the Jungle or Magilla
Gorilla?"

"Up and up."

"Maisie," Blu says, "Evangeline's Uncle Paulo no look
like Davy Jones to you? I mean, he Filipino, but he no
look like one kinda haole-ish Monkee to you?"

She shrugs her shoulders.

"You like Davy Jones the best, Ivah? He my best Monkee. Me and Maisie like Davy the best."

"No," I tell Blu, "I like Mike Nesmith the best."

"He my second. The one I no like is Mickey Dolenz. He
get sakushi mouth." Blu demonstrates by moving his bottom teeth in front of his upper teeth. "Thass ugly when
your mouth like that. Just like Henrilyn Reyes. And Peter
Tork, I no like his hair. Thass how Mr. Shaw use to be,
yeah, Ivah, with liddle bit hair like that, and the next year,
he was getting bolohead. And this year, he really getting
bolohead. I think Peter going be side-bolos pretty soon."

"Ssshhh! 'Colour My World,'" I yell at Blu. I raise the
volume on the little radio. "Get Maisie's tablet, quick,
quick. We only need the end part. Listen good, eh." Blu
scurries around the table and sits down with his ear near
the radio.

"I dunno why you rushing me, Ivah, got that long piano
part in the beginning anyway."

Then Poppy walks in the door. "Whatchu guys doing?
Sheez, almost nine-thirty, you betta go sleep right now.
Whassamatta you, Ivah?"

"Poppy, it's Friday night."

"Oh." Poppy shuffles slowly to the rice pot and lifts the cover. "Tamago meshi—whass this in here? Kamaboko and tofu? Eh, Ivah, you getting to be one A number one cook. What you guys doing?"

"Sing for Poppy, Blu," I tell my brother. "Colour My World."

"Beautiful girl," Maisie whispers to Blu.

"What you said, liddle girl?" Poppy asks. "Since when, Maisie, you talk so much, hah? You make Poppy happy when you talk, you know. Sing her that song, Blu."

My brother doesn't need to warm up; he just opens his mouth and the sound of notes comes pouring out, so sweet, so strong, my brother's blue notes, but Blu never listens.

Moon River, wider than a mile.
I'm crossing you in style someday.
Old dreammaker, you heartbreaker,
wherever you're going, I'm going your way . . .

There is a moment of silence. I remember wind drifting into the room, the smell of ocean mud and puakenikeni. I remember Maisie holding on to Ka-san, wiping the tears from the dog's eyes. Mostly, I remember the silence. Blu's waiting face, hanging on the stillness of no one's response.

Poppy stands and walks toward the curtains, draws them back, and looks outside. Without turning around, he says, "Get to sleep, Blu. You too, Maisie. Call the cat in the house. Ivah, you get me one tall glass water and one bowl of the tamago meshi. Move it, all of you." All of this he says without once turning around.

d-jerk Maisie and Blu down the hallway and get
s dinner to the table. "Here, Poppy. Time to eat."

turns toward me, so sad, so sad. He looks on the
fridge for the words to "Moon River" and peels the tape
off gently. He holds the words written in Blu's handwriting, then folds the paper into a very small square and
tucks it into the pocket of his jeans.

He doesn't eat. He stares at the scars on his hands for
a long time. Draws them close to his eyes and then holds
them up in front of him. I just sit there and watch. "I neva
going say this again, Ivah. I going draw back the veil one
time and one time only for you—and maybe later on, you
be big enough to tell Blu and then Maisie."

"What veil, Poppy? What you talking about?" I ask my
father.

Poppy doesn't answer me for a while. And then he
says, "The veil I talking about ain't like one curtain. I
talking about the veil that hide our eyes from what we
no can see." Poppy moves my hair out of my eyes. "Just
like that—when I move your hair away, you see things
that maybe you miss otherwise." My father shifts in his
chair and moves out of the light.

"I dunno," he says, "just one thing stack on the other
thing and I walk in tonight, I see you and Blu, doing the
things your madda did and how happy that make you,
just like her.

"And your bradda's voice—thass your Mama singing
right out his throat, you know that, eh, Ivah? What I going
do? What I going do? Ivah, I pray to God every day that
I be release from some of this, but He no hear me. I
walking every day of my fuckin' life with her tie to my

back, so heavy on me, sometimes, but I no can cut the rope. And I feel so bad, every single day of my goddamn life, that one foot no like go in front the other one.

"I ain't eva going ask this of you again, Ivah. And you been doing so much shit around here, make me sick to think I gotta lean on you. But I only going ask you once. And I only going take you once: I like you go with me on the other side of the veil, so maybe you help me lighten my load. Help me walk on liddle bit."

And then the veil lifts, and I start to see the other side, ropes that we need to tie ourselves with, to these chairs in the kitchen in the house in Kaunakakai. So, as Poppy says, we can find our way back from the place of memories, so good and so strong, or so bad that you want to stay to fix them, or, sometimes, forget to come back. On this night, I hear, for the only time in my life, the secrets that Mama and Poppy and all the adults whispered all through the years.

"My teacha in Hilo," he says, "she the one first see the spots. She the one been turn me in. Same with your madda. I was born Hilo, you know that, right? Your madda was from up Kalihi Valley. Ivah—this hard for me say 'cause been one secret for so long from you—me and your madda, us had leprosy. I like your promise that you neva call us lepers. Don't eva define us again by that disease.

"Was right before World War II that I went the Kalihi Receiving Station. I was eight. You see how this hit me tonight? Blu eight years old, right? I was his age when I went all by myself to Honolulu with the red spots on my hands and face. Was inside my nose too.

"I was suppose to be playing with my small sista, grow- ing up catching swordtails in the stream, raising fighting chickens, and writing the words from songs too. And singing um to my fadda, but I was yank from the world, and put away all by myself. Betty neva even come to the door say goodbye to me. Then like now, I no was one strong person. I no could handle nothing. I was eight years old. And I was lost.

"Your madda was Maisie age. Only one five-year-old girl. I like you imagine you the one gotta give Maisie to the doctors and nurses and know you ain't *eva* going see her again. Eleanor's madda came see her when she could have visitors on Sunday, but me, my family all in Hilo— was pretty much the last I seen of them when they ship me to Honolulu. I no can even tell in words the way it feels for one child be yanked away from the arms of his madda. How you keep reaching your small arms but they only get mo' far away.

"My family, they write me letters all the time, and I write them back all the time, all those years I was down Kalaupapa. Why your face look like that, Ivah? You no asked your Poppy, eh? No mo' nothing already. See? I no mo' leprosy no mo'. We was imprison down Kalaupapa, and now, no mo'."

I want to turn away and hide my face. I want to put my head down on the table, cover my ears, make Poppy stop. At the same time, I want to hear more, all of it, every word, to keep for myself in a shoebox forever. And it seems like forever for me to say, "And then what, Poppy?"

"They tell me before when I was one small boy down

there, you talk like this about your past life of happy childhood days while you in this sad place, Kalaupapa, you tie one rope around your body before you take back the veil and step out the window for your dream walk. Bumbye you no like come back. The rope, he help you make your way back to the room you was in when your mouth started for tell your story."

My father's hands linger on the rusty legs of the vinyl chair. I watch him dream-walking.

"When the Japs bomb Pearl Harbor, the government came scared that all us leprosy patients was going break out of the Kalihi Receiving Station. So fast kine, one day in May, they wen' put all us kids on one boat going straight to Kalaupapa. And we was all scared. I thinking: This is it. It's all pau. I going there for die. Was mostly all kids on that ship and the sad part was, Eleanor's madda neva said goodbye to her, and afta that, was like Eleanor was on her own. Not one more word from her madda. Us heard years and years later that Eleanor's madda had plenny mo' kids and was shame that had one kid with leprosy in the family. Thass how was—you no like nobody know had one *pilau leper* in your family. Best you keep um one big secret."

Poppy wants to go on, I know he does. Poppy wants to stop, I know he does. *Hold on to the rope, Poppy. Not too far. Take your time; catch your breath.* "How come you came up from there, Poppy?" I ask him. He seems startled, but, slowly, he continues.

"Was 'cause of you. By the time came 1949, the sulfone drug finally came Kalaupapa, late 'cause of the war, but on some people, the bugga made changes overnight. The

department was still fumigating our mail, but the
was working. I told your madda take the sulfones
when she flare up. Bumbye she get immune, but she
no listen. She no listen. She no like *eva* get leprosy again.
And the bugga been eat up her kidneys.

"I dunno. The way I talking make you think I hated
Kalaupapa. No get me wrong. I mean, your madda and
me made one good life for ourself down there. The people was good, we had good friends down there, and us
was away from the staring eyes of the world. But we
wanted for prove to the world, everybody, that we could
make perfect children, perfect.

"By the time came 1956, I was declared negative and
got paroled. But I wen' wait and pray for Eleanor. Then
God came answering in 1958 and your madda too got
discharge and parole. Thass why we came Kaunakakai.
We wanted for start over. I neva like go back Hilo 'cause
Aunty Betty them was scared I taint their good name. And
my madda and fadda, they was still alive. They love me,
but I no like bring them no shame. And your madda, the
poor thing, nobody claim her in her family. Not even one
bradda or sista and got ten of them.

"I make it clear to Ella and her to me: I got her and
she got me. Then Sonny and Cher sang one song about
Eleanor and me. And every song she hear that make what
we get more strong, she write the words for me and sing
in that voice that make the angels stop and listen. My
father pauses long in the still night. "What I going do,
Ivah? What I going do?"

Poppy's gone far. *Come back. Come back.* Blu appears
in the kitchen light. He's been sitting in the hallway the

whole time. He squeezes himself next to me on my chair and I hold him. He stares at his own hands. Shame, so much shame under his skin. He rests his head on me. It brings my father back.

"Your madda died 'cause each one of your faces starting with you, Ivah, made um mo' and mo' clear to Eleanor that she was neva going back Kalaupapa. So she kept taking, and taking, and taking the sulfone drug even way after she was declared negative. And the bugga wen' eat and eat at her kidneys—wen' nag her for years—but she kept taking the sulfones so she would neva have to go back there without you kids, so that she neva abandon her kids like her family did her.

"And look at us—what was the use? We no mo' her with us here. She gone. She so stupid. I told her no take um till she flare up bumbye she get immune to the sulfones and look. The thing wen' kill her slow. And she abandon us anyway. Was love wen' kill my Ella. Love for you."

Shame under his skin, my brother puts his face in his hands.

I stand up to reheat Poppy's dinner. Ka-san comes into the kitchen, head bent low and tail wagging. She rests her head on my Poppy's knee and looks up at him with red eyes. "Blu," I say softly to my brother, "go close the window for Poppy."

My father begins to eat his dinner slowly. With each bite he takes, I wind the rope from the dream walk around and around in a coil on the floor. Lower the veil. When Poppy finishes eating, he drinks two glasses of water. He doesn't shed one tear.

After Poppy goes to bed, and Blu curls himself into Maisie's body, I stay in the kitchen. The rope that Poppy tied to his body for his dream walk lies spiraled in a heap on the floor. I wrap it around my brother: keep him close to me always. I wrap it around Maisie: come home to us with words. I wrap it around Poppy: dream-walk, but come back to this kitchen.

I wrap it around me:

The dog drops her head.

The light flickers on outside.

Mama, let go of the rope.

11 Blu watches too many cartoons. That's where he gets the idea to tie knots in a sheet, tie it to the leg of his bed, and throw it out of the window for an easy escape. A perfectly good sheet, one that wasn't thinning into cheesecloth in the middle like some of Poppy's BVDs. But after Blu's full weight, hanging on the sheet thrown out of his window, I couldn't even loosen the knots with my teeth.

"You goddamn fuckin' stupid jackass kid," Poppy yelled, "now we one sheet short in this house." He hit Blu on his head with the knot at the end of the sheet, over and over.

It's Blu's fault. He's obsessed with cartoons, TV and movie stars these days. This is what he told me about the knotted-sheet episode: "I was pretending I live in one tree house kinda like the Swiss Family Robinson, but more like David Carradine—you know the *Kung Fu* guy, and his wife, Barbara Hershey. She change her name to Seagull, you know, 'cause she seen one seagull at the beach and was so free that she wanted the spirit come in her. And speaking of free, thass what she name her and David's first son, you know, Free. Free Seagull Carradine."

"How you know all this shit, Blu?" I ask my brother. I mean, I am truly amazed at this. "You reading all this someplace? Where?"

"Blendaline," Maisie says. She looks at me and tightens her lips.

"What? You hanging around Blendaline Reyes? Since when? I neva see you two guys together. What the hell, man?"

"Blendaline," Maisie says again as she sits down next to me on the orange chair.

"Shut up, Maisie, you bigmouth. Ever since you talk, you only talk for—"

"Shut your fuckin' mouth, Blu, you hear me? Why you think she telling me all this shit? You stupid or what? You know what them Reyes sistas is all about."

"Why, Blendaline nice to me," Blu whines. "She lend me Evangeline's *Tiger Beat* and *Seventeen* in school and sometimes she mo' smart than me on movie stars. She know everything. And she share her stuffs. So thass why I like her."

"You irritating me bad, Blu. But you do whateva you like do. Just no come crying to me when Blendaline cut off your balls and serve um to her sistas for after-school snack, you dumb asshole."

"I ain't going come crying to you. I going invite you come eat human mountain oysters too. Evil mouth."

❀

Blu writes on Miss Ito's board with purple chalk:
    Blu = Flier Mynah = Flier Dove = Flier Mejiro
            OR
        Flier Sparrow

❀

My new names for the spirit of birds in me!!!!

❀

It all started with Blendaline's Uncle Paulo. Uncle Paulo in Da Sun, the yellow Datsun truck with the "t" sanded off, a 76 orange ball, and a black panty lace tied to the radio antenna. Uncle Paulo who looks like Davy Jones, even the hair, which Uncle Paulo flings around like Davy does as he plays the tambourine for the Monkees.

It was a Saturday afternoon in May. Hotter than a hot day in Kaunakakai. Blu, Maisie, and I at the county pool. Along comes Evangeline, Blendaline, Henrilyn, and Trixi Reyes with their Uncle Paulo and stupid Mitchell Oliveira. Uncle Paulo doesn't even shower but dives like a jack-knife in the pool like all the cool high school boys do. Except Uncle Paulo is about twenty.

You don't see him surface for a long time, and then on the shallow side of the pool you hear Blendaline shriek, and Uncle Paulo comes up for air, flinging his hair out of his face big time. He splashes water on Evangeline and Blendaline, swims around and around them, and occasionally one of them shrieks as if they're being pinched. Henrilyn sits on the stairs that lead into the pool with her knees pulled tightly together. Trixi's on the pool deck shivering. Then Uncle Paulo surfaces and does the hair fling.

Mitchell holds Evangeline from behind her on the shallow side of the pool. They look like two fools, the dumb haole-for-a-Portagee hugging stupid Evangeline in the pool. And slowly but slowly, Blu's bobbing toward their side of the pool.

"Where you think you going, dummy? Think I stupid, eh? I know where you like go, traitor. Go, go then," I tell him. "You think me and Maisie like you here with us when us know you rather be over there with them? Beat it, Blu."

"Why, we only playing Marco Polo. I just going say hi to Blendaline."

"What for? You going with her? I can see you going for say hi to her if you going with her, but if not, then butt your big ass out. Think they like you over there?"

"Why maybe I *am* going with her. And maybe they *do* like me over there. Why, bodda you, hah?"

"Yeah, bodda me."

"Well, don't let it." And with that, Blu bobs toward the splashing, screaming, and laughing Reyes sisters and their Uncle Paulo acting like a human shark going under the water.

Blendaline and Blu splash at each other. I don't know what she sees in him, but he's starting to lose weight. Then the huge commotion. Uncle Paulo circling everybody, including Blu. Blendaline, Henrilyn, Trixi, and my brother. Circle, circle, and sink.

"Stay here, Maisie." I swim over, head above water. As I approach them, I see Uncle Paulo's hands between Blendaline's legs, pinching her vagina underwater. Blendaline screams but laughs at the same time, a sore scream and a sore laugh.

Then he heads toward Trixi, his long hands and seaweed hair moving in the water like a mermaid's. "No!" She kicks Uncle Paulo in the head and his chin hits the bottom of the pool. He starts coming up with a big push off the floor of the pool.

"No! No! Stop it!" Henrilyn screams at her Uncle Paulo. The lifeguard's whistle is screeching, and Uncle Paulo comes up for air, flinging his hair out of his face, coming at me; I'm right there in his way, backing up with my brother behind me. "Stop it, Ivah," Blu says. "Move. You spoiling all the fun."

❀

Leave, I want to leave.
At Mid-Pac, no laundry, no cooking.
No Blu.

❀

After they swam in the pool, Uncle Paulo would drive Evangeline, Blendaline, Henrilyn, and Trixi in Da Sun to buy magazines from Misaki's and shave ice up at CPC. Blu would hang on to the tailgate for one last look at sakushi mouth Blendaline before the truck skidded out of the parking lot. Then he'd wave at her from inside a red dust cloud as the truck skidded out onto the road.

That is, until the day Uncle Paulo stuck his head out of the driver's window and said, "Blendie, tell your boy-friend he can come if he like. Couples in the back. Henri and Trixi ride in the front with Uncle. Eh, brah," he tells Blu, "tell your big sista come ride on my lap in the front if she like. How old her?"

"Thirteen."

"Perfect fit."

"Fuck you, Blu," I scream at my brother. "Wait till I tell Poppy what you doing, stupid shit."

"Aw, shut up," Blendaline hisses at me. "Scram."

"Yeah, scram, Ivah. Tell um, Mitch," says Evangeline to back up her sister. Mitchell doesn't say anything but looks at me with that sorry-I-know-we-were-friends-but-now-I-choose-love-over-friendship look, and he makes me sick.

"You wait, Blu, they going eat you alive."

"No—" Maisie says, and holds my hand tighter than knots in a sheet. She looks up at me and says slowly, "Eat cats."

Da Sun drives off toward town. Blendaline sits between Blu's legs, copying Evangeline and Mitchell, and I quickly look at my mother's Seiko watch, something Maisie stole for me from Mama's drawer with her itchy fingers and something I wear on my itchy wrist. Most of the time, I keep it in my pocket so Poppy doesn't see it.

4 p.m. Poppy's gone by now to the truck barn.

Maisie and I take the slow walk home past Mr. Iwasaki, who bangs his Saloon Pilot cracker cans and waits for us to look, past the Kuro-chan's, the hungry dogs begging to be taken home to live with Ka-san, past Elena Gaspar's, hanging her new panties on the line to dry, past the Reyes house that smells like rats.

I fry some Spam and green beans for dinner and cook three cups of hot rice. Feed the dog and sweep and mop the floors. Maisie's bathed and in her Buster Browns. It's so hot that I let her sleep in panties only. She has summer school tomorrow with Miss Ito. By seven o'clock, Blu's still not home.

"Where he stay, the mento fool?" I tell Maisie. "We gotta work tomorrow, me and him." Blu and I have found another job on Mondays and Fridays, helping Miss Ito tutor the Special Ed kindergartners in reading for the summer. Five dollars a week, plus we still iron on Wednesdays and groom dogs on Saturdays.

Maisie draws back the curtains and peers out. The sky is indigo already. She turns away from the window, holds her breath, slides down, and leans against the wall. Ka-san's whining.

"Maisie, Poppy ain't home, so no worry. We not going get lickens from him for Blu not being home. Go put the rope on Ka-san. Us gotta go look for Blu. He probly stay Blendaline's house eating adobo or something."

Maisie's eyes want to believe me but don't. She whistles for the dog and we head out the door. The streetlights softly crackle above us.

When we see the Reyes house around the bend of the gully, the lights are all off. "Blu, Blu," I call. Ka-san pulls on the rope, and Maisie lets her go. Da Sun is gone, everybody's gone, but I hear chickens and crickets, the crunch of mango tree leaves under our feet.

"Blu," I whisper. "Presley, Presley. Where you stay?"

"Ivah, help." But it's not Blu, it's Mitchell. Ka-san barks and yelps at him as Maisie pulls her hard by the rope around her neck.

"What the fuck's going on?" I yell at Mitchell.

Then I see my brother tied to the clothesline with sennit, the knots pulled so tightly that Mitchell has to use his teeth to loosen them. An old T-shirt gags Blu's mouth. All of the ropes around Blu's body, his arms, and his feet cut into his skin.

Mitchell tells me, "We were playing a game of cowboys and Indians with Uncle Paulo, who suggested that we take a hostage, so he looked around and said, 'Grab the fat ass, he make good stew,' and proceeded to tie up your brother. Uncle Paulo told him not to worry—Blu was actually Clint Eastwood and the hero of the movie, so they'd get F Troop to set him loose in no time. But they didn't.

"Then Uncle Paulo yelled, 'One mo' time,' and I knew this time it was me, so I ran for the gully and hid. Then

Vangie and Blendie tickled your brother's feet until he cried, and Uncle Paulo said something like they had to go get their mother Agnes from the airport, so they all jumped in the truck and left."

The rag tied to Blu's mouth is full of saliva. I take it off. He's got deep rope burns from all the struggling. "Run home and get a knife, Ivah. Hurry up before they all come back."

I get up and cut through the Reyes' oleander hedge. Turn back and stop. I hear my brother say, "Ho shit, why you guys acting all nuts? We was only having some fun."

❀

The next morning, there are rope-burn scars on his wrists and ankles like he had around his neck after hanging on the mango tree. I mix aloe sap from the huge plant we have next to the gully with some honey and put it on his burns just like my Mama did when the rice pot fell on Maisie and burned her chest.

"They wasn't being mean, you know, Ivah. They was going get their madda and then they was going make me eat dinner their house."

"Yeah, right, Blu. You go on dreaming."

There's a knock at the door. Maisie opens the door and Mitchell Oliveira walks on in.

"What's new? What are you guys doing today?" he asks as he sits at the kitchen table.

"We gotta go work down the school," I tell him. "Why, now that you seen the real Evangeline, what—you scared silly, hah, Mitchell? You one stupid Portagee if I eva seen one."

"See, Ivah," says Blu, "you get one evil mouth and you

use um on everybody, right, Mitch?" We get up to go to the school and Mitchell starts walking with us down the dusty driveway. "Stay, Ka-san, stay," Blu tells her, and she sits at the end of the road. Blu and Maisie walk ahead of Mitchell and me.

"So what, Mitchell? How come you was all tight with Evangeline and now you back hanging around with me?" I know it isn't love, and to tell the truth, I like this haole better as a kick-around-the-block kind of friend. "What made her so good to you?"

"Ivah, you cannot tell anybody else if I tell you, because if my Aunty Mary found out what I did, she'd send me back to El Segundo on the next flight out." Mitchell takes a deep breath and looks around as if there are spies all around us. "Vangie licked and sucked my—"

"Ivah, hurry up," Blu yells. "We going be late for Maisie's school."

"You take her fast, Blu. Go, Miss Ito waiting. Mitchell gotta tell me something. What? What you said about you and Vangie?"

"Fuck, I hope she didn't tell anyone. Oh jeez, she must've told everyone. What'll I do, Ivah?"

"Go on. What she did to you that made you stay with one girl who look like one baboon? Sorry, Mitchell."

"Sometimes it was her and Blendie sucking me and sometimes they used the Jergens and one time blueberry yogurt, which they licked up."

"Stop. Stop."

"It feels like, like—"

"Stop. I no like know."

"It feels like—like no pain. Like flying."

After he was tied up, Blu made lots of Dymo labels with Miss Ito's label maker. All over his black marble composition tablet was stickered:

BLU -N- BLEN
LOVE HURTS BABE
BLEN LUVS BLU
COLOUR MY WORLD
BLACK -N- BLU = BLEN -N- BLU
IF BLEN LIVE ACROSS THE SEA
WHAT A FINE SWIMMER BLU WOULD BE
U -N- ME
4-EVA

✽

It hurts.

Not because I loved him in the past. It's not about Mitchell. I need to know how the Reyes sisters take away pain.

My Mama used to blow on a cut. Mama used to sing. But it never felt like flying.

✽

Mitchell and I go to his Aunty Mary's one day after the summer-school bell rings. They raise canaries in a huge aviary filled with yellow, black, white, and gray birds all in the upper branches of a dead guava tree.

There are birdbaths with clean water, canaries wetting themselves furiously and shaking their feathers into yellow balls and revealing the shine of clean bodies. Papaya rinds sit on the floor of the aviary and waiwi cut in half, bird-pecked to the skin. Aunty Mary has bird swings and bird toys hanging from the top of the aviary at different lengths, mirrors and sticks of birdseed and grit tied to the guava branches.

"Here, Ivah, stand here and look up."

I look up. Sunlight and feathers. The quick flit and skitter of birds.

"Close your eyes."

Singing trails of notes sweet and high.

"Hear them all at once."

I hear the play of colors.

"Now listen to only one. Concentrate. Keep your eyes closed."

I hear my brother singing.

I look up. My eyes behold a light rain trapped in sunlight and the falling of yellow down. There has never been another moment like this one.

❀

Mama said: "If you dream of rainfall all night in your dreams, something will happen to make you worry."

Now I lay me down, down,

let me go, let me be normal.

Don't wanna be a Mama too.

❀

Blu's back playing with Blendaline again and there's nothing I can do to stop him. He's home by five like I ask him, but he says nothing to me about what they do.

Mitchell's back with Evangeline again and there's nothing I can do about that either. He calls me on the phone at night and goes to work with us at Miss Ito's on Mondays and Fridays. I'm his only friend-friend still. And he tells me everything. Even what I don't want to know.

"Ivah, I gave Vangie two canaries from my Aunty Mary," he tells me.

"Rats eat birds too, you know."

"Huh?"

"Neva mine."

"Vangie's Uncle Paulo made this huge birdcage that's like a miniature version of Aunty Mary's aviary. I mean, you can't walk in it, but it's huge. And nice."

"So?"

"I just thought you might want to know. Aunty Mary said you could have a canary too 'cause of all the papayas we've been picking from your trees in the back of your house."

"I don't have a cage."

"Oh."

They keep going back and back and back. To the Human Rats who suck and lick.

❀

During one summer-school recess, Blu sits with Maisie on the dusty stairs. A palmful of M&M's sorted by color melts in his hand and mouth. And one by one, he puts reds on the tip of Maisie's tongue. He tells her:

"I going be Free Canary. No, change my mind. I no like copycat David Carradine and Barbara Seagull. I like be Flier Canary."

Maisie holds out her tongue and closes her eyes.

"Blendie my girlfriend, you know."

Tongue out and nod.

"Who is *more* than a girl who is a friend, unlike Ivah's boyfriend Mitchell, who is a boy who *is* a friend. Blendie get two canaries name Sam and Mary. She wen' name um that 'cause all Portagees name Sam or Mary. You like know why I Flier Canary?"

Red dye bleeding into the taste buds on her tongue. More, give me more. In the quick wag of her tongue.

"I cannot tell 'cause Blendie said not to."

Saving all the green M&M's for himself.

"You know what Ed the Big Head Endo told me, Maisie? His bradda Eugene told him about wet dreams. I get um, you know. And every morning I wake up, ho, I get one boner. Make your penis look big, you know, when you get boner."

She turns her head one way and looks at him, eyebrows cross.

"Gimme your tongue." He gives her a whopping three. "Sometimes, I see Blendie's panty, I get boner. I see ovary in the health book, I get boner. I read her poem, I get boner." He crunches hard, the green M&M's. "I just thinking about this now and I getting boner." Maisie looks at his crotch. "So much boners, I get, if had feathers on my penis, maybe I fly away dick-first."

"No," she says. "Stay."

"But what Ed told me," he says, placing the rest of the candies from his color-stained palm in Maisie's waiting mouth, "nocturnal emis-shuns, thass one waste of good sperm."

❁

Friday after summer school, Mitchell and Evangeline meet at the pool. She's with her Uncle Paulo, Henrilyn, and Trixi. "See you later, Ivah," Mitchell says to me as he runs off toward the swimming pool. Blu, Maisie, and I continue to walk home.

"I going Blendie's house, okay, Ivah? I come home by five."

"No, Blu. No go if only you and her home. Bumbye she blame you for something and going be her word against yours, then what?"

I have been dreaming of constant rain.

"Why, what she going blame me for? I her boyfriend. You no blame the one you love."

Blu runs up the Reyes driveway and goes right in the kitchen door without knocking. Maisie and I walk on home. We sit in front of the TV with mayonnaise bread full of paprika.

"Scared."

"Of what? Blu going with Blendie?" I ask.

Ka-san comes running up the back stairs. I hear her barking and the scratch of her nails on the door. Maisie runs to the back door and Ka-san's yelping wildly, running in circles and whimpering. "What Ka-san, what?" I ask her. The dog scampers down the stairs and stops in the middle of the driveway. "Just like Lassie," I tell Maisie. "She like us follow her." The dog turns to see if we're following, then runs toward the bend in the road.

❀

My body is running to the Reyes house.
I know it as I follow my dog.
My body is running up the Reyes driveway.
Into their kitchen door.
I stop.

Trixi's alone in the living room playing with the canaries. She looks up at me for a moment and smiles. Her hair's still wet. She looks like Maisie, baby eyes, wide and teary. And she says nothing to me. But she shifts her eyes toward a laundry basket, upside down on the couch. Inside: Hoppy Creetat, crouched low and panting.

I know my brother's here.

"Let my cat out," I tell Trixi.

"I neva do this to your cat," she tells me.

I believe her. She lifts the basket off of Hoppy and my cat panic-runs around the living room, until Trixi opens the back door and the cat dashes out.

"Where my brother?" I ask her.

"I dunno," she says. "I just came home." Then she head-jerks me: Down the hallway.

I move down the hall.

I hear the bath water running behind the closed door. Burst into the bathroom.

I see my brother, naked, sitting on the edge of the bath tub, his legs spread. Blendaline kneeling between them, her mouth around my brother's penis.

He doesn't even see me until I say, "Blu. Blu!"

I see his pain leave his face, his whole body sink and sigh. And Blendaline spits into the tub, then runs into her room and slams the door. "Get out of my fuckin' house, Ivah." Her voice sounds muffled from behind the closed door. "Wait till I tell Vangie. We going kick your fuckin' ass."

I don't care. I look down at my brother, putting on his clothes. "What the fuck you doing, Blu? What you doing all naked, letting her—letting her—" The words don't come and my brother never looks at me. "Why you gave her our cat?"

"Blendie hate the canaries. They make too much noise."

"Why, Blu, why?" I want to hit him. I want to hold him.

"She said she suck me as many times as I like if I put our cat in the birdcage later on."

"Why, Blu? What you doing to us?"

It's a moment in my life that I will remember against my will forever. Him, tied on earth to me. There's no way for him to escape the house without a mother, the days and nights without a father. No money, no food. He pulls Lila Beth's old T-shirt over his head.

"I gotta fly, Ivah, anywhere in this world." My brother walks to the living room of the Reyes house like nothing happened. "Bye, Blendie," he yells down the hallway. The birdcage on the coffee table is full of feathers wind-sucked to the wire and empty birdseeds. Blu turns to me. "Flier, get it, Ivah, Flier? Why you no can just let me fly, hah, Ivah?"

The rope burns on his wrists and ankles aren't even healed. At night, he hangs on to a knotted sheet dangling from his window. The sky turns purple, then indigo. The cat cries in the gully. The rains spill endlessly in my dreams. But tonight, I loosen the knots in the rope that tie him to me, and let the rope fall away. Fall from my brother, who has learned how to fly.

12 The sun hovers near the horizon. Off the wharf, halalu run in silver schools. The whole town's down there with bamboo poles and buckets, Styrofoam ice chests, frozen shrimp, and fishing tackle. The halalu swim in mad circles in the shallow bucket water. Fresh fish for dinner.

Blu carries our bucket with seven fish and Maisie the bamboo poles down the long wharf right outside town on our way home. We walk past the electric company, the loud churning, cranking, the wheezing of machinery, past the Dairy Queen and the Baptist church, past Kaunakakai School, the baseball field, the fire station, and the gym.

I gut the halalu with a dull knife. I'm not too good at this, but I pull out the stomach and the red lacy gills and then place them in a margarine bowl for Hoppy. Blu takes her onto the porch for her fresh fish dinner and listens to her crunch the guts.

"Maisie, come," he yells into the house. "You gotta watch how nice Hoppy eat and no get no blood on her hands and mouth."

I hear him talk to the cat. "You the cleanest cat I eva met. Ai, Maisie, come quick, Maisie. I see lumps in Hoppy's stomach. You pregnant, yeah, Hoppy? No wonder you so hungry."

Maisie opens the door slowly. And Blu points.

In their sleep without rain, how could they not hear her crying in the gully, night after night, a cat crying that sounds like a baby?

I fry the halalu the way Mama taught me. Get the heavy cast-iron frying pan and heat the oil. Salt and pepper the fish, coat them lightly in flour, and fry them crispier than crisp. So crunchy that you can even eat the head and not worry about the bones.

"C'mon, eat. Maisie, you be careful. If you get bone stuck in your throat, what you suppose to do?"

She shrugs her shoulders.

"Swallow one ball of rice whole," Blu says.

"Your name Maisie?" I ask him.

"No, my name Presley, why, bodda you? What my name, Maisie?" She doesn't answer.

"Eat nice," I say to Maisie, ignoring the wise-ass Blu. I set her plate down. "Here, Blu, I made you two halalu."

"Ivah," he says, "you wen' fry fish for Poppy yet?"

"What for? He coming home eleven o'clock. I make um when he come home so the fish stay crunchy. Go, eat. Bumbye the bugga wilt and taste junk. No worry about Poppy." Blu saves the head for last and starts on the tails and fins, fried so well they taste like expensive fish flakes that melt on the tongue.

Poppy hasn't spoken to me for days. Nothing. Hasn't played the piano or made small talk about the neighbors. Hasn't asked about TV or the weather, Blu, Maisie, or the dog. When he does speak, it's to ask the most basic things, like "Get tea?" Or "Where the shoyu?" He doesn't do much, but once in a while he asks me softly, "I miss

Eleanor, you too, Ivah?" And I nod yes very slowly. I get tired hearing the same thing over and over.

We're halfway through dinner when the phone rings. "I get um, I get um," and Blu runs to the phone. Hallo? Yeah, this Blu. Fine. She fine. Yeah, he fine. We all fine. She over there eating dinner. Ivah, come quick. Big Sis like talk to you."

"Hi, Big Sis." It's been a few weeks since her last letter to me. "No, he at work still yet. Six days a week, he work. About eleven he come home."

"I put in one request for student-teach at Molokai High, math, and I got um," she tells me. "I going be in the cottages. I already sent my truck. You think Uncle Bertram can pick me up this Sunday? I like come early so that I can set up my classroom."

"Yeah, Poppy can go airport on Sundays 'cause he no work. I tell him." My heart aches. I'm so happy Big Sis will be here with us in a few days.

"I get plenny stuff for you guys too. Sheez, Lila Beth go through clothes and girly shit like nothing. She gone already. Went Seattle University, some small-ass college mo' small than UH and Hilo College, but 'cause she went mainland, she one hot shit, eh? You know how Hilo people—you go mainland college, you automatic one hot shit. You get the Kiwanis scholarship, you double hot shit. And you know Lila, she was already one stupid shit, so I guess that make her three times one big shit."

Big Sis and I laugh over the phone. "What cottage you get? Us can help you set um up like that?" Blu and Maisie sit against the hallway wall. "Go finish your dinner," I tell them, but they don't move.

"I got assigned to share cottage with somebody name Sandra Ito. They said her haole roommate wen' pack um up back to the mainland. Only wen' handle one year."

"Yeah, that was Miss Owens. That was Maisie's teacher, the one wen' put her in—"

"Special Ed? Where Maisie?"

"Right here. Thass the one, I was telling you, Big Sis, the one, she act all big time, fast-talking, sassy mouth haole, but her panty was all over town."

"Yeah, I rememba. But how's this Sandra Ito?"

"She Maisie's teacha. The one me and Blu work for this summer. We went sleep her house for Maisie's birthday. She the best. When summer school was finish, she treat us three at Pau Hana Inn to lunch and then we went beach after that." I want to tell Big Sis about Miss Ito helping me to get into Mid-Pacific, but I don't.

❀

So much I want to go.
So much I want to stay.
She sees it in me.
What nobody, only Mama saw.
Something not lost to sight.

❀

"Ivah? Ivah? You there? So you was saying that I get one good roommate? Whatevas. Tell Uncle three o'clock Sunday. I see you guys then. And eh, Ivah, anytime this year, my place. We make slumber party every night, you like."

"Okay, Big Sis." After we hang up, Blu hugs Maisie sitting against the hallway wall. Then he looks at me like I should hug the both of them, but I don't. I don't know why.

I walk to the picture window and draw back the curtains and see the moon, a white hook hanging in the purple sky, housetops and treetops; lights in every window on our street.

How can I leave them?

❀

With the new school year, I enter the ninth grade and Blu starts the fifth. Maisie is back in a regular first-grade class, Mr. Anson Shaw's class. Back with the sharks and piranhas preying on and eating the weak ones at the edges of the schoolyard. Miss Ito tutors her twice a week. "She's very, very bright—don't let her fool you, Ivah," she tells me all the time. "She's reading at the third-grade level."

Blu has Mrs. Doris Ota. The same old buck I had in the fifth grade. And always comparing Blu to me. "Oh, I hope you're as creative as your sister!" Blu's way more creative than me.

"Oh, I hope you're as helpful as your sister. Always staying late to help me close the windows." She *made* me do it for extra points for not finishing my sentence diagrams the way she wanted.

The first long weekend in October, Big Sis picks us up in her truck early Friday evening. We're going to spend a couple of nights at the teacher's cottage. I make a big pot of chicken feet soup, mostly for Maisie; Mama claimed that chicken feet gave you strong muscles.

Their kitchen finally knows what it should smell like. Japanese. After we all have dinner, Miss Ito has a screwdriver and Big Sis a baby Miller. They bring out all the sleeping bags and we lie down on the floor. Maisie's asleep already next to Blu. We watch *Gidget Goes Ha-*

waiian on Channel 4. Miss Ito falls asleep on the couch and Big Sis covers her with a quilt. She walks to the front door and douses the mosquito punk, which is clipped with a clothespin to a tuna can.

"We go beach tomorrow, Ivah," she tells me. "You and me can talk some more about Mid-Pac. Sandi told me all about it. You like go, right, Ivah? Go. Just go. I know you get plenny other stuff fo' consider, but if I was you—"

"Whass that, Mid-Pack?" Blu asks. "Whass that?"

"We tell you later, Blu," Big Sis says. "We talk some more when only me and you can talk," Big Sis whispers to me.

"Okay," I tell her. My heart races.

"Presley," she says.

"What? Whatchu like?" He's acting cocky because we didn't answer his question earlier.

"You know what I glad about?"

"What?" Blu asks again, more wise than the first time.

"You ain't treating your blood like shit no more."

Blu pulls himself close to Maisie and kisses her forehead. He looks at me and smiles, his lips pulled sideways into his cheek. " 'Cause they my bestest sistas, thass why." He turns his body to the TV. "Ivah," he says looking back at me straight in the eye, "I neva hang our cats. I just wanted you for know. Wasn't me, okay? I promise."

❀

With the new school year, we see Poppy less and less. It's him who is there on the orange chair, but he seems to be a two-dimensional picture of our father staring blankly at the TV before falling asleep in the living room. Night after night, Poppy sits in front of the TV.

One evening as I help Maisie with her math, Poppy says, low and tired, "Ivah, pour me some o-cha." He's brewed it in the old dented teapot that Mama used every night to make gen mai cha popcorn tea after dinner. I walk slowly to the coffee table and pour him some tea backhand style so I can get back to Maisie's homework.

"What the hell with the backhand, Ivah? I dead to you too, eh?"

"I sorry, Poppy." I remember Mama saying don't pour tea dead-man style. When I did, she hit my hand with chopsticks, which was also bad manners, but I guess less bad manners than pouring tea that way.

The smell of the tea is sweet and strange. I lift the cover and inhale the steam. The liquid is bright yellow and thick. "Poppy, this popcorn tea?"

"Yeah, why? Something boddering you about the tea?"

"Smell different."

Poppy says nothing for a long time. He gazes off, glassy-eyed, at the television. Then he gets up to play the piano.

"I miss Eleanor. You too, Ivah?"

"Yeah."

"I mean, I *really* miss Eleanor," Poppy says to me.

"Yeah," I tell him, with the tone of: Yeah, I heard you the first time.

"You too?"

"Yeah," I say again.

"Why you no can talk little bit more about your own madda?"

I think about her every day.

Every day of my life.

He's so fucking lost.

"I dunno," I tell him.

"I dunno too. Sometimes I feel so sore for her, stay all over my body again. I see the lesions all come out on my body. And Eleanor helping me with the bandages."

I swallow hard and look down.

"Pour me some more tea and talk to me about Eleanor."

"Like what, Poppy?"

"I dunno," he says. "Why I gotta be the one start um off?"

He's off. What's he talking about? I look at Maisie and she at me, and she shrugs her shoulders.

"What you said, Ivah?"

"I neva say nothing. I said something, Maisie?"

She shakes her head.

"Oh."

We both pause for a long while. Then Poppy says, "Well, talk to me about her, fuck, what you waiting for?"

I talk about the smell of her hair, he yells at me, "What you talking about her *hair* for?"

I talk about her honohono blooming in March, the leaves covered white with rice water, he yells at me, "Fuck the flowers. Talk about Eleanor."

I talk about the tripe stew she made, he says, "Thass all you think about is food."

I say nothing, I get "You fuckin' cruel, Ivah, you cruel just like your madda's side, and you just like my sista Betty. You no like talk to me, no need then. Get outta my fuckin' sight."

I take the lid off of the teapot and breathe in deeply. "Whass this, Poppy? C'mon, tell me." Poppy says nothing for a long while. So tired from being mad.

He says at last, "Thass the brew we made down there. For make the sore go away. All kine sore go away with this tea. We give um one dignified name. Call um hemp tea."

Hemp? My mind scrambles for a meaning.

"Furtado them only like the kolas. He give all the leaves to me. I dry um in the aku drying box, then cut um up for the tea." Poppy leans back in the orange chair. "You no drink this shit, now, Ivah. Thass for me and Eleanor only." His mouth seems dry.

Pretty soon his mouth slacks open and Poppy snores softly in the orange chair. I cover him with a blanket. This takes place every night. Poppy drinking thick yellow tea, staring at the TV, and falling asleep curled up in the orange chair, the best chair in the house.

❀

One night, Blu's knotted sheet tears, and he falls out of his window. But Blu's done a lot of stupid things. Things I couldn't stop or help. Things that I've stopped helping altogether. And he tells me lots of things. Things I couldn't even dream of knowing. No Mama, no questions answered. A Poppy so far gone he talks in bubbles, all nonsense. When he drinks the hemp tea, there are many things I cannot stop or help.

Now, I hear my brother praying under the house with sister Maisie. Brother Blu playing communion soda cracker and grape juice like we had in Vacation Bible School.

"Dear Heavenly Mama, Highest Queen of Queens, I pray to thee today like the Baptists teach us, yeah, Maisie?"

"Yes," Maisie says, all holy.

"Well, my heart of hearts is broken asunder. My girl-friend, you know her, Most Heavenly Mama, Blendaline Reyes, our neighbor? Maybe she my ex now, because she cannot stand the sight of Ivah. Well, she was doing some-thing with her Uncle Paulo which I saw when I went to her house to say sorry for Ivah, which is a whole 'nother prayer.

"I was pretty heartbroken. I was scared when Blendie's uncle said, 'What the fuck you like, punk? Shut the fuckin' door.' Sorry about the F-words, but I wanted you to hear the real thing. Oooh, Poppy came home. In Jesus name us pray. Amen."

"A-men," says Maisie.

They heard my footsteps. I cannot even imagine what it was that Blu saw. So I ask him. And this is what he finally tells me:

"Okay. You no can tell nobody. Not even Mitchell, but I know that he know this too, 'cause he was in the house that time that I came in. But he was in Vangie's room."

"Stop calling her Vangie like you guys close or some-thing, Blu," I tell him.

"Shut up or I ain't going tell you the rest, Ivah."

"Okay, go on."

"You know Mrs. Agnes Reyes work two jobs since Kan-cho Kaneshima, the daddy, wen' go fool around her sec-ond cousin, Florence Tanaka, right? So she ask her bradda, who is Uncle Paulo, for watch the girls."

"So what all those details got to do with this story, shit?" I ask Blu.

"I thought you wanted the whole scoop? Well anyways, I wen' open the door slow kine 'cause I heard Blendie making the love sound she make when she do that kine stuff and they was on the bed. Blendie and her Uncle Paulo was on the bed all naked and oofing each other, for real, Ivah, I seen um. Mitchell and Vangie was in the other room probly doing the same thing."

"Where Trixi was?"

"In the living room playing with the canary that no mo' one feet. But thass *another* story. Bugga hop around on his stub, you know."

I don't know what to say. I don't want Blu near their house. I look at him: the more I tell him no, the more he goes back and begs like a dog at the door.

"Thass when Uncle Paulo wen' stand up and yell at me, 'What the fuck you like, punk? What, you fuckin' shithead, eva heard of knocking? Eh, what the fuck you staring at, mothafucka? Shut the fuckin' door.' I was looking at his boto, Ivah. Was big and ereck-shun. Thass why he no mo' girlfriend, you know. He no need. He get Evangeline and Blendaline. Pretty soon, maybe he going oof Henrilyn and Trixi."

"Henrilyn? And Trixi too? You lie, Blu."

"I ain't lying. Maybe right now he only stay touching around their chingching, but pretty soon—Henri and Trixi might get oof too, Ivah."

I feel sad. And sick. Trixi's eyes are wide and scared like Maisie's.

"And when I was just about for go out the house," Blu

continues, "I heard Uncle Paulo calling Trixi. 'C'mon, Trixi Treat. You going be the best. You the tightest. Uncle neva come yet.' And I seen Trixi stand up, she look at me long time—she was scared, Ivah, her mouth, her whole face was crying, and she run down the back steps and hide in the bushes by the gully."

Blu looks at me for an answer, but I have none.

"C'mon, Ivah, say something."

I have nothing to say. Why do they all need me to say something? I'm afraid for my brother in a way that hurts my body and makes me mute. I look toward the window.

"I dunno why Trixi gotta cry, sheez," Blu says, "wen' look like Uncle Paulo and Blendie was having good fun."

How do I make the world stop for Blu? Hang on to this earth, I want to say. But there's no more rope to hold him.

13 Poetry Unit
English Workbook Series Red Level
Presley V. Ogata
Mrs. Ota
Room 8

> Roses are red, violets are blue,
> how does your garden grow?
> Roses are red, violets are blue,
> I like to see you in your red church
>   dress.
> Roses are red, violets are blue,
> your garden grew long eggplants and
>   wild violets.
> Roses are blue violets,
> you gave the red dress to Ivah when you
>   died.
> Roses are red violets,
> I miss you.

Mama read the instructions off a package of seeds and planted the border of the whole front yard with wild violets. Dug the red dirt with her garden spade and mixed in hapu'u fibers and red cinders, then lay the seeds down like babies going to sleep. White violets, purple violets, and white violets with purple centers. Leaves shaped like hearts. And to find the flowers, we searched the violet plants and cut the thin stems long so that Mama could tie a tiny bunch together with white sewing thread for the teacher to put in a vase on her desk.

I remember finding flowers pressed by Mama between the pages of the World Book Encyclopedia. There, between the old, yellowing pages, in wax paper, were wild violets thin as dragonfly wings. In the Webster's Dictionary, the King James Bible from the Baptists, and the thick Betty Crocker binder from Aunty Betty, as well. And every time I find one, I put it in the shoebox under my bed. My mother's violets. Do you know that violets are not blue until they've been pressed for months, thin, without air?

❋

On Mother's Day, Maisie, Blu, and I go to her grave in the cemetery hidden in a grove of kiawe trees on the outskirts of town. Over Lawrence "Bullseye" Santiago Rest in Peace and Maria T. Santiago INRI. Around God's Grace Aboundeth Hazel Mitsuyoshi and past Julius Corpuz Mercy Be Thine Sayeth the Lord.

Mama's stone is plain. *Eleanor "Ella" Yumiko Ogata. Loving Mother and Wife.* Maisie places the thread-tied bunches of wild violets all around Mama's name like a lei.

And there I see the pie pan with the childbearing stones. Perfectly round stones of all sizes, smooth and shiny. Maisie sticks her hands in the pan to feel the stones and runs them through her fingers. The sound of tiny coins falling into a can.

Blu sits on the gravestone next to Mama's, God's Glory Itsuko Nakagawa Full of Grace, pulls kiawe thorns out of his rubber slippers, and swears.

"Sorry, Mama."

"You better be, Blu," I tell him.

"What's this, Ivah? What the stones doing?"

And there under the shade of the kiawe trees, I see, in the pie pan missing from our house, the stones giving birth to stones. The same strange stones I had seen in Poppy's bedroom while sweeping under his bed, and I know in that moment that he has been here before me.

The shape of a pigeon's eggs, the stones are streaked with white and red marks. When the mother-stone is about to give birth, I see the child-stone inside her with my own eyes.

"I scared."

"No," I tell Maisie. "This one miracle."

The child-stone spins inside the mother-stone, a red and white swirl. "Look."

"Ai-ka, omigod," Blu gasps. "I gotta send this to the Ripley's Believe It or Not for cash prize."

"You no send miracles from God for cash, you moron."

"Mama," Maisie screams.

And when the child is born, there are no scars left on the mother-stone. The wind stops moving the leaves of the kiawe tree. Maisie holds her hands over her mouth. She looks at me, not believing what we have seen with our own eyes.

Blu gathers up the bunches of wild violets and places them all in the pan. Maisie weeps.

"Thass the miracle," Blu says. "Even after all that, the
Mama-stone no more scars and the babies perfect. Gotta
keep um warm. Cover um with blue violets."

❀

Roses are red, violets are blue.
Roses are red violets.
Red violets, blue.
Roses are violets.
Red is blue.
Heavenly God the Father,
bless Marcella, Gunther, Prudence, and Simon. (dogs)

❀

The dogs in the basement are dying.
We find Prudence dead on Saturday. Freshly dead.
I think Mrs. Ikeda knew she was dead but waited for
us to find her so she wouldn't have to take her out of the
cage. And Mrs. Ikeda acts overly shocked when we open
the cage and see Prudence's body. Matted and full of
gray, scaly lesions, bald spots with thick, red liquid.
Her blue tongue sticks out of the side of her mouth; a
bloodshot-blue membrane partly covers her sad cocker
eyes.

Mrs. Ikeda makes us bury the dogs in her back lot.

Blu tries to comb Prudence's hair first while I carry her
dead body, but it's so tangled it's no use. He works on
grooming her face and head only. He pulls the last blood
ticks off of her eyes and out of her ears, gently combing
the tangles out. She's limp and heavy.

It takes so long to dig the hole. Maisie, Blu, and I take
turns using the shovel with the broken handle to dig the
hard red dirt. Ten shovelfuls each, and while we wait for

our turn, we hold Prudence and say nice things to her about her life, her personality, her children, and how sorry we are that we didn't help sooner, but it's too late.

Her death hits my brother hard. When it's his turn to hold the dead dog, he squeezes her body tightly to his and rocks her. "Listen good for when they call your name in heaven. Thass why you need clean ears," he says. He wipes the apricot wax from the inside of Prudence's ears with the bottom of his T-shirt.

Maisie lays newspaper in the grave so it's clean. Then she puts an old Give a Hoot T-shirt she found in one of the Salvation Army boxes in Mrs. Ikeda's garage beneath Prudence's body.

Blu lays her down. He carefully arranges her legs and head, bent this way, looking comfortable, as if Prudence is sleeping for the night on a T-shirt, on a newspaper, in a hole, in the ground. While we throw clumps of hard, red dirt over her, he says:

"Roses are red, violets are blue,

"Our most heavenly God, Father of Jesus, and Uncle to the Holy Ghost, please bless Prudence, a dog full of grace and mercy. Loving Mother, Sister, and Wife of Many Brothers."

At home Maisie makes a cross out of sticks tied with sennit to bring with us the next Saturday. She finds the best sticks in the schoolyard, and with them, brings back another bunch of wild violets tied with white thread.

The next Saturday, we bury Simon.

"Dear God, Boss of the heavenly cherubims and angels choir, bless Simon, a dog full of energy and long black hair. Loving Brother and Protector of his Sisters."

Then Marcella.

"Heavenly God, first in command, bless Marcella, a dog who borned deaf children. Always a Kind Mother to the Deaf."

Gunther.

"O God on high, bless Gunther, no more blood ticks on his balls."

Mignon.

Claudia.

Burl.

The dogs are dying in the basement.

❋

"Roses are Choward's Violets," Blu tells me, back on the porch of our house, where he sits with Ed the Big Head Endo. "The one in the purple-and-silver wrapping."

The ones he eats because they're mints, actually, and taste like powdered perfume.

"Mrs. Ota eat them all day. Stay in her desk drawer and she eat um 'cause they mints and they battle halitosis. She get stink mouth, yeah, Ivah? She had stink mouth when you was in her class? Just like she no soak her dentures in Polident nighttime or something. Kinda greenish gray, her teeth, yeah, Ivah?"

It's his latest favorite food, these Choward's Violets, and after melting the powdered perfume squares on his tongue, he cups his hands in front of his face and goes, "Hhhaaa." Then he inhales deeply. Blu and Ed eat their Violets and smell each other's breath.

"So okay," Blu says, "make Merv Griffin. Ask me one question."

"Okay," Ed the Big Head begins. "What is your favorite food?"

"Well, Merv, you ask what my favorite foods are. Well, if you're talking school lunch, I might say Shepherd Pie and Mash Potato. I also like can Green Beans with Butter, Chill Pineapple, square Shortbread Cookies with fork holes in the top. I like Hot Cross Bun and Creole Macaroni. Sometimes Maisie wrap her Shortbread Cookie or Peanut Butter Cookie in school napkin and let me eat hers after school."

My sister giggles.

"But if you're talking favorite food but not school lunch, then I might say it use to be Violet Crumble but now it's Choward's Violets."

They all laugh, and Blu, the boss of the Violets, places one on each tongue.

"This is my body," he says, "eat it in remembrance of me, sayeth the Lord Jesus Christ."

He's taken a handful of the child-stones from Mama's grave and packs of Violets and starts putting them in the mouths of the dead dogs before placing the dogs on the T-shirts, on the newspaper, in the holes, in the ground.

In remembrance of me.

To all the old dogs who are still alive, he slips the Choward's Violets that he loves so much to make their day sweet, powdery, and perfumy, their breath minty and fresh.

This is my body.

Always a kind word or two, my brother, full of mercy and grace.

He pets the old dogs, telling them about heaven, God,

and Jesus with heavenly blankets, who's there waiting for them, and how his Mama went there and could probably help the angels feed them. The Holy Ghost, God's nephew, will take them for daily walks in Central Park. No more cages and lots of fresh air to breathe. Outdoors, a garden with fresh water from a spring, not pipe water poured from an old Malolo syrup gallon with green moss on the bottom.

No more white powder on toenails cut too short.

No more sores.

No more howling when the cage door shuts.

Lots of Milk-Bones.

And skipping stones to chase into the water.

The one he put in their mouths.

Chasing stones across the River of Heaven.

❀

One night, a few weeks after we visited Mama's grave, I ask Poppy about the childbearing stones.

He sips his hemp tea, loaded, on the orange chair.

One thing I notice about stonies is that if you repeat things to them without periods or in between other thoughts, you can really mess with their heads childbearing stones and they cock their head sideways like confused dogs, one way, then the next childbearing stones way and pretty soon, you have them so confused, they say, "What?" And you get a better answer sooner.

"The childbearing stones?" he says. "How you know about them? You been snooping under my bed? Shit, what I told you about itchy fingas, hah?"

"Poppy," I tell him, "we went to Mama's grave the other day and saw the stones making babies in the pie pan."

"Oh. I put um there."

"How come?"

Blu sits next to me at the dining-room table. Poppy takes another sip of his tea. Maisie has her coloring on the carpet; she listens without looking.

His answer is simple:

"Down Kalaupapa, the stones, they was me and Eleanor's babies. We had plenny, plenny babies with elegant kine names and grandchildren and great-grandchildren all in pie pans and muffin pans and bread pans in the house. When we came topside, I took with me my favorite mother-stone, Philomena Leiko Ogata, and Eleanor took her favorite mother-stone, Zinnia Violet Ogata, and we started one family all over again. Starting with Ivah Harriet, blue rock, hard and strong. Presley Vernon, porous like the aʻa. And Maisie Tsuneko, little cinder. But the childbearing rocks, they remind your Mama and me of the days when you guys was one far-off dream for two people with leprosy in one house full of stones." Then he rubs the ache in his body, the rivers of scars, and goes back to drinking his tea in the dark living room, alone.

❀

I find Mama's treasures in her drawer. A box full of what Maisie, Blu, and I can keep in our own boxes:

The fingernail kit for Maisie on a night after dinner and a bath to anoint herself with rich oil.

❀

I see my sister taking care of her long, beautiful fingers.

❀

A picture of Mama and me as a baby and written on the back in her script: *"This I made with my body."*

❀

I see a full moon in the sky.

❀

Photos of Mama—
"Me and Alice P. outside Bishop Home for Girls."

❀

Dream, and I see Kalaupapa, girls with Hansen's disease, sun in their squinting eyes, on a porch, alone.

❀

"Me, 5." Mama's naked with her hands across her chest, looking with a girl's sad eyes into the camera, and the numbers of a criminal in front of her.

❀

I see my Mama alone.

❀

"Me, 5." Mama on a table in a dark dress with a lacy white collar. Front view, side view, the numbers of a criminal.

❀

Little girl alone.

❀

Then smiling with red lips, and Poppy, handsome in a vest, tie, and suit. "Discharged! Bertram my love and me."

❀

I see my Mama, dreamy, in love, Kalaupapa '58.

❀

And at the bottom of Mama's box—
Mama's Bible? For Blu? Maybe she knew God. And in it, a piece of parchment paper with the words of Father

Damien de Veuster: "I am no longer necessary; I am going to heaven."

❀

Poetry Unit
English Workbook Series Red Level
Presley V. Ogata
Mrs. Ota
Room 8

❀

My rewrite for higher grade:

❀

Roses are red, violets are blue
The dogs are dying, a-choo! God Bless You!
Roses are red, violets are blue
Where do they go? 1 + 1 = Two!
Roses are red, violets are blue
they smell like Clarabelle Siu! (Stink)
Roses are red, violets
are the best candy for dying dogs
won't you have some too?

❀

C–/D+. Presley, Did you look at my example on the board? It goes:
Roses are red, violets are blue,
Sugar is sweet,
And so are you!
Do you see how poetry should flow and rhyme? Work on this at home. Ask your sister for help. Maybe she remembers doing this in my room. But DON'T copy Ivah's poems. Do try your best. I know you can do it! Good luck. Mrs. Ota.

❀

"Mrs. Ota make me mad," Blu tells Ed the Big Head. "I creative and I get minus points. I no *like* my poems be like hers one."

"You the loser," Ed says.

Blu and Ed the Big Head raid the wild violet plants. They tie seven bunches with white thread. Three bunches for the bud vase on Mrs. Ota's desk. Three bunches for her to wear as a corsage with a little safety pin. One bunch pressed between the pages of English Workbook Series Red Level. Blu really wants a good grade for this part of the Poetry Unit.

So Ed the Big Head helps my brother write good poetry like he wrote in his tablet named Edson, Son of Ed, because he already earned an A on his first try.

❀

"Roses are Red, Violets are Blue"
  By: Presley V. Ogata
Dedicated to: My favorite teacher, Mrs. Ota
Roses are red, violets are blue,
  here are some violets I picked for you!
Roses are red, violets are blue,
  they smell sweet like morning dew!
Roses are red, violets are blue,
  honey is sweet, and so are you!
Roses are red, violets are blue,
  I think they're nice, what about you?

❀

And Mrs. Ota writes, "Wonderful! I see your sister helped you with this. Your rhymes are perfect! A+. Keep up the good work! Smile! Mrs. O."

❀

Back on the porch of our house, each with a pack of Violets, Ed the Big Head and Blu smell each other's breath. "See," Ed says, "I told you for kiss Mrs. Ota's ass for betta grade. Now you gotta pay me back 'cause I wrote um for you. I like see your fadda's stones, brah."

"Okay," Blu says. I know he thinks he's getting a good deal because it's a payback that's free. "Thass all I gotta do, right, Bob? Let you see the stones."

"Yeah, Pep. I only like see the stones," Ed says.

"Stupid Pep and Bob shit. I thought you guys gave that up?"

"Shut up, Ivah, Evil Mouth of the World," Blu says. Pep and Bob run into Poppy's room and lie down on the cool wood floor. Blu reaches under the bed and pulls out the pie pan of childbearing stones.

He's named them all, all the new child-stones. And introduces them one by one to Ed:

Gunther

Simon

Mignon

Prudence

Marcella

Claudia

Burl

When Chloe dies the next day, Blu stands in front of the crosses made of sticks and sennit and points his finger at all of the graves. He doesn't bite his finger, as I tell him. "Follow me home," he says.

This is the day we get fired.

That morning, I remember Blu stuffing his pockets with

tiny stones and candy to sneak to the dogs as he'd done for the last few weeks. It was 6:45 and we had to hurry. Maisie was doing the dishes and Blu ran back to the dining-room table to lick the yolk off his plate.

"Hurry up, you Blu," I tell him. "Or you gotta do your own dishes."

"Yeah," says Maisie.

"Ho, getting brave, eh, you, small girl," Blu says. "Just like your big sista but you Evil-lyn Part II." And he licks the yolk clean off.

We head out the door. Past Elena Gaspar picking up cat shit from her yard. Past the Kuro-chan leaning on his porch rail with the peeling white paint. Past Mr. Iwasaki sliding around the side of the house to get to the front full of Saloon Pilot cracker cans. Up the road to Mrs. Ikeda's.

The smell comes right to us on a kona wind. A backwards wind. Clothes hanging on lines tug in the opposite direction. Dust picks up in reverse swirls. Icky's waiting for us near a stack of beat-up towels and the dog clipper that she's spraying with WD-40.

"Another day. Another ten dollars for Christmas," she says. "I guess we start with Chloe today, Ivah," which is my cue to go down to the dark, airless basement and prepare Chloe for grooming. "She's been crying a lot lately. Dogs mourn their dead too, you know," Icky says to us, as if we're imbeciles. "Poor, poor Chloe girl. When she lost her mother, Claudia, I think she went over the deep end. But she's in for a treat today because she's first in line for a good grooming and all of our attention, right, crew?"

"I go with you, Ivah," Blu says, and walks toward the basement door.

"Maisie dear," Icky says, "go pour the Sulfodine into the old VO5 bottle from the gallon jug in the garage. And don't spill a drop of it, precious, because it costs Mrs. Ikeda an arm and a leg from that detestable little vet clinic here in town."

Maisie lugs the heavy jug to the washbasin and pours very carefully. Thinks she might end up in a cage in the basement too. No air, no light, one cup of dry food every night, and one hour in the house with the house favorites once a month. Or in a shallow grave in the backyard. A stick cross and dry violets.

Blu reaches into his pocket. "Here Burnaby and Constance." He places the lavender squares in front of them, which they lick out of his palm. "Hi, Patricia. How you stay, my small baby? You look sleepy. Oh no. Ivah, where Chloe?"

I come down the stairs slowly and look up at the little window on the ocean side of the basement. "Ai, look, Blu. She get the window open for the dogs. How come?"

"For the smell, she gotta open the window. I dunno," Blu snaps, "maybe she finally figga they need fresh air too. Where Chloe? Chloe, here, girl!"

"There her, by the wall." She whines and whines; it's so pitiful to hear her name called in the dark. I walk up to the door of the cage. "C'mon, girl. Your turn. Blu"—I begin to panic—"she ain't getting up. What the fuck, Blu!"

My brother swings the door open so hard, the top rusty hinge breaks and the door hangs. "C'mon, Chloe." She attempts to make her way up, struggling to pull herself out. It's her only chance. Her claws get caught on wire as she tries to drag her weight out of the urine- and shit-caked cage.

Finally, I grab her under her front legs, and Chloe screams. "Ivah, stop it, stop it, you hurting her."

"I just pulling her under her legs little bit. Stop yelling before Icky come down here, you fuckin' stupid Blu."

I get her out of the cage to the sound of whimpering and I pass her to Blu. Chloe's so excited to see him, she whines and licks Blu's face, trying to reach him with her tongue. He lowers his head to make it easy for her. Green mucus oozes out from her eyes. Blu pulls back her ears and looks inside.

"Ivah," he says, and looks at me with a face so helpless and afraid. "Ivah, look. Her ears are swollen shut. So red, I can see um throbbing. No mo' one hole, Ivah, stay swollen shut." And he holds Chloe, pets her head, and says, "It's okay, baby girl, it's okay."

Chloe lets out a stream of urine all over Blu's shirt and whines as it comes out, golden yellow and thick. When I look at it, there's blood all over his shirt. And there on her vagina, sandy white grains and dried purple blood. She's crusted shut as if with paste; urine can only pass through a tiny space at the top.

"What's going on down there?" Icky shouts from the top of the basement stairs. "Maisie and I are waiting so patiently for our first customer." Fake-cheerful as ever.

"We coming, Mrs. Ikeda," I tell her. "Try wait. We trying for wipe up some spilled food."

"My patience is wearing thin. I don't want you to be here all day. Spit, spot."

This is when we get fired.

Blu stands up with Chloe in his arms. He stands in the square of sunlight cast from the open window and looks up toward the sky for a brief moment. All of a sudden, he bolts past Mrs. Ikeda in the doorway.

She falls and hits her back on the counter.

He screams like a wild animal, holding Chloe in his arms, a fat madman screaming, out of the garage and down the driveway.

He falls on the street, still holding Chloe. Once back on his feet, he turns and sees Mrs. Ikeda coming after him. He screams and runs all the way to our house.

I grab Maisie and go after him. Icky yells, "Give me back my dog. My baby! Chloe girl! Chloe girl! You're all fired. Ivah, you're in big trouble. I hold you responsible. Come back here! All of you! I'm calling the police. You goddamn filthy kids got leprosy in your veins."

When we get home, I call for my brother, but he doesn't answer. I find Blu in our bedroom closet, holding Chloe. And I look at my brother's face:

❀

He's full of grace, telling her all about heaven.

Who's there and what she'll have to eat.

How his Mama went there and could probably help the angels feed her.

No more cages and lots of fresh air to breathe.

Outdoors, a garden with fresh water from a spring.

No more white powder on toenails cut too short.

God the Father.

No more sores.

Jesus, Son of Man.

No more howling when the cage door shuts.

Holy Spirit.

Lots of Milk-Bones.

No swollen ears.

No blood in her urine.

He wraps her in one of Maisie's old baby blankets, tight like swaddling, and holds her close, rocking her, so gently that when she dies, there's no crying at all.

"Chloe, rest in peace," he says.

Then Blu pulls a lavender square from his pocket, a childbearing stone, and places one in the center of the dog's mouth. "Play catch with my Mama."

That's when the police start knocking at our front door.

14 Blu spent all of the dog money. He didn't want a penny left to remind him of anything that had to do with Mrs. Ikeda. For Maisie he bought two Mattel Perfume Blossom Baby Dolls, Lilac and Violet, from Molokai Drugs. They smelled just like his favorite candy. For Poppy, a bottle of Aqua Velva and a bottle of Brut. He also bought packets of seeds—green onion, mustard cabbage, won bok, sugar snap peas, cherry tomato, Singapore beans, zinnia, marigold, black-eyed Susan, and impatiens—so Poppy could be in the garden out back where he was most happy.

And for me, three yards of purple corduroy and quilt batting from Misaki's. "Make the softest cat bed you can, Ivah," he said, "so that when you find the black one, she get one soft place for sleep."

His half of the dog money nearly gone, he bought three packages of frozen laulau, salted salmon, and tomatoes for a big bowl of lomi salmon, haupia, kulolo, day-old poi, a strip of pipi kaula, and a slab of the reddest piece of sashimi—for a dinner no longer a part of *anyone's* dreams.

❀

On the night that Hoppy Creetat births her kittens in the gully, Ka-san howls long and round but won't follow us down into the cave which Maisie has lined with newspaper. Hoppy cries as she pushes out four kittens, each in a dark green sac that she eats away. Then she licks her babies clean with a rough tongue.

The first is a Siamese colored white. We call her Miss Anna. The second is a calico like Hoppy, a lucky cat as the Japanese say, especially a rare male. We call him Fortune Cookie. The third is a plain and grouchy orange. We call him Morris the Cat. And the last, a black, tiny ball, I call Kingdom Come. I know it's her from the moment I hold her in the palm of my hand and her small head moves toward the sound of her mother.

"I get the box, Ivah. I left um next to Ka-san at the top," Blu says. He scurries up the rocky ledge to get the apple box, lined with a purple corduroy pillow that I made for the kittens.

Then Blu looks at me for a confusing moment. I watch as he unties the rag nooses from the kiawe tree branch near the cave, and he lays them across the palms of his two hands. He puts them under Hoppy's nose. "Thass why you gotta stay in the house, Creetat. Bumbye they hang your babies and feed um glass in their milk. You like that, hah, Hoppy?" She seems to be listening, afraid, as she sniffs the rag nooses, then nuzzles her head in the palm of my brother's hand. "Then you listen to Ivah," he tells the cat, "and bring your babies tonight inside the closet. Or they going hang um high and the Human Rats going make manapua for feed their canary with one leg."

Maisie leans her body on mine and faces the Reyes house.

"Their porch light went on," Blu whispers. We put the

babies and Hoppy in the box, gather up the newspaper, and burn it in the dirt as if nothing ever happened. Blu reties the rag nooses to the kiawe tree to remind all of us of the kittens that hung, not too long ago, over the gully.

❀

Blu still writes poetry in school. He tells me today in his best Mrs. Ota impersonation, "Here are a few tips, class, to remember when composing a haiku."

"You betta listen to the way she like um, Blu, and just do um her way," I tell him as I rinse my hands at the kitchen sink.

He disregards my remarks and continues in Mrs. Ota's voice, enunciating each syllable in a false British accent. "The haiku should be about nature. The first line must have five syllables, then seven in the second, then five again in the last line." He flips through the pages of his tablet to act as though he were reading from a teacher's guide.

"Haiku does not rhyme like our other poems," he scolds. "And finally, class, it came from the Japanese." Blu puts his two palms together and bows. "Now the poet need silence," he says. This is what Blu writes:

Creetats
Born one full moon night
No like die you sleep inside
On the purple bed.

❀

His poem scares Maisie. She leaves the table to check on the kittens in the closet, but since Big Sis and Miss

Ito are coming over tonight for dinner, I continue preparing the huge pot of nishime. Big Sis once told me, "Chop everything big, throw um in one big pot and half cup sugar, shoyu, and water. Boil the bugga." Tonight is our turn to cook.

Poppy grows most of the vegetables we need out in the back, but I spend some of my dog money on pork belly, dry seaweed, konyakku, and carrots. Blu and Maisie are in the back lot digging up the gobo, the araimo, and the daikon. I tell them to pick some green beans and okra too.

The part I hate most is peeling the araimo. All that slimy white sap after I start taking the skin off, and the way they shoot out of my hands when they're wet. My hands and arms are itchy afterward. But after the nishime cooks, the araimo melts in your mouth.

Big Sis comes over early so we can cook together and talk. Maisie and Miss Ito play with her perfume dolls on the living-room floor and Big Sis helps me peel the gobo and daikon. "Afterward, show me the black cat," she says. "I like see if you guys found *the one* for real. 'Cause not any old black cat can cure the sadness, you know. Gotta be *the one*, know what I mean?"

"Go get Kingdom Come, Blu," I tell my brother. And he runs down the hallway to our bedroom.

"Kingdom Come?" says Big Sis, and then she laughs. "Whateva, Ivah. You heard that, Sandi?"

"Nice name, Maisie," she says, and they smile at each other.

Blu comes back into the kitchen. "Hoppy the best mother, yeah, Ivah? Ho, when her babies drink milk, they stick their tiny claws in her stomach and push and push just like for get mo' milk out, and look so-wa, but she no care. And she get four babies too. Thass almost as much as Mrs. Nishimoto, and Hoppy ain't screaming at her babies." Blu holds Kingdom Come close to his cheek and kisses her nose and pretend-bites her ear.

"Let me hold um," Big Sis says. "Sandi, try come. You hold um too and tell Ivah if this the one going help Uncle Bertram." Miss Ito and Maisie walk into the kitchen. They both hold her and smell the baby-cat smell, but she doesn't cry for her mother or claw their clothes.

"Feed um good, Ivah," Big Sis says after a while.

"I told you," I tell her.

"Yeah, but I tell you something. You gotta let this little bugga come old first—the older the cat, the more wise her, thass what Nancy's fadda told me. Bumbye you put this one on your fadda's stomach and this small baby absorb all his sadness, but the bugga too baby yet. No can handle all that, know what I mean, Ivah? Maybe she too small. You asking her do something that going hurt this little thing. So you gotta wait and let her grow mo' old and mo' wise."

I've got no time.

Heal my Poppy before I go.

Fly.

"No worry, Ivah," Big Sis says, and she hands the kitten to Miss Ito and Maisie, who play with the other kittens on the floor. "This one going do the job in due time." Big Sis scrubs the rice pot and washes three cups of Calrose rice. She stares at me.

"What?" I tell her.

"Me and Sandi got the application from Mid-Pac, Ivah. Sandi's sista sent um in the mail." Miss Ito stands behind Big Sis. "Sandi, tell Ivah what you know, 'cause look her face—can tell she all nuts about this."

My face must show yes; my face must show no at the same time.

"Ivah," Miss Ito begins, "we got you an application to enter next year, your sophomore year—that and an application for financial aid."

"Poppy cannot pay for me, you know," I tell her.

"I made it through on a Work Scholarship Program," she says. "It was easy. You'll live there on campus in a dormitory, and I promise, Faith Ann and I will send you home every long weekend and holiday."

I want to go but the words leave me slowly. I don't look at Maisie or Blu when I say, "Okay." Even the sound of the word coming from my mouth doesn't sound like my own. "You guys can help me fill in the application?"

"Of course we will," Miss Ito says.

"You promise, Big Sis, you going send me home?"

"Yeah, I promise, Ivah."

"Going?" Maisie comes into the kitchen and leans on me.

"See what I mean?" I look at Miss Ito and Big Sis and shake my head no. I can't do it.

"We be here for Maisie and Blu—all the way," Big Sis says. "And about time Presley be the man in this house, take care his small sista for Ivah so that when he come ninth grade, he can go Mid-Pac too. And then Maisie after that. You guys all gotta help each other out. Only get us now thass the blood, know what I mean?"

"And, Ivah," Miss Ito says, "there's a long weekend every month, and Thanksgiving, Christmas—all the way through the year. We'll call you and write you every day and send care packages. My sister's right there in town if you ever get stuck. Go. It's a good college-prep school—it's the only way the three of you can make something good come of all this."

"Go," Blu says.

Maisie wants to cry. She's holding on to the edge of my T-shirt. "No cry, Pidge," I tell her. "Us three, you, me, and Blu, gotta talk about this, okay? No worry." Maisie nods.

"What time Uncle coming home?" Big Sis asks, to change the subject.

"About nine," Blu tells her. "He cleaning at the Bank of Hawai'i tonight with Felix Furtado."

"Ooohh, thass the one checking you out, eh, Sandi?" Big Sis teases. The mood lightens up. That's how Big Sis is just like Mama. "He get bubble eyes and bubble ass and he need one comb for Christmas."

"Faith Ann, you wait till we get home," Miss Ito says, and laughs as she shakes off the thought of ugly old Felix Furtado loving her.

"Sandi get the whole island, all the young guys checking her out still yet. But lucky thing she sharing cottage with me, so I run those horny buggas outta our yard, yeah, Sandi?"

"*Faith Ann*," she says, like she's pretending to run out of patience, "you're asking for a dirty lickens when we get home."

"Ooohh, I scared. I shakin'," says Big Sis, laughing.

After a dinner of hot rice and nishime, Big Sis and Miss Ito share a bottle of Miller in the living room. "Tell your ghost stories, Faith Ann," Miss Ito says. "You guys eva heard this one tell her stories?"

"Nah, bumbye they no can sleep and Uncle Bertram be blaming me. Then they be ova our place every night, Sandi, how you like that?" Big Sis nudges Miss Ito with her elbow.

"That's fine by me," she says. "I would've taken them all in long ago when I first fell in love with Maisie." My sister smiles at Miss Ito.

"C'mon, Big Sis, tell your ghost stories. Neva mine all this love-Maisie stuff," Blu whines. "You not scared, yeah, Maisie?" Maisie nods no. "See, she handle. Plus I sleep with her every night."

"You the worse one, you big chicken," I tell him.

"Shut up, evil mouth, before the ghost go in your mouth and come out your anus and then haunt your eyebrows."

"No even make sense, Blu."

"For real, yeah?" says Big Sis. "In your mouth and out your anus? Sheez. Okay—so Presley no get all nuts, I tell you small kine ghost stories. All this I tell you is true 'cause wen' happen to me. I start with the obake lady.

"Eh, all my life, I been seeing this lady and I dunno who her, but before, she use to stay in the corners of the ceiling. I seen her plenny times up there when I was small. She was one obake, the real Japanee kine—thass what Nancy's fadda told me when I told him about all those years this lady been coming to me.

"She get the kine obake long white hair. But when I

told Nancy's fadda that the bugga get legs and walk toward me in the hallway, he tell me no worry 'cause obake with legs is harmless. Not like the kine that no mo' legs —they out to get you. But he tell me, good or no good, *not right* that one obake stay bothering me. No good. She suppose to go to the light.

"So Nancy's fadda, he tell me, 'Leave the porch light on at yo' house for the lady find her way to heaven. And every time you come my house, we make one extra offering rice at the living-room shrine and light some senko for the lady.'

"So good enough, we was doing all that but she was still coming around, pulling my blanket nighttime, hovering like one cloud in the crucifix I get in my room, pounding on my bedroom wall all night, shit like that.

"Then when Nancy's fadda died, thass when everything started fo' go downhill and I mean downhill fast. I was sleeping over her house every night 'cause she was having hard time handle him being gone. Then maybe no mo' than two weeks afta he died, she started fo' go out with this real asshole Chinee guy from Food Fair. She neva even like the guy and there I was—going up her house every night. And there she was—leaving me there every night like I was a piece of yesterday's shit.

"So anyways, she went out with the prick the night of the forty-ninth-day service. I beg, beg her for stay home, but she neva like listen. I wen' light senko like Nancy's fadda always do and turn on the porch light and I wen' light some votive candles that I brought from home. I was lying there thinking about him when the weirdest thing wen' happen.

"I reach out my hands to the candles and the light rays went straight inside my fingas, you guys know what I mean? Was like the light was going inside me. And I move the light all ova the room with my fingertips—in circles, front and back, and I move um right on my face. And there he was.

"He gave everything he had, all his light, to me. Me. You can believe that? And when I wen' turn and look by the porch, he had the obake lady with him. He look at me, and I know he telling, 'I help her find the light. I help her, Faith Ann. And I help you be rid of this lady foreva mo'.'

"And he wen' leave. I neva seen him or the obake lady from that night till now."

Big Sis takes a swig of the Miller, then looks at the back door, which opens slowly, creaking, the porch light leaking onto the wood floor of the kitchen, and she screams! Blu screams, Maisie screams, Miss Ito screams, I scramble to the corner of the living room. "Hi, Uncle Bertram," Big Sis says, as calm as can be. And we all throw pillows and rubbish at her for fooling us so badly.

"Eh, howzit, Big Sis? Sandi," Poppy says as he walks through the back door. "How you guys doing? What you buggas screaming for—like you seen one ghost or something." Poppy sits down on his yellow chair. "Ivah, make Poppy some tea for drink with dinna. How was the nishime? Ono?"

"Yeah, was ono. Ivah one good cook, Uncle."

"Blu and Maisie—you two kids betta have bafe and go sleep pretty soon, eh."

"Ho, Poppy," Blu whines.

"No ho-Poppy me," my father says. Lucky thing Big Sis is there to save my brother from getting it.

"Uncle, I can take them three sleep the cottage tonight? Get good movies on TV, and I get couple more ghost stories tell them."

"Yeah, yippee," screams Blu.

"Up to you, Faith Ann," Poppy says. "Sandi, you let me know if this niece of mine imposing on your life with these kids of mine, you hear me?"

"Don't worry, Mr. Ogata," Miss Ito says, "your children are very special to me. You know that."

Poppy smiles. The first time in months. √

❀

The following Wednesday, we show up at the Nishimotos' to iron as usual. I need to make lots of money. I watch Mrs. Nishimoto cook a pot of chili over her hot stove in her hot house full of sweaty children. Jonathan fights with Richard over the pieces from the Battleship game that he wants to play with Blu.

Mrs. Nishimoto holds one-year-old Matthew while she stirs the bubbling meat; the two-year-old, William, plays with a roach motel on the kitchen floor.

Christopher stares at cartoons with the TV on volume ten; he wears his dirty baseball shoes and hangs his legs over the arms of the chair.

Maisie plays with Richard's twin, Michael.

All the while, I iron Mr. Nishimoto's aloha shirts in the living room, doing the "Banana Splits" with Fleagle, Bingo, Drooper, and Snork.

❀

And she had so many children
She didn't know what to do.

❁

"Goddammit, William," Mrs. Nishimoto screams. "Drop that damn roach trap. It's full of filthy germs." She bends over with Matthew on one hip, grabs William off the floor by his armpit, and smacks his hand hard. "Don't you cry, William, don't you cry." But he does, loudly. And her floors haven't been vacuumed in so long that his tears and his sweat make long blond hair and fuzzballs stick to his face and shirtless body.

"Oh dammit, Matthew pooped," she says to no one in particular. Then she screams, "Jonathan and Richard, stop fighting! Christopher, turn the goddamn TV down. Christopher Allan Nishimoto, did you do your homework? William, you stop your crying now. Michael, get me a diaper for Matthew and a Kleenex for William. The chili—oh Lord, Lord, what have I done?"

❁

So many children.
What to do?

❁

I finish the ironing and fold up the ironing board. I put the iron back in the hall closet. Pick up William and take him to the kitchen sink to wash his face and stop his heaving sniffles. Wash all the lint off his body and the lines of red dirt caught in the folds of his sweaty neck.

"Blu, take Jonathan, Michael, and Richard to see our kittens, but teach them how be gentle with um, especially Kingdom Come," I tell my brother as I stir the chili and lower the flame on the stove. "Is that okay, Mrs. Nishimoto? Our house stay right over there." I walk to the picture window and point down the street. She knows this. Every day, she passes us as we walk home, in her station wagon filled with boys.

Mrs. Nishimoto looks at me mad but relieved, with blue eyes the color of Brach's mints. And I stare back for every remark I've had to take from her haole mouth about my sister, my sister who wet her panties every day in Miss Owens' class—while Mrs. Nishimoto, church sister and haole-to-haole friend, sat in the Teachers' Lounge full of cigarette smoke and coffee cups—laughing, I know she was, laughing at my sister, my brother, and me.

"Kingdom Come?" Mrs. Nishimoto doesn't even have the energy to tell me how heathen the name is to her Christian self.

"Maisie, take Matthew and change his diaper," I tell my sister. "If you start his bath water, I come help you bafe him, okay?"

Maisie lifts Matthew from Mrs. Nishimoto's arms. "Stink," she says into his neck.

Mrs. Nishimoto smirks, but lets it go, she's so tired.

I hold William on my hip and he plays with my hair. "As soon as I pau cook you guys' rice for your chili, Christopher, I help you do your homework at the table. I help Blu and Maisie every day since my Mama die."

Christopher looks at me. "Mom, can Ivah help me?" Mrs. Nishimoto nods. "Okay, Ivah. I'll go get my school bag," he says as he runs down the hall. "I just gotta write some haiku for English."

"Blu and me are good at that. And take off your dirty base-ball shoes and put um on the porch, okay, Christopher?"

"Okay, Ivah," he yells from down the hallway.

I quickly walk over to the TV and say, "All right, William, big boy, turn off the TV for Ivah." And with his two-year-old's clumsy hands, he slams the TV off, so proud, he claps for himself.

Maisie bathes Matthew in the bathroom. Blu plays out in the front yard with the three boys around the apple box with the corduroy pillow and the kittens. Making cat games with twine and bells, bowls of milk, and a handful of cat chow. At the kitchen table, William bounces on my knee, reaching for Christopher's pencils and erasers as he writes a haiku about the "Banana Splits." Mrs. Nishimoto sits with her head back on the sofa, eyes open, staring at the ceiling, crying without making a sound. The meat bubbles slowly on the stove.

❁

The porch light is on by the time we get home that night.

Da Sun is in our driveway.

I hear the TV on volume ten.

The back door creaks open as the three of us walk slowly up the driveway.

"So anyways, Bertram, I bring you couple mo' two-finga bags on Friday. But none of this 'I pay you later, Paulo' jazz. You get the cash or you no mo' the grash." Uncle Paulo looks happy that he made a rhyme on the spot.

"Where you kids was?" Poppy asks as we all try to get past Uncle Paulo without being noticed. All of us, that is, except Blu.

"Hi, Uncle Paulo," Blu says. "How's Blendaline? Ivah said I no can hang around her no mo', so thass why I no come over as much."

"Why, why," Uncle Paulo says to me, and I smell the liquor on his breath, "whass wrong with my niece playing wit' yo' bradda? What, he mo' betta than her 'cause he Japanee? Fuck, Japs for think they mo' betta than everybody else, fuckas. Especially the Filipinos. Fuck, everybody for spit on Filipinos, shit. You fuckin' snipes."

"Where you was?" Poppy asks again, but not mad, just a little louder.

"We was helping Mrs. Nishimoto."

"Thass another one," Uncle Paulo mutters. "Fuckin' haoles. They mo' worse than the Japs the way they act like we just a truckload of fuckin' brownies picking pineapples for minimum wage. Fuckas all hate us Filipinos. Thass why I say, Bertram, 'They cannot take one joke, take one toke.'" Uncle Paulo staggers into Da Sun and leaves.

"Get inside and bafe. All you guys," Poppy says.

When I walk in, all over the kitchen table, kolas in a small pile, stems and leaves in another, Zig-Zags, a couple of matchbooks rolled up, a Ziploc bag, and a ripped-open bag of Doritos.

"Stay outta the kitchen," Poppy says to me.

"But we neva eat or do homework or nothing, Poppy," I tell him.

"Then why the hell you was fuckin' doing slave work for that highfalutin haole? You shoulda been home cooking for your own family."

"But."

"Eh, no but me. Boil saimin and eat in the living room. Then go do your guys' homework in the bedroom. Now. And stay off the kitchen table." Poppy sits down and sprinkles some of the kolas onto a thin sheet of Zig-Zag.

Moves it gently between his fingers and licks the edge. "Get outta here, Ivah. I no like see yo' face for the rest of the night."

"Okay, Poppy." I turn to walk away.

"No okay-Poppy me."

"Huh?"

"You heard me. Trying for make me feel all guilty. You no think I know your game, hah, Ivah? Eva since Eleanor die, I know you been trying for make me feel like one guilty piece of shit."

"What, Poppy?"

"No what-Poppy me. I ain't going let you make me feel bad about smoking a joint, just *one* joint a night after work. I ain't. 'Cause after I smoke, I not snapping at you kids for screwing up or acting stupid. You like me be pleasant? Then no look at me like that. You turn the odda way when I light up or drink my tea. You just turn the odda way. Now beat it."

From my bedroom, I smell the sweet smell of marijuana. It wafts through the walls. I hear the sucking, deep and long. The orange chair creaks and then it is silent.

"Okay, Maisie, you pau page five of your math? Blu, you wen' check um for her?"

"Yeah, all correct."

"Okay, go sleep, Maisie. Blu, you did your workbook?"

"Yeah. I tired, Ivah."

"Go sleep then."

The sweet smell, the night so still, I hear the crushing of the roach in the ashtray. The soft mewling of the cats in the closet. Ka-san's low breathing.

I creep into the dark living room. The TV colors the whole room a fluorescent gray-blue. Poppy's asleep in the orange chair. I put the afghan Mama crocheted over his body, and he stirs like Maisie does when I cover her at night. I turn to go to sleep. And there, in the stretch of orange streetlight across the floor of the living room, sits the black cat.

Kingdom Come.

Thy will be done.

Ka-san cries in her sleep. I put the black cat on my father's belly and watch her settle in, curl herself into a tight ball, there on my father's stomach, absorbing all of his sadness into her little body.

In the morning, Poppy's still asleep in the orange chair, but the cat's not there. I find her on the front steps, Kingdom Come, licking her paws with that rough tongue. When she looks at me her eyes glow white. The slit of her irises widen, then disappear in the sunlight.

15 When school ends, Mitchell Oliveira talks me into signing up to be a Junior Leader for Vacation Bible School. Mitchell's born-again. Full-blown-born-again, Sunday-School-and-Morning-Service, Evening-Service, Wednesday-Bible-Study kind of Christian, his last hickey from Evangeline Reyes barely faded as he took the plunge that Palm Sunday into the bathtub built into the pulpit of the church.

"I felt like trash because of what I was doing with Vangie," Mitchell tells me. "But when I accepted the Lord into my heart, all that guilt went away. I'm through with being a sinner. And I'm saving myself for marriage. Thanks for signing up to be a Junior Leader, Ivah." And every time we talk nowadays, Mitchell steers the talk to God and why I need to be washed by the blood of the Lamb.

Blu and Maisie sign up every year for the Baptists' Vacation Bible School and free swimming lessons, plus this year a volleyball league. Homemade Okinawan fried donuts, Rice Krispie marshmallow squares, and powdered-sugar-sprinkled lemon bars donated by the church ladies led by Mrs. Nishimoto. Homemade snacks with a waxy paper cup of red Kool-Aid every day at Vacation Bible School. Blu's in cookie-and-punch heaven. Maisie, in Ivory-soap-sculpture heaven. Every summer in Vacation Bible School, she carves an Ivory soap cross.

Mitchell begs me to attend one of the Wednesday Bible Study classes. "Please, Ivah. I promise I'll do anything you ask," Mitchell says. "I'll help you clean Miss Ito's and Miss Fukuda's classrooms on the last day of school. I'll help you iron shirts on Wednesdays. I'll ask my Aunty Mary to teach you how to make Portuguese sweet bread. I mean, you're getting a pretty good deal here in return for your eternal soul."

I sigh heavily so he knows that I don't really want to go. "I gotta take Blu and Maisie with us 'cause my fadda working tonight," I tell Mitchell over the phone. Sometimes, just the mention of Blu coming along makes Mitchell think twice.

"That's okay. I'll be there at six-thirty. What're you having for dinner?"

"I made meat loaf. My cousin taught me how."

"I'll be there at six, then. I'll bring the sweet bread."

After dinner, the four of us walk to the Baptist church. Blu's fuming mad. Maisie has pomaded her hair. "I thought we was Buddhist," Blu says to me. "How come now we 'coming Baptists? We was only pretend-be-Baptist for the free swimming lessons and cookies. You Buddhist like me, yeah, Maisie? 'Cause Mama was Buddhist, you know."

"Japanee," Maisie says.

"We ain't nothing, Blu, so no worry," I tell my brother. "Jeez, you act like you go down the Buddhist temple every Sunday and pray, I doubt it."

"This Mitchell's idea, right, Ivah? How come we following Mitchell now? What, you not going with Vangie anymore? Ivah, he the number-one traitor of ours, and we following him. How come? First he was all our friend, and then he don't know us, and now he know us again. Sheez, brah, make up your mind."

"Shut up, Blu," I tell my brother. "Evangeline and Mitchell pau already."

"So what, so what, now you like check out my sista, hah, Mitch? She ain't no second place to Vangie Reyes, brah," and Blu shoves Mitchell.

"Oh, please, Presley," Mitchell says. "Stop pushing me before I have to make you sorry. Ivah and me have been friends since I moved here two years ago. Where've you been, man? Oh, I forgot. You've been with Blendaline in the bushes."

Blu shoves Mitchell some more, yelling things like "Stupid Portagee punk, stink ass, traitor with hickeys up his ass," but by that time, we're walking up the sidewalk to the church. Blu shuts up fast. He peers inside the big doors.

Up front, there's a circle of metal folding chairs near the piano. And nobody's there. Blu runs to the piano and starts playing "Moon River." He sings the first few lines to the song my father sang too many times.

"How you wen' learn that song, Blu?" I ask my brother.

"Poppy been in good mood lately, right, Ivah? He been teaching me when you and Maisie not around 'cause he said this father-and-son time. I one fast learner when come to music, you know. But I only know the first two lines." Blu plays them over and over until a tall haole man walks into the room.

"That's very nice." There in front of us is the God Almightiest Handsomest Christian man from here to Kingdom Come.

"Hi, how's everyone doing?" he says. Nobody says a word. I watch his Adam's apple swallow nervously. Blu slides off the piano bench and stands next to me.

"I'm the Baptist church's summer missionary, Jim Cameron." We all stare at him except for Maisie. She has her face pressed into the small of my back. Blu looks at me as if to tell me: Say something. So I look at Mitchell and nudge him with my elbow.

"It's not quite summer yet," Jim continues in an effort to ease the silence, "but I'm here early to get things started."

Oh my God.

Nobody speaks.

"Jim Cameron." He holds out his hand to Mitchell.

"Mitchell Oliveira," he says at last. "I'm saved." Blu rolls his eyes.

"And who's this young man playing the piano?" Jim asks.

"These are my guests," Mitchell says in perfect English. "Ivah, Presley, and Maisie Ogata."

Blu copies Mitchell and shakes Jim's hand. "They call me Blu," he says. "I not saved yet."

"Well," Jim begins. He doesn't quite know what to make of Blu's remark. "We have the start of a fine Youth Group right here. Why don't we all sit together and open in prayer." We sit on the cold metal chairs. "Let us bow our heads." I look around to see if anyone else is coming. Nobody but us. "Dear Heavenly Father—"

So I stare at Jim from the corners of my eyes.

Auburn hair.

"Bless this gathering—"

Blue eyes, flushed cheeks, dimples.

"As we come together in Your holy name—"

Tight Levi's, huge pink hands.

"To serve You and honor You—"

The handsomest haole I've ever seen, which contradicts the idea I had that all Christians were ugly, doofus weirdos.

"In Jesus' Mighty and Holy name we pray—"

Mrs. Jim Cameron.

"Amen."

Mrs. Ivah Cameron.

Amen.

❀

Jim is a fisher of men. He goes to the high school campus. He goes to the elementary school campus. He bats his brown eyelashes all over town.

Pretty soon, we're the most popular church in town and being born-again is in, starting with the captain of the boy's volleyball team, Raymond Quinores, who was Jim's biggest fish caught in the net of Christian fishers of men. Raymond Quinores, also Senior Class Vice Prez and last year's Homecoming Junior Class Escort and Winter Ball King, makes it his goal to have an entirely Christian team by the start of the next season.

So the starters of the boy's volleyball team, Glenn Perreira, Rhoyden Medeiros, Billy Wong, Teddy Takata, and Dwayne Kahele, start coming to the Baptist church, which attracts the popular cheerleader girls, Teresa Kabalis, Paulette Iwahashi, Cynthia Low, and Connie Peralta.

Which brings Uncle Paulo.

Which brings Evangeline, Blendaline, Henrilyn, and Trixi Reyes, who are Catholics.

Which brings all the studly intermediate and elementary boys: Winston Wang, Scott Fukushima, and Darren Ota, who are Buddhists. Ed the Big Head Endo. Kingdom Hall.

Pretty soon, Jim's planning the greatest-ever Penny Carnival to benefit Muscular Dystrophy.

Pretty soon, we're a Youth Choir, auditioning for parts in "He Is Alive," a five-part musical with tape accompaniment.

❀

In the Youth Choir's production of "He Is Alive," Blu auditions for the part of the singing narrator and Evangeline auditions for Mary Magdalene.

"You sing like an angel, sweetheart," Jim tells her.

"Yeah, a Catholic angel," I whisper to Mitchell.

"Presley is a little young, but he certainly has the strongest, most beautiful voice I've heard in a child in all my years in the church—so we need to pray for him in the lead role as the singing narrator," Jim says. "Let us bow our heads and pray."

Raymond Quinores and Glenn Perreira play the lead male parts of Jesus and Judas. Cynthia Low and Connie Peralta play the other girl parts of Mother Mary and the prostitute who anoints Jesus and almost gets stoned.

The rest of us are the chorus and have to pray for the lead singers. Uncle Paulo runs the ancient sound system, the bent-up mikes, and the scratchy tape.

Act One: Jim makes Blu sit on the railing of the choir box and lean against the wall as he sings one of the songs. "Lean back. Look cool and relaxed," Jim tells Blu. "You're hip. You know the score. You're righteous, man. Snap your fingers as you sing."

Act Two: Blu sits on the stairs leading up to the stage part of the pulpit for another song. "Put your elbow on your knee and your chin on your fist. Look casual—like hey, I'm in the groove."

Act Three: Jim adds a few dance steps to the "He Is Alive" reprises, which makes fat, stupid Blu think he can boogie, when it looks like a six-foot-four haole missionary taught dance steps to a fat Japanese boy with no rhythm whatsoever.

Evangeline starts playing the "Ooohh, I getting nervous for the performance, I like give up the part, I no think I going make it" shit, and all the cheerleader girls gather around her and kiss her ass and beg her to stay, like "Yes you can, you can do it, Vangie. We need you. Stay, please stay."

Raymond and the boys gather around, and Raymond says, "Let's all bow our heads and pray that Jesus give Vangie the strength to perform." And Evangeline starts crying, saying, in between Raymond's pauses, "Amen, praise You, Lord, hallelujah." Shit like that.

Uncle Paulo looks for the girl wearing black panties. Running the tape, checking out asses, but looking holy for Jim.

It was pretty much routine for Maisie and me to be down there as part of the chorus. Mitchell too didn't seem to care that since Jim started catching bigger fish in the sea of sinners, we were just a bunch of tilapia chorus members, while Blu was King of the Youth Choir and Son of Jim the Missionary. We rehearsed Wednesday nights, Saturdays, and Sundays for a month.

Before rehearsal one Wednesday, Blu confesses: "Sometimes I think maybe I rather be Baptist than Buddhist. I mean, I no like burn in hell, and if you not Baptist, thass where you going, right, Ivah? And all that sins Mitchell did with Vangie, I did too with Blendaline, but you know what, Ivah, Mitchell said that Jesus wipe his slate clean 'cause he got baptist in the bathtub by the choir box. He shown it to me. But Jim said if you ain't save, then you going on a one-way ticket to hell when you die." Blu pauses and looks at me.

"So that mean our Mama went hell, right, Ivah? And what about Chloe and all them dogs? They wasn't Baptist, they was Buddhist too, like Mrs. Ikeda."

"I scared." Maisie.

"Shut up, Blu," I tell my brother.

"Then tell me what you think, Ivah. Mama in hell, gotta be, and if thass where she stay, then thass where I like go too. I ain't going be Baptist."

"You gotta sing the main part this Sunday, Blu. Poppy said he going church with us. And Big Sis and Miss Ito."

"I know. What you think, Ivah? Thass Jim's fault or Jesus' fault that Buddhists cannot go heaven? You know what—when Jim told us close our eyes last Sunday and see Jesus on the cross and feel the nails go inside yo' hand and yo' feet, and feel the crown of thorns on yo' head, I felt um, you know. Thass why when I sing the end part, I know what Jesus feel like hanging there all sore and thirsty and how he like go see his fadda 'cause he miss um so much. But was Jim or Jesus who said

Buddhists cannot go heaven? Ivah, Mama ain't with Jesus—"

"Hate you." Maisie runs into our room. She knows about hell too from her Sunday School teacher.

Mitchell's been sitting outside on the porch. "Sorry, Ivah. I didn't mean to make them confused."

"C'mon, Maisie, let's go," I call toward our bedroom. Her tiny feet come padding down the hallway.

❀

On the Sunday of our performance, the whole town turns out: mothers and fathers, grandmas and grandpas, sisters and brothers, cousins, aunts and uncles, girl-friends and boyfriends, the curious. Even Poppy puts on his one dress shirt and striped tie, pomades his, Blu's, and Maisie's hair. French toast for breakfast, then he drives us to the church. "You sing good, you hear me, Blu? I still no can believe you got the main part. Maybe your Mama was right. You get music in yo' blood. And she be listening all the way in heaven, I know, 'cause you her boy."

"*Heaven,*" Maisie says as she looks at Blu.

"Shut up, Maisie, you Japanee Buddhist," Blu snaps.

"You shut up, Blu," I tell him.

"You guys all shut up before I turn this car around and all your Mama hear today is the sound of you three fight-ing, then getting dirty lickens from me at home. You like that, hah?"

Poppy sits in the last pew at the far end with Big Sis and Miss Ito. Everyone smiles at the next person, nodding once, the way holier-than-thou people say hi.

In the Sunday School classroom turned dressing room,

Blu gets to look like Rebel Without a Cause—white T-shirt, Levi's, and a black leather jacket. "Jim, I can make one Waikiki wave with my hair in the front?" Blu asks. "Somebody gimme one comb now," he demands.

Evangeline, Cynthia, and Connie get the see-through scarves costumes. "Jim, try come, try come," Evangeline says, like there's a big panic crisis. "I can pull the Jeannie pants down little bit and show belly button?"

Raymond wears the Jesus robes and jute sandals and Glenn as Judas puts on disciple high-water pants with a rope belt. "Glue the beard on good," Raymond complains. "Eh, hurry up. Where the bag of fern fur? Somebody bring me the bag of fern fur, hurry up."

The rest of us chorus members wear the maroon satin robes that smell like ten years of mothballs, sitting on the cement stairs outside like little extras.

And then "He Is Alive" begins.

Uncle Paulo adjusts the squeaky mikes.

But Blu doesn't even need a mike. In his duet with ✓ Evangeline, his voice rises and falls in a sound so clear, church ladies wipe tears from the corners of their eyes. My father's face glows.

At the end of Act Four—before the big production number of "He Is Alive" in Act Five, in which all of us whisper to one another first, "He is alive, ssshhh, He IS alive, ssshhh, He is ALIVE (scream it), HE IS ALIVE—is the sad scene of Jesus, Raymond Quinores, nailed to the cross, and Judas, Glenn Perreira, hanging himself on a tree limb pounded into the wall of the choir box.

Then the congregation is still as Blu steps up to the pulpit and the tape begins to play. His head bowed, he looks up slowly at Jesus. I know he feels the nails in his own hands as he turns his palms upward, fingers trembling. He looks at Judas, touches the rope around his neck, shivers slightly as he holds his throat. Blu looks at my father for a long time, his voice rising to heaven. Then he turns to look for me. He raises his arms—that's not the way we rehearsed it—he's a cross, singing so chilling, with his head bowed and sad, then he wraps his arms around himself.

Jim looks nervous. It's not the way we rehearsed this; and when the tape jams, Jim freezes. But my brother sings a cappella as if it was part of the whole performance all along. And when the branch breaks off the wall of the choir box, and Judas tumbles to the ground with the rope stuck around Glenn's neck, the branch dangling from it, the whole Youth Choir scrambling around him, my brother sings on, like it was meant to be. He moves to the feet of Christ Jesus and falls there weeping for himself, for my mother, for a place for all of us in heaven.

"Sweet Jesus," he whispers, "my Mama ain't with you."

My father is in the last pew and wipes his eyes. Maisie leans into my body and buries her face in the maroon robes. The congregation stands and applauds for Blu.

❀

It was meant to be. Jim said Blu should've dedicated his life to Christ. Blu was not Baptist material. But Mitchell and I get closer and closer, and he wants me to be Baptist so, as Jim says, we can be equal yokes. Maisie and I still go to church. Blu stays home with Poppy and gets his piano lessons.

Mitchell tells me one night before Bible Study, "On top of planning the Penny Carnival, there's lots of money we can make, Ivah."

"Like how?" I ask him.

Blu comes over to the kitchen table, plops himself down, and echoes, "Like how?" He looks at his fingernails really cocky-like. "And how come we still letting this Portagee tell us what for do, hah, Ivah? How much money? Better be plenny, Mitch, 'cause Ivah this close to being one Buddhist or maybe just nothing again." Blu holds up his fingers with a small space right in front of Mitchell's face. "And I already back to being one Buddhist."

"I'm talking to Ivah."

"Well, if you in this house, you talking to me too," Blu says, " 'cause this my house too and one plus one equal two, so two against one, brah. Plus Maisie equal three and blood run thicka than water, you hose pipe."

"You're not even making sense, Presley," Mitchell says.

"Yeah, Blu, shut up. We go hear out Mitchell's plan," I tell my brother, who looks at me with hurt in his eyes— like he's backing me but I'm not backing him. He's really into this blood-runs-thicker-than-water jazz that Big Sis has been pounding into his head. And after the "He Is Alive" performance, Blu completely stops going to church. He and Ed the Big Head quit the Youth Choir, Sunday School, and Bible Study. But they're still signed up for Vacation Bible School, free swimming lessons, and the volleyball league.

"Well," Mitchell continues, "before I was rudely interrupted, I was saying that I was watching *The Lucy Show* last night, and I saw Lucy and Viv find out that some pennies are worth a lot more than other pennies, so they went to Mr. Mooney's Danfield Bank and traded in ten bucks for ten bucks' worth of pennies. Then they went to the Danfield Library and looked up books on rare coins, and you know what? They found a penny worth six dollars."

"Six dollas for one stupid penny?" Blu leans in on the conversation.

"I thought you was Buddhist," I tell him.

"So what? Buddhists can collect six-dolla pennies too."

"Anyway, Lucy and Viv take the penny to the Coin Shop, but Lucy drops it in the rain gutter and then her and Viv have to act like county workers so that they can go down in the rain gutter to get the penny while a police officer watches them suspiciously—well, you know what I mean."

"No, we dunno what you mean, you stupid Portagee," Blu says. "What this got to do with us?"

"Call me stupid Portagee one more time, you fat shit Jap Presley and I'll beat the fat out of you so bad that—"

"Okay, okay, so what that got to do with the Penny Carnival?" I ask Mitchell.

"Jim wants me to run the games, and I got a few of them figured out, but I wanted you guys to help me plan the rest of the games. Then we give the other members of the Youth Group their jobs—but the trade-off is, we tell Jim that we want to give him twenty dollars for twenty dollars' worth of pennies."

"Whose twenty bucks?" Blu asks sassily. "Jeez, I wonda. Only us get money, Ivah."

"No, we all chip in five dollars—Ivah, me, you, and Maisie, and we split the money if we find a rare penny. I already went and borrowed coin books from the library, so we know what's worth what." Mitchell's sure this will work, and since the end of our dog-grooming days, our money's been getting lower and lower.

"Okay. Sounds painless enough," I tell Mitchell. "Go get you guys' fives. Maisie, get five for me too."

"Mitch get his five too, then. Cannot be trusting these Baptists now'days."

"Shut up, fatso," Mitchell says.

"You shut up, Pocho."

❦

We find more of them in the ashtray of the Malibu, in the bean garden, next to the patch of chives, under the backseat of the Malibu, under the cushion on the orange chair, in our toy drawer, in the washing machine. Useless pennies, worth a penny each.

❦

Mitchell, Blu, Maisie, and I plan some of the games.

Blu: Sink the paper cup with pennies that are bombs in the washtub filled with water.

Me: Penny Toss in the clown's mouth that we painted on cardboard.

Maisie: Make the penny float down into the baby-food jar at the bottom of the 100-gallon aquarium.

Mitchell: Guess the number of pennies in the jar.

Raymond and the cheerleaders plan lots of other games, like Penny Roulette, Penny Tiddlywinks, and Kiss Your Favorite Volleyball Player or Cheerleader for fifteen pennies. Uncle Paulo's there all night until Jim comes over and tells Uncle Paulo to keep the kissing Christian-like; in other words, keep your tongue in your own mouth.

The night is brimming with excitement and the church hall is packed. We're at the Penny Toss booth right across from the Kissing Booth, where Evangeline and Blendaline have the second shift. Mitchell's born-again, but watches as Evangeline opens her mouth like a cave for fifteen pennies, even with her Uncle Paulo, when Jim's not looking.

And before she does it, she looks straight at Mitchell.

"I no care about the six-dolla penny," Blu says. "I going get me one fat kiss from Blendaline. I miss her."

"No, Blu. You stay right here. Jim going bust them and then they going force for be Catholic again," I tell my brother. Mitchell wants to go over there, I know he does, and he looks at me with those sorry eyes and turns to go get his fifteen-cent kiss, but right there in front of him is Evangeline Reyes.

"So what, Ivah, you bitch," she hisses in the large crowd that swallows her voice. "Like steal my boyfriend, eh? Step outside so me and Blendaline can show you what we do to pussies like you who steal from their neighbas."

"I, I," I stammer, and my brother rushes over.

"Ivah neva steal your Portagee from you. Was Jesus wen' steal yo' boyfriend from you, you slut, go blame the right one." And Blu steps up to Evangeline. "Plus that, you ugly, Vangie, you damn cat killa, Human Rat, dick-sucka."

Evangeline rushes Blu and shoves him into the clown's

mouth, his face scratched and mouth bleeding from her punches. Blendaline jumps in, biting and scratching more, pulling hair and punching Blu's head, as Mitchell grabs Maisie and pulls her to the side. I kick and step on Evangeline.

It pretty much ended the festivities.

Uncle Paulo drags Blendaline away.

Jim Cameron ministers to Evangeline.

Jim tells Blu to always turn the other cheek.

"For more fuckin' slaps? I no think so," Blu yells.

The two oldest Reyes sisters are thrown into the back of Da Sun, Evangeline screaming F-words and crying. Henrilyn and Trixi sit with heads hung low in the front seat, so ashamed they don't look back at anyone. The following Sunday, it's back to the Catholic church.

❧

The two thousand pennies are worth two thousand pennies. And it takes us all of the next day and five library books to figure it out.

But Blu says nothing's ever a waste. He tells Maisie to stand in the yard and hold up her hands, and he sprinkles the pennies onto her face as she spins and spins; she gathers the pennies in the scoop of her T-shirt like Easter eggs she finds in the grass.

Blu takes the pennies to the county pool in the orange marble bag and throws them on the glass surface of the water. They fall in slow motion through my fingers, tumbling to the bottom, where the three of us, cheeks full of air, gather the pennies in the orange marble bag. When we rise to the surface, we see an explosion of pennies in the sunlight.

Blu lays all the pennies on the cool sheet of our bed and tells Maisie that it's gold, now roll in it; the two of them laugh in the tinkling money, rich in the pennies that are golden in the strip of orange streetlight that crosses our bed at night.

❀

"I not Baptist, Blu. I with you."

"Japanee," Maisie says.

" 'Cause we gotta see our Mama, right, Ivah? And she waiting in heaven with all our favorite dogs. And she heard me sing. Otherwise, if we turn Baptist, she burning in hell and we neva see her again."

"We nothing," I say to Blu and Maisie. "Nothing but us."

"Us," Maisie says.

"God ain't Buddhist or Baptist. He God," Blu says.

"Mama said you was born on the night of one full moon, Blu," I tell my brother. "Thass why you so strong."

"What about you, Ivah?" Blu says.

"What about me?" I ask him.

"When I see Mama," he says, "I going ask, 'On the night that Ivah was born, was the moon over the wharf so big and full that nobody in Kaunakakai knew why that night felt like day?' "

"Thass what the Japanee say about the full moon," I tell them.

My brother, the Buddhist. My sister, Japanese. Me, I'm with them, Ka-san, Hoppy, and four kittens. All of us sleeping on a bed of golden pennies.

16

"Poppy, I going," I tell him. He leans back in the orange chair. "I got accepted. Poppy—talk to me, please."

"When you coming back, Ivah?" says Blu.

"Who going pay the tuition and room and board? Who going take care these two kids?"

"Ivah," Maisie says softly.

"You think you too good fo' Moloka'i High, hah, you kid? Like all the odda rich Japs on this island, every island, the Japs think they big time. You listening, Ivah? I said, who going take care these two kids, hah?" Poppy gets up and walks toward me.

"Me," says Blu, getting between Poppy and me, "I the second main man of this house when Ivah go Mid-Pac. I going take care Maisie."

"You gotta be kidding, boy. You cannot go, Ivah, you betta think this one out good. This not one good idea. Maybe later on you can go. Way later on."

Big Sis's truck pulls up the driveway. She comes quietly into the back door, alone. "Whassup, man? So what, Uncle, Ivah told you? Pretty competitive, you know, Mid-Pac. That mean she up and up with all those Honolulu kids. If Ivah go now, she can make things smooth for Blu when he go, and then Blu can make things smooth for Maisie when she go Mid-Pac."

"C'mon now, Big Sis, we gotta be fo' real—who going take care the two small kids when I working two jobs? Who going cook for them and take them school? Who going help them with their homework? Who going sleep with them?" Poppy has *no* written all over his face.

I don't know what to do.

Why can't I take care of myself for once?

I watch Maisie creep toward Blu. I watch him put his arms around her. Her face relaxes.

"Uncle, Ivah got one of the biggest scholarships at Mid-Pac—that plus Work-Study. How you can pass that up? Thass free college-prep education. Ninety-five percent of their grads go college. I going pick up Maisie and Blu for go school every day, and I pick them up after school. And they ain't going play till I check their homework every day. I going watch them on the nights you work, no problem, come pick them up my place after you pau—and they be fed and bafe by that time too. What, they stay my house now, what three, four times a week anyway. We blood, Uncle, and I staying on Moloka'i. Me and Sandi."

"Staying? Right. Like all them other teachers. Staying till you get tenure, then splitting back to the city," Poppy says to Big Sis.

"I here for the kids, for Sandi, and for the job. Even you, Uncle, I promise. This going be our home." Big Sis and Poppy look each other in the eye for a long time.

"And when we going see you, Ivah?" Poppy asks at last.

"Me and Sandi get um all work out," Big Sis says. "We bringing her home on the small commuta airplane every long weekend and holiday. No worry, you going see her once, sometimes twice a month. C'mon, Uncle Bertram, let her go."

Poppy says nothing for a long time. He looks out the window, then at Blu and Maisie. At last, sadly, "Up to you, Ivah, but I swear, you betta think on this and be able fo' live with what you decide. No only think about yourself." Poppy stares again at Maisie.

Big Sis shakes her head. "She *neva* thinks about herself. What Ivah choose is for all of us."

"No," Maisie says. "I die," and she runs to her room, Blu chasing after her.

❀

Later on that day, Blu and Maisie sit under the house with Ka-san, the three of them eating raw Pop-Tarts and Tiger Milk bars for Blu's diet. He's reading her something, which makes me nervous. The last time, he was defining dictionary words for her. Words like Vagina, Reincarnation, and Masturbation.

I listen from the porch.

"I glad Mrs. Ota not giving us any more worksheets," he says. "Where Ivah, Maisie? You seen Ivah? Sometimes she spy on us, you know." Blu pauses, peering left then right.

"Mrs. Ota told us to remember when saying goodbye to our journals that parting can be such sweet sorrow. What is sweet sorrow?" he asks Maisie in a teacher voice.

I hear him thumbing through the tissue-paper pages of the dictionary. "Okay, sorrow mean (n.): a deep distress and regret. How that can be sweet?

"Parting sometimes just sweet, like when we left Aunty Betty house in Hilo. You know, the other day she told Big Sis her choice in life going only bring regrets. And fo' make us all shame, saying things like we was rude with no manners and Big Sis or nobody could change that.

"But parting was sweet, no, Maisie? 'Cause after Aunty went hang up the phone, we all went Midnight Inn, and Big Sis treat us chocolate sundae and Coke float.

"And remember, Maisie, Big Sis said we only should talk about good things like what we all going to do this summer like camping with her and Miss Ito, swimming, fishing down the wharf when the halalu run, and what kind bait work best."

I see the cat squeeze her way under the wooden slats for her piece of a Pop Tart. "And we get Vacation Bible School and maybe working in Miss Ito's Special Ed class. 'Cause if me and you make half the plane fare and half the hotel room, then we can go Honolulu at the end of summer with them for help Ivah go in the dorm.

"And we can stay at the Pagoda Hotel and go to the Honolulu Zoo and shop for next year clothes at Ala Moana. Plus go to Waikiki Twin to see movies and go Sea Life Park.

"So, what I'm trying to say, Maisie," Blu says in his teacher voice, "is that if you talking about Aunty Betty, then parting is sweet. If you talking about Mama, then parting is only sorrow."

"Mama," Maisie says.

"If you talking about Ivah going Mid-Pac, then it's little bit sweet 'cause I going follow in her feet and lots of sorrow for Maisie 'cause Ivah is her second mother."

"Ivah," she says. "Sweet sorrow."

❀

Poppy went back to work the night shift at Del Monte. For the last couple of nights, he smoked joints from a bag that he bought from Evangeline's Uncle Paulo. But Poppy doesn't say a word to me about my leaving.

"If Paulo come by when I not home," he said before leaving for the truck barn early one evening, "give him this twenty and make sure thass one two-finga bag Paulo giving you. No tell Blu and no tell Maisie what get in the bag and hide um under my mattress, you hear me, Ivah?"

"Poppy, but I thought you said that—"

"No Poppy-I-thought-you-said me. You like me be one fuckin' rag and take um all out on you kids, hah, Ivah? I get plenny on my mind right now, and I just gotta make it through the next coupla weeks. So you no question me nothing, you hear me? Betty right when she say that you think you one adult, but you just one kid, and I should treat you like that. Maybe she right."

"Poppy, you mad 'cause I going?"

"So what, just like that—you made up your mind already? I no can believe you, Ivah, how selfish you. Blu, he no need you—the boy going make it in this world come what may, couple slaps from life here and there. But the small girl—you like her come all mute again? And then what, hah, Ivah? Tell me now—what *you* going do?" Poppy makes a long pause for the guilt to settle in. "I gotta go work."

He pulls on his work boots, snatches his dinner in a paper package off the table, and slams the door behind him. "And Blu and Maisie," he yells from the porch, "you betta wash this goddamn stink dog before you let her in the house tonight." But I hear Poppy say softly, "Bye, Ka-san." And then out of the Malibu window, "Now, Blu!"

Blu runs out of the back door with his bottle of Herbal Essence. Maisie shoves past him with the dog towels, both of them waving goodbye to Poppy. "Bye, Poppy, see you tonight. We going wash the dog now," Blu yells to the car pulling out of the driveway.

And as soon as Poppy's out of sight: "Phew. Okay, he gone, Maisie. No need act no more. I ain't going use this Herbal Essence on Ka-san. Sheez, she impo-tant, but I no like waste this on one dog. Ivah, get me the Suave Strawberry from the bathroom, please. You go get Ka-san, Maisie."

"Get um yourself," I yell to him from the kitchen window. "Stop bossing us all around. We no more Suave already. Only got the VO5."

"Please go get um, Ivah, I said please, jeez. I getting the washtub from the back and the bugga stay heavy and dirty." Blu hoses down the washtub and fills it with cold water. The late-afternoon sun heats the whole garage, as Maisie pulls Ka-san into the water. Then Blu and Maisie scrub Ka-san with Alberto VO5 shampoo. Ka-san shakes her whole body and makes Maisie laugh and scream. Maisie gets inside the washtub to hold the dog still, then Blu shampoos her hair too. "No need wash Maisie's hair tonight, Ivah," he yells.

"Get her out of that dog water now. Hurry up, finish washing the dog, going get dark pretty soon. Blu, you betta listen to me. No wash Maisie's hair with that pilau water."

The two of them giggle. The dog shakes off the water all over the garage and runs around like a pup. Maisie chases her with a towel. And Blu washes his own hair in the cool dog water.

❀

As the month of June wears on, it gets hotter. I don't understand why Blu and Ed the Big Head Endo decide to make a plateful of S'mores with marshmallows on chopsticks over the stove. Hershey bars and graham crackers. Maisie grins at the kitchen table, warming the chocolate in the Easy Bake Oven. All three of them perspire in the kitchen.

"You know Winston," Blu begins, "the damn Twinkie King who always get at least three Hostess Twinkie or HoHo in his Pan Am bag? Ever since I was the lead singer in 'He Is Alive,' then quit the Baptist church fo' be Buddhist again, Winston call me hee-then and sinner, you know, Bob."

"Like Bob even care," I whisper to Maisie.

"He care, right, Bob?" Blu screams. "M Y O *f-ing* B, Ivah." He turns back to roasting the marshmallow over the stove with Ed. "But thass not the worst part. That part I no care too much about, as much as I do when he make everybody tease me that I the boy with breasts," Blu says.

Maisie and I giggle.

"Not funny," Ed yells at us. "M Y O damn B."

"Yeah, not funny. Maisie, no laugh befo' I no give you one S'more." She covers her mouth with both hands and peers into her oven window.

"Well, like I was saying, Winston said to Darren Ota and Scott Fukushima that I have love handles and two-inch pinch on my stomach and if you counting my breasts then I got a five-inch pinch. Just 'cause he skinny and Baptist, plus the captain of the ten-and-under volleyball team for the church, he think he hot. Was he the lead singer in the big show of 'He Is Alive'? I don't think so," Blu says sassily.

"Well, anyway, Winston also told the class that he saw

that I had stretch marks on my stomach part and by my underarms part too. I not going take free Baptist swimming lessons if Winston take swimming lessons 'cause he might make everybody see for themself all my stretch marks."

"Eh, you promise us was going take swimming lessons together," Ed whines.

"You better listen to Poppy and go on one serious diet this summer," I tell my brother. He looks at me and pulls one side of his lips into his cheek.

"Then," Blu says, bringing his chopstick loaded with brown marshmallows to the table, Ed behind him, "somebody put in my desk some AYDS candy, which is for curbing the appetite. Like one time I was reading Dear Abby, and this lady had one co-worker who had rotten B.O., and Dear Abby said to sly put a small bottle of deodorant on her desk. Well, that what someone, who I know is Winston Wang, did to me. He sly telling me that I'm a fat pig."

"Whass the big secret when he already told everybody you had zillion stretch marks?" Ed says. "Ooohh, sorry, Blu."

"I really sad, you know. Why all you guys not taking this serious?"

Maisie puts her hand on Blu's. "Shit, some of the boys saying I get tar on my neck 'cause I so fat. As the Filipinos call it, cubcub, that no matter how much you scrub, even with the Japan washcloth that feel like Brillo, the cubcub no come off.

"But the worse is that Winston said I get upepe nose which is like God chewed one big bubble gum, plop um on my face, and stuck his two fingers to make nostrils. This not very Christian, if you ask me."

Blu puts his face in his hands. Maisie taps his shoulders with the palm of her hand. "I ain't eating N'more of my S'more," he says. "I on one diet."

❀

Blu wants the trip to Honolulu bad.

"I like go Sky Slide and Gibsons and 'Checkers and Pogo Show,' plus maybe see Steve McGarrett, DanO, and Zulu, plus that go the zoo and Gems for Edible Creepy Crawlers. Oh yeah, and help you get all set for school, Ivah."

But he's spent all of the dog money he earned, and with his half of the ironing money, he's been buying Tiger Milk bars, Pop-Tarts, Archie comics, Herbal Essence, and plastic jewelry for Maisie.

"I figga I work six weeks for Miss Ito," Blu tells Maisie and me at dinner one night. "Thass five dollars a week. Five times six is thirty bucks. Okay, thass half my plane fare." He puts his head down.

"But I not going have nuff for the hotel plus spending money. Ho, man, only you and Maisie going." Blu heaves in deeply and puts his head on his folded arms—full of drama. Those acting lessons from Jim Cameron for "He Is Alive" really made Blu into a drama ham.

"Give me some of your dog money," Blu says to Maisie. Slowly she nods yes. Blu looks up grinning like his little act paid off. "Okay, okay," he says. "I get one idea—we go put all our money together and see if—"

"Wait, wait, Blu," I tell him. "We work hard too, you know, to save that money. I ain't putting in all my money for you, sheez. I mean, I can see if we give you *some* of our money for help out, but brah, we like spend money on clothes for next year at Ala Moana. I gotta save all my money from now on for plane fare and take care myself in Honolulu."

"Then what I going do, hah, Ivah? I about fifty bucks short. Ho, man, and I wanted for buy that Freddy Fender album 'Wasted Days and Wasted Nights.' You know what Ed told me? Get 'Before the Next Teardrop Falls' on that album too, you know."

"Blu, *we no mo'* one phonograph," I tell him for the hundredth time.

"Well, maybe I can buy one when I go Honolulu."

"Yeah, with what? You no mo' even your hotel money yet," I tell him.

"Me help," Maisie says. It's kind of a good thing that Blu's so caught up in the whole idea of going to Honolulu. Maisie's getting caught up too. I haven't really talked to her yet, and I see her scared eyes all the time.

Mama leaving. Ivah's leaving. A silent mouth.

"See, Ivah. At least one of us is with me," Blu says. "C'mon, Maisie. We go in the bedroom and make our plans for money." And the two of them walk down the hallway, Blu with his arm around Maisie's shoulders. He turns back to smile with his lips pulled into his cheek and nodding as if to say: No worry, no worry, I show you.

Maisie runs and gets the Elmer's glue and scissors. Blu runs out and gets scrap paper and pens. Both act like the big secret of the year is happening and I have no part in it. I saw on *Get Smart* how to spy on someone in the next room: you get a glass and put it to the wall and listen. I think about doing this to Maisie and Blu but decide that I don't want them to feel good about my wanting to know what they're up to.

Pretty soon, Blu and Maisie come out with a handful of homemade tickets, all crookedly cut. One of Maisie's reads:

BLu'S CaR aND DoG CLeaNiNG SeRViCe
WaSH   WaX   CLeaN THe iNSiDe
CLiP ToeNaiLS aND SCRuBaDuB 2 TiMeS FReSH
"i Do WiNDoWS aND eaRS"
$3

"I got this idea from *Henry Reed's Babysitting Service* and those Homer Price donut books that me and Maisie been reading together, what you think, Ivah?" Blu says. "Henry Reed made plenny money, you know."

"Thass *fiction*, like the librarian tell us every year," I tell Blu. "You *nonfiction*, you moron. I no think going work. Who you going sell all these tickets to anyway? Poppy? He make you wash and clean the Malibu for free."

"Miss Ito get one car and Big Sis, thass two," Blu says.

"And why you figga thass fair to them?" I tell my brother. "Sheez, they the one saying they going take you to Honolulu and you going sell car wash tickets to them? No class, you Blu."

"Why you making this so hard, Ivah? You no like me go Honolulu with you guys or what? I like see what my future school look like too, you know. And plus that, everybody get dog over here. We shoulda thought about this one long time ago." Blu pauses and I feel bad for a moment.

"I dunno," I tell him. "Maybe I still get Aunty Betty inside my head, know what I mean? How we no mo' class and we do what we like, how we like, with no manners. Thass kinda low-class to sell tickets. I mean, if we work for somebody, thass one thing, but for sell tickets? Thass the part I no like. Who else you going sell those tickets to? I sorry, Blu. I like you go with us, but I dunno if I like you do this car- and dog-wash plan."

"Church," Maisie says.

" 'Cause Jim get the pastor's Volkswagen Bug and Mrs. Nishimoto's station wagon and all the deacons. Thass at least five," Blu says. "And no forget Raymond Quinores and Glenn Perreira. See, Ivah, get plenny guys who get car at church. And you know church guys no like seem like they all tight and un-Christian, so they pretty much force for buy."

"I know but—" I pause and feel kind of disgusted and ashamed.

"I know. Thass real shame, but I ain't Christian, so why should I feel nothing? Plus that, I gotta go Honolulu, 'cause if you guys go and I no go, I going die. I just going have to die."

Blu and Maisie move their ticket-making operation to the kitchen table. Maisie draws soap bubbles with a blue crayon and Blu makes clouds around the words. The stack of tickets gets higher. I start to trim the edges.

❀

I hear Blu's pitch to Jim Cameron over the phone. "Hi, Jim? Blu. Presley. Presley Ogata. I'm calling to tell you about my car- and dog-cleaning job which I charge three dollars and wash, wax, clean the inside, and 'I DO WINDOWS AND EARS' is my motto.

"I Ajax the tires too. I bring all my car- or dog-cleaning supplies to your house when you like the job done. All you gotta do is call 553-BLOS which I was shock was almost my name perfect for my job as car or dog cleaner."

"He talk so haolified, no, Maisie?" She giggles as Blu grits his teeth and shakes his head at me.

"By the way, Jim, could you ask Mrs. Ota, your church treasurer, if she would like her car cleaned? And please tell her I'm not LAZY, LAZY, LAZY when it come to money. I already asked my last-year teacher, Miss Torres, if she wanted her car or dog clean and lucky she was in the office at the time and did not want to look like a tightwad, so she said why, sure, anything for you, Presley."

He's nodding.

"Three dollars."

And nodding.

"Car and dog."

And nodding.

"Thank you, Jim. Okay, bye."

Blu hangs up the phone, then sits at the table.

"So?" I ask.

He *hhhhaaaa*'s on his fingernails and buffs them on his shirt like a big shot. "Five tickets, if you please." And Maisie smiles as she counts them out. "Aloud, Maisie, count aloud," Blu says to our sister.

❧

By the Fourth of July, Blu's making a great killing as a car and dog cleaner. He's cleaned about three cars a week and three dogs a week since the beginning of June and saved about sixty dollars. He goes to church, now, every week to clean out the Baptists.

He has plans to go to church with Ed the Big Head Endo, who's back at the Kingdom Hall. Planning to be Jehovah's Witness next, and after that, the big one: the Church of Jesus Christ of Latter-day Saints. "I going be one Mormon, Ivah. Just for three weeks in August right before our trip. I figga I can do maybe one, two cars and dogs a day, except for the Sabbath. And *maybe* you can get in on my riches, what you think?"

When I don't respond, don't even change my expression, Blu snubs me, his money folded in half. He fans himself like a fat Mr. Mooney. "Count it and weep," he says. "C'mon, Maisie. We go in the bedroom and count my money." Blu walks down the hallway, swaying his ass and waving his money, Maisie and Ka-san behind him.

❦

The night Big Sis and Miss Ito take the three of us to the Fourth of July fireworks display at the wharf, we sit waiting on the porch. Blu has made egg sandwiches with the six eggs he picked up from the coops out back. Maisie holds a Tupperware full of green mango we sliced and soaked in shoyu, vinegar, and pepper. Mitchell Oliveira comes up the driveway with warm Portuguese sweet bread in a paper package. "Thanks for inviting me," he says. "When's your cousin coming?"

"When the moon turns blue," Blu says.

"Oh, shut up, Presley."

"Same to you. One plus one equals two," Blu says.

"Knock it off, Blu. You ruining our night," I tell my brother.

"Come sit by me, Maisie. No sit by Mitch." Blu always has to get in the last word.

When Big Sis's truck pulls up the driveway, headlights moving into the black space of the garage, we hop into the bed. She's made it into a real bed—with foam padding, sleeping bags, pillows, and her Igloo full of Diamond Head sodas and Millers. Miss Ito and Big Sis both get out of the front to settle us in.

"Howzit, Mitchell. Sit down in the bed, now, Maisie. Put the sandwiches in the cooler, Blu. Us get musubi like that," Big Sis says, "and fried hot dogs and egg roll. Sandi said the JayCees take long time for light the next fireworks, so we might be down the wharf for couple hours."

"Right, Ivah?" Miss Ito asks. "They take forever every year just to get a few firework displays up. But it's worth the wait, I guess. I mean, the whole town's down there every year, waiting for the next ooohh and aaahh."

"Yeah, they take long time, every year," I tell Big Sis.

"Except the year the whole thing blew up," Blu says. "Remember, Ivah? The whole place was light up. Ho, had about ten of um in the sky one time, and all the JayCees was diving into the water. That was the best one yet."

We drive slowly through the main drag of town, then down the long road to the wharf lined with sweet kamani trees. The air smells of muddy banks, ocean brine, and fermented pineapple. A sliver of moon hangs in the sky. Stars, lying low, and gray-blue clouds linger above us.

Big Sis parks the truck by a bunch of other trucks. It's the Youth Group gang from the Baptist church—Raymond Quinores' Toyota and Teresa Kabalis. Glenn Perreira's Ford and Connie Peralta. Rhoyden Medeiros' CJ-7 and Cynthia Low. Everyone's equal yokes. And off in the darkness, Da Sun, I can barely see. It's Uncle Paulo with Paulette Iwahashi. I suspected that out of the group of cheerleaders, she would be the only one with black lace panties.

"I going make Paulette buy one car-wash ticket for Paulo," Blu says as soon as he sees the two of them in Da Sun. "Look, you guys, two heads, one driver." And Blu reaches into his pants pocket for his tickets.

"Goddammit, Blu. No tell me you wen' bring your stupid tickets to the fireworks," I tell my brother.

"No take the Lord's name in vain, Ivah, you creep," Blu says, and before I can respond, he hops out of the truck and starts running toward Da Sun with his tickets in his hands, the first explosion of fireworks making his hair, his back, neon white and gone.

"Betta go watch him, Ivah. Look like Paulo and Paulette getting real close in that car, know what I mean, and Blu going piss him off," Big Sis says. I get out of the truck.

Blu's already knocking on the passenger-side window, and Paulette leans over to crank the window open. "Hi, Presley," she says, full of cheerleader grace. "How you been? I neva see you in church long time. You still washing dogs and cars? My madda said for tell you that you did one good job on our fox terrier. What you like?"

"Paulette," Blu says, real innocent, "you like buy one ticket for me wash your boyfriend's truck?"

"Paulo," Paulette says, turning to Uncle Paulo's mad face, "like buy one car-wash ticket from Presley, please, honey, please, sugar pumpkins, my baby muffins," and she tickles Uncle Paulo, who laughs a stupid chortle without once looking at Blu.

"How much?" he asks.

"Only three," Paulette says. "And Presley come your house with all his stuff for do the work. Can come tomorrow, Presley?" Paulette asks. " 'Cause I going be down Paulo's house before I go Bible Study, so I can pick you up."

"Okay."

"Here, three bucks. Beat it." Uncle Paulo wraps his arm around Paulette's neck and licks it as she passes Blu the money. Blu puts the ticket in her hand.

He walks away and I stand up from where I was sitting. "Thass some Christian," Blu says. "She suppose to wait till she married fo' do that with Paulo. And they ain't equal yokes, yeah, Ivah, 'cause Paulo wen' quit church after he got Paulette."

"Whateva, Blu," I tell him. The slow fireworks explode above us in the cold sky, stars dissolving in the gray-blue clouds brightening with neon white for a moment of ooohh, for a moment of aaahh, then gone forever.

When we get home, I put Blu and Maisie to sleep. Then I go outside. I remember nights, Mama and me, sitting on the porch. She'd light a cigarette and drag in deeply. Smoke fingers creeping along on the humid air. How many thoughts we thought on the porch at night.

Who I would marry. — mother + Ivah

No only think about yourself. — father's voice

Be a veterinarian, a taxidermist, a zoologist.

You like her come all mute again?

Who do you trust and why?

You selfish, selfish, selfish.

Relive a memory:

The best sekihan I ever ate. I was twelve the last time the red rice stuck to my teeth.

Who going cook for the two of them?

Who comes first in your life?

Family always come first.

Should I stay?

I want to go.

You betta live with what you choose.

Mama, teach me how to be Ivah too.

Me, Me, Me, thass all you think about.

Mama, we never go in without an answer.

Only you and I can figure this one out.

You're the one with all the answers, remember?

"Where is heaven, Ivah?"

What, Mama?

Is that why you can't go?   (still Ivah talking)

The answer's so clear.

Over there.

You gonna live with your decision forever.

How long is forever?

I put my face in my hands. I don't know what to do. Ka-san nudges me with her cold nose. She sits in front of me and stares up at the full moon. And then I remember: On the night of a full moon, many children were born. Ivah Harriet, Presley Vernon, Maisie Tsuneko, a litter of kittens, and a dog with red eyes.

I open my eyes so I may truly see the answers to the questions I have asked tonight: I rub Ka-san's tears in my own eyes, my mother's tears, inugami's tears, spirit eyes with which I see the dead among the living, see from the eyes of a dog come to save us.

Smoke hangs on the still night. Mama's a cloud shape that moves into the form of a mother, a shape that funnels as it forms. I've seen this with my eyes open and clear.

"Go, Ivah," my Mama says. "Save yourself."

I don't know what to say to my sad Mama who cannot find the true light. "Go, Mama," I want to tell her until she feels the heart inside me.

❀

Paulette comes to get Blu in her mother's Celica at about five the next day. He waits on the porch with his laundry basket full of Blu's car-cleaning Supplies. A chamois, Turtle Wax, Ajax, a coconut brush, some Palmolive in a mayonnaise jar, a bucket, a sponge, a whisk broom, and old towels.

"I bring him home before I go Bible Study," Paulette yells at Maisie and me, standing in the garage. "So he betta do one good job fast. You know Paulo and that truck," she says, like we're supposed to know exactly what she means, but we don't.

"Yeah, okay, bring him home after he pau," I yell back to the cheerleader, with my brother, sitting in the front seat, acting like the big shot with the high school cheerleader, Mr. Mooney with the plans and big bucks in his briefs.

So I cook dinner. Then we watch TV. Then Maisie does the dishes. I bathe Maisie. We watch more TV. It's 7:15. And Blu should've been home. I call Mitchell. He's gone to Bible Study. 7:30.

I get on my bike and Maisie gets on Blu's bike. We pedal furiously to the Baptist church. Bugs in my mouth,

I crunch; in my eyes, they tear. The night is so humid, termites swarm around the orange-white streetlights. I stand by the jalousies on the ocean side of the church and try to grab Paulette's attention.

Everyone's there, it seems. When Jim sees us, he says, "C'mon in, Ivah. There's lots of room for you."

I feel an airless frenzy inside. "Paulette, where my brother? You said you was bringing him home before Bible Study. Where he stay?"

"Why you panicking, Ivah?" Paulette gets up and walks over to the window. "I cooked dinner, so we ate first and Presley ate with us, and then he started for clean Paulo's car. So by that time, I had to come church, so Paulo said he take Presley home for me after he pau clean the car. They probly still up at Paulo's house. Sheez, Ivah, why you acting all nuts? I mean, I trust Paulo with my life."

"Fuck you, Paulette. Fuckin' slut."

"Ivah, wait," Mitchell yells. "I go with you." He knows what Paulo's done to all the Reyes sisters.

I turn around and see Mitchell running down the street behind Maisie and me, but I cannot stop to slow down. It's uphill to Paulo's house, about four roads above ours. My legs are pumping furiously, but I don't feel them or my body. The lights are all on, in the garage, in the house, but Da Sun's gone.

Maisie skids to a stop next to me. "No mo' Blu's stuff," I tell her.

Without speaking, we pedal off to our house, downhill and fast. The lights are off. "Blu, Blu!" I yell.

Maisie drops her bike and scrambles into the house.

Then the porch light goes on and Maisie steps into its flicker. She rotates her hands: nothing.

Maisie and I ride our bikes back to the church. No Da Sun. Past Midnight Inn, Pascua Store, the Dairy Queen. Nothing. The pool, the gym, the baseball field.

And there, right down the street from our house, in the parking lot of the Kingdom Hall: Da Sun. I throw my bike down and run toward the truck, see the laundry basket of car-cleaning supplies in the bed and pull the door open.

The smothering heat of bodies in a closed car, steam on the window. My brother's gagged mouth and tied hands, his face neon white in the light of Jesus Coming Soon.

And in that moment, Paulo's left hand around his own penis, his right hand around Blu's, the slapping of flesh, Paulo spitting in his hands and the quick jerk over skin, over skin, over skin.

I grab my brother, who stumbles out of Da Sun, and Paulo spurts out of himself, white mucus, all over the steering wheel, and leans back, moaning.

I drag Blu through the parking lot, Maisie on the other side of him. We run to the church and hide in the darkness between the church buildings. Maisie tries to undo the knots. Blu's eyes are scared eyes. "Undo his hands," I whisper to Maisie, "so he can put his penis back in his pants, put his penis in." I peer around the corner. "He getting out of the truck. Omigod, no."

Maisie and I bite at the knots in the rope. I yank them off Blu's hands and it burns his wrists. Maisie throws the ropes to the ground. She peers around the corner.

"Coming."

I rip the gag from Blu's mouth to his neck. He's breathing hard and weeping. Then for a moment, only a moment, he rests his face on my shoulders.

"Run, run!" The three of us move silently along the walls of the Kingdom Hall, the shadowy outline of Uncle Paulo behind us when I turn. Then he's gone.

❀

In the night, we go from backyard to backyard, darkness to darkness. Da Sun cruises the street, up and down, up and down in front of our house. Cruising with its lights off. We sit behind the mock-orange hedge in Elena Gaspar's yard, run across the street, then skid down the gully to the ledge, cool dirt and darkness.

A rustling in the bushes, and Ka-san whimpers. "We not going home until we see Poppy turn on all the lights," I tell Maisie and Blu. Da Sun continues to search our street. Paulo leans out the window, whistling for us like dogs.

Ka-san sniffs Blu and then I see my brother's bleeding slightly down the legs of his pants. He falls onto my lap, his whole body shaking with sobs as Maisie leans down and puts her face next to his, stroking his hair.

"What my name?" he whispers to her. She says nothing. "What my name? Tell me."

Maisie touches his hair then presses her mouth to his ear. "Blu."

❀

I don't know what to do.
Never was a Mama.
Never will be.
How to save myself.

I have to save myself.

Me.

❀

Ka-san moves right by me and sits upright, stares into my eyes, red to red.

"Mama," and Maisie turns.

Mama knew this would happen. So I take her tears, hold my brother's face in my hands and wipe them into his eyes. And for the only time, all three of us see:

❀

Kingdom Come.

❀

Blu drops his head again; I move aside. Maisie recoils and gasps. So when Blu looks up, he sees our mother's white face, her white hair, a spirit's tender smile.

Blu's hanging, hanging on, locked in a cloudy embrace with all of us, and for a moment it feels like lost forever in our mother's arms.

The kitchen light goes on and Poppy yells into the night, "Ivah! Blu! Maisie!" My mother's body moves toward his voice, toward the house that she's mistaking for heaven, but Blu hangs on to her thighs, her knees, her calves, her feet: "No, Mama, no."

"Blu," she says, "there's heaven for me."

And my brother, my brother full of grace and blood, says, "No, Mama." He closes his eyes and sees a grassy hill, a river, fireworks in the sky every night, beautiful dogs with beautiful names. "Mama, go," he says. "Mama, you gotta go to the light of the Buddha, the light of Jesus—both feel same, feel warm, you cannot miss um."

How did my brother know? Was he there listening that

night I sat on the porch? "She gotta go heaven, right, Ivah?" Blu says to me with sweet, sweet sorrow.

"And we gotta go home."

I hold his hand in mine.

The sweetest sorrow.

My brother gets up, dusts his pants, and leads Maisie and me back to our house.

17 On the walls of Uncle Paulo's house in dog shit, warm and foul; cat shit, sweet cinnamon rot; and the red, red dirt that stains our heels, Maisie's up-down handwriting:

> MaLeSTeR
> HaNG
> i KiLL You
> HuMaN RaT

Uncle Paulo scrubs with Brillo, fast and furious, checking to see who's looking, his walls stained for life.

❀

I hear my brother praying on the back porch under the yellow bug light on this night of no moon. A mosquito punk is clipped to a tuna can, and senko—where did he buy it?—in an old bud vase from under the house.

❀

"Dear Heavenly Mama, hallow be thy name:

Blu's prayer

"I know you probly thinking like everybody else what a big fat fake liar I am, but I wanted to tell you what Poppy told me. It's very hard to tell anybody who ain't blood and you blood to me, Mama, you let me hang on you the longest. Okay, here goes. And this is the exact words of Poppy to me:

What?

What you said?

I no can believe.

When? Where? How in the hell?

What you was doing over there nighttime?

You stupid or what?

You get stink ear or what?

Why you no listen sometimes, hah?

Where was your sisters?

Why the hell they neva go with you?

You walk around this town like it's nobody's business.

You think this town is your oyster.

You wrong, you damn hardhead kid.

I knew this would happen.

Your mother told me this would happen to you, Blu.

Told me, watch out for the boy, 'cause he the one with his own mind but no common sense.

But did I listen? No.

I never shoulda have you.

Look what I get letting my dick lead my brain.

Now what am I gonna do?

What the fuck am I gonna do with you, Blu?

"Now, Dearest Mama on earth as it tis in heaven, I want to tell you what hurts me inside and outside but DO NOT tell anyone, especially God the Father, Commander in Chief.

"Outside: Every time I use the bathroom for number two, it bleed little bit but I put toilet paper over there and pray to Jesus, Buddha, and you to make it not sore anymore.

"Inside: Now Poppy hate me the most. He don't talk to me or look at me. I got *no parents*, and when I woke up, it *wasn't* a dream. It was real when Poppy no even say my name no more.

"I wanted to tell you my inner feeling of I cannot sleep. I scared when I see Uncle Paulo's Da Sun. Mama, please no hate me, but I wanna tell somebody the truth. When Uncle Paulo did that to my penis, wen' feel good 'cept for the ass part. Maybe I like do um again, but not the ass part. Is it wrong when something feel good?

"But I wish with all my soul that Poppy forgive me. Until that happen, I trying to act brave because men are the stronger sex. And I have to be the second man in the house when Ivah go to Mid-Pac.

"In Jesus and all them odda guys' name I pray, Amen."

&

He comes in the house. Into the bed. Dirty feet. Maisie and I hold Blu to help him fall asleep. Ka-san lies curled at his feet with the family of Creetats. We cover him with the soft corduroy blanket. Maisie strokes his hair while I rub his back.

I tell Maisie my plans once Blu is asleep. In the strand of orange-white streetlight that falls across our bed, his face looks cut up. "We gotta tell Big Sis. She going know what for do," I tell her. "Poppy not going do nothing. Thass why Paulo act all hot shit when he see us in town. Maisie, we gotta tell somebody or else he coming for you. Maybe Blu again. We gotta protect him from himself. Uncle Paulo eyes tell me when he look at us on the street that he hungry for meat still yet." Blu's body stirs, his arm covers his eyes, a twist of his head, left, then right, the kick of a foot, a small grimace.

"Tell," Maisie says.

"Yeah, maybe I should tell Paulette. I like smash her face bad, that Sunday School slut. But all I know is that you and me gotta stop doing all that revenge shit to Paulo. He going catch us and then he going mess us up bad like—like Blu. Maisie, he eva touch you, I dunno what I would do. I dunno what I was thinking letting Blu go there. Thass all my—"

"No go," she says. "Stay."

"Stop it, Maisie."

Her face changes. She's silent and still for a long time. Then she gets off the bed and scampers into the kitchen. She comes back with the Molokai Drugs calendar and a big red marsh pen. She says nothing and shoves them at me.

"This is today," I tell her. "Tomorrow we going Honolulu with Big Sis." I mark the calendar for her. Turn the page. "Labor Day." I mark it in red. "I come home on Friday night and leave Monday night." I turn the page again and again. "Discovery Day, Election Day, Veterans Day, Thanksgiving, Christmas vacation, Presidents' Day, Easter vacation, Good Friday, Memorial Day. See how many times I going be home? Going be betta for the three of us, you gotta get that in your head, Maisie. And Big Sis and Miss Ito going take care you. And Blu."

Maisie looks at me, then takes the calendar and clutches it to her chest. We hold each other on the warm bed. "Thass all my fault, what happen to Blu." Maisie shakes her head no. "It is."

"I dunno why Poppy not helping Blu." I pull some of Blu's blanket and cover Maisie. "I scared talk to him," I tell her. "He blaming me, I know. And I know that he like slam my head into the wall for not being there for Blu. I can see um in his eyes the way he look at me, his hand ready for crank me into the counter."

"Poppy," Maisie says.

"*He* suppose to help Blu, but too late. Me and you gotta think pass Poppy already."

The back door creeps open and I hear Poppy's tired footsteps trudge into the kitchen. The squeak of pants on his vinyl chair. The heavy lean of his arms on the table. I get slowly out of bed so I don't wake Blu. He stirs again in his restless sleep. Maisie follows me to the kitchen.

"Poppy," I say. He looks at me, startled.

"Huh? Oh, Ivah. What you doing up, little girl?" he asks Maisie. "Where the boy?"

"He sleeping," I tell him.

"Ivah, go make me one tall glass ice water. Plenny ice."

I look at Poppy for a long time before I move. He *knows* something that he's not saying. There is a calm over his face. Deep breaths held and then released from his lips. A glaze over his eyes. By the time I bring him his water, he's at the piano, playing "Moon River."

Stop.

❀

I'm crossing you in style.
Someday.
No.

Maisie looks at me with a wild look. Then she screams, "No! Stop! Stop!"

❀

Old dreammaker, you heartbreaker.

✿

Poppy turns around on the piano bench and faces Maisie and me. Then I turn. I feel Blu leaning on me. He's rubbing his eyes and holding on to me. So Poppy finishes:

✿

Wherever you're going, I'm going your way.

✿

"No, Poppy," I whisper. I know *exactly* what he means. I've known this all along. "Please no. I cannot be one Mama. I dunno how. I going school in Honolulu. Poppy, stop." Blu crumbles onto the floor. He puts his face in his hands.

My father doesn't even turn around when he starts his dream walk, like we're not even in the room, the veil drawn, no rope for him to come back on. But he goes.

"I knew we neva was going fit in topside. I knew we shoulda stayed Kalaupapa. I tried for talk Eleanor out of it for months. The world had um out for us the moment the teacha been spahk that red spot on my arm.

"Even then I thought: This not fair. How come bad stuff only happen to me? I thought: How come this no happen to Betty? She was one shithead all her life. I was one good person. Always was. I was betta than my sista. How come God no make this happen to bad people?

"All those years, all those years, we was nothings to nobody. Neva had one hope or one dream. Until me and Eleanor got together. Me and Eleanor. She was my best girl. I dance with only her, all night. She could read real good too.

"Then today I was coming home, I thinking: I shoulda take the sulfones with Eleanor. I shoulda gone all the way, fuck the kidney failure, all the way, if she was going all the way. What I was thinking? I no can live without her. This one cruel joke, me here by myself, dying one cruel death. Every day I dying. She my backbone. She my rock. I no mo' nothing to lean on when the bad things come now'days. I only get me and three kids I no can even feed.

"And now, I get one boy who all fucked up. Fuck, I get one boy who going be homo 'cause of me. Then I think no, 'cause of Ivah. Was all Ivah's fault. Then I think no, this all Eleanor's fault for coming topside and making these babies and then taking those fucking sulfone drugs. Then I think no, Eleanor would blame me. Was my fault. Where I was? How come I no could protect our boy? What the fuck's wrong with me?

"Then I think: I no can take all this. I gotta go back. I gotta go back. I dirty still yet. This is only some more of God's punishment on me for being one leper. I no deserve good things in this life. I neva even deserve one good wife who was just like me. I was going spend the rest of my days with Eleanor. But now, she gone. I gotta go find her. I gotta go where she stay. Maybe she over there, waiting for me."

❊

I'm crossing you in style.

❊

Poppy's dream-walking. I want to tie him with the rope to the vinyl chair, his chair, in the kitchen in Kaunakakai. He shakes me off of him. The veil's drawn; the curtain to the other side opens. "Throw away that rope. I neva want to find my way back from the place of memories. I like forget that I gotta come back. Hey there, Ella—where you going? Wait for me. I like walk with you tonight. Get one nice sky, whatchu think? Where you got that red dress? You going catch cold you no cover your shoulders."

Poppy gets up and walks to the back door. I panic. I close my eyes. Maisie grips my hand. Blu holds on. Nobody breathes. Nobody asks, "Where you going, Poppy?" Nobody can speak a word.

"I gotta walk back," Poppy says to us. "And I gotta stay there till I fix what I did wrong the first time. I gotta take my sulfones too with Eleanor. Wait—hey there, girl in the red dress—I like walk on the beach with you. You can read good, eh? Wait fo' me. After the dance tonight, teach me how fo' read."

Ka-san comes out of the bedroom and sits at Maisie's feet. She's whimpering and Blu gets on his knees to hold her.

Then Poppy dream-walks out the door.

Down the driveway and out to the street.

He's not looking back.

"What time you coming back, Poppy?" I call into the black night. "We leave the door unlock." I turn to my brother and sister. Blu holds Maisie. She's shivering. "No worry. He be back," I tell her. "Tomorrow, maybe the next day. But he ain't going be him for long time. We make him tea and foods he know only us cook. And he come back to us slow by slow. And when I gone, if he like talk about Mama, you guys talk all you can, the nice stuff you rememba about her, till he come back to his old self again. Cover him with the afghan Mama made for

Poppy. Cover him when he go sleep on the orange chair. You can, right, Blu?"

Blu nods a confident yes.

Maisie and Blu step out onto the porch with me. Blu's turned the porch light off. "He going fo' be with her fo' one last dance," Blu says.

"Might not be his last," I tell him.

"But Mama right here," Blu says, holding Ka-san's face in both of his hands. There is a moment of deep silence. The three of us look at each other but no one has an answer. Maisie puts her tiny hand in mine.

"You gotta put Poppy to sleep with the warm blanket," I tell Maisie. "And, Blu, you lock the doors and shut the lights every night. Us all can be Mama."

"Us three, we always was," Blu says, kicking the porch railing with his dirty feet, then leaning his warm body on me.

I don't know what to say. I look at Ka-san. She looks at me with feverish eyes. I've seen those eyes on this porch whenever I needed to see. Always with me. Never near enough. And then I know.

"We gotta call Big Sis," I tell them. "Explain this whole thing to her." Poppy's getting smaller in the distance, as far away now as the Reyes house.

I look at my brother in the wave of night. Ka-san whimpers all of a sudden, then squirms out of Blu's arms, frantic, running in circles out of the garage and barking.

Blu and Maisie call Ka-san back. Then Blu reaches for Ka-san's tears. One more time.

"Mama."

"No, Blu. Thass all for Poppy. Let her go." Ka-san scurries down the driveway and stops. She takes one last look at the three of us, her eyes red, a fire, a light. Then she runs down the street after Poppy. In the distance, he turns to greet her with a gentle hand.

He's going to find her, to walk with her, to dance with her, but she's walking behind him. Poppy, turn around so you can truly see. "Leave the porch light off, Blu. The priest had um all wrong when he told us for leave um on so she find her way. Mama gotta find her way to heaven, not *home*. She couldn't tell the difference."

"Mama," Blu yells into the night. "Heaven ain't here."

❀

Blu sits at the piano and plays songs my father taught him to read. And when he sings, notes pour from his throat in a sound so clear, I hold Maisie close, shut my eyes, and sleep. In the morning, I call Big Sis.

The three of us wait for Miss Ito and her at the kitchen table. Poppy's asleep on the orange chair. Hemp tea from Felix Furtado brews on the stove. The freezer is full of frozen dinners.

In a little while, we'll board the plane to Honolulu, and I carry on a shoebox full of treasures I've kept under my bed: a tablet, a pan of stones, wild violets pressed thin, pictures, sweet oil—stories that keep forever of a girl born at the time of a full moon, a sister with God's wonder in her silent mouth, and a brother who sings songs with the long, deep notes of his sweet, sweet sorrow.

A C K N O W L E D G M E N T S

*After a day of dark clouds
and fever of humidity,
an evening sheeted in lightning and sky
pulled across with rain,
the morning lifted blue.*
''ANNUNCIATIONS,'' MEREDITH CARSON

To my friends and family who know the lightning and
rain of these days, the humidity and dark, know the blue
of my mornings exists through you:

To the Bamboo Ridge Study group for a place to share
my stories; lifelong friends, your eyes for clarity, thank
you.

To Melvin E. Spencer III for your sense of intuition,
powerful and giving, you make me bust laugh, piss my
pants, only you make me think this world ain't gonna do
no shit to me.

To Nora Okja Keller, Cathy Song, and Juliet S. Kono,
for shared lives and your wisdom; for egging each other
on always and the wonderful house in the middle of 'ohi'a
where *"Everywhere I look, the blue mountains, / blue
flowers, blue stars . . ."* Juliet's resonance.

To Wing Tek Lum for being *you* all the time for *all of
us*; for restoration and friendship.

To Ge-wald "Turn around and never return" and Steve
"Oh, it's the customer from hell" of DATA-1. May you

never see me sitting outside your Aiea Shopping Center doors again with a broken computer.

To Morgan Blair for sturdy faith.

To Susan Bergholz for possibilities I can hold as my own; dreammaker, seeing and saying so that I may choose.

To John Glusman for pulling out the seeds of my doubt with honesty and rewrites, separate eyes, and good English.

To Molly Giles for a fall in a poet's aunt's house in Manoa.

To Mari Ann Arveson, Kristi Lucas, Joy Sakai, LuAnn Ocalada, Janice Simon, Cheryl Lamb, Pauline Kokubun, Miss Mercedes, and Naomi Grossman for my son's freedom, hearing the softest notes of his voice, for dignity; I am writing you into the stories of our lives.

To Makia Malo, brother of PiliPili, keeper of stories, my treasure, *solid as a rock*. To Ann Malo for your insight, two of you—searching with me and finding in a rain, years I looked, and the marking of a single tree. My thank-you.

To Glenn Nakaya and Ross Yamamoto for stories that made me laugh and cry; an Obake Bridge I will never forget.

To Ivah's namesake, Ivan Kong Jr. of Waimanalo, Hawai'i—I got you in my heart forever because you said it would be so.

Houdini